Totally Bound Publishing books by Jaqueline Snowe

Out of the Park
Evening the Score
Sliding Home
Rounding the Bases

Classic Curves
Whiskey Surprises

Cleat Chasers
Challenge Accepted
The Game Changer

I0681186

Cleat Chasers

THE GAME CHANGER

JAQUELINE SNOWE

The Game Changer
ISBN # 978-1-83943-746-5
©Copyright Jaqueline Snowe 2021
Cover Art by Erin Dameron-Hill ©Copyright October 2021
Interior text design by Claire Siemaszkiewicz
Totally Bound Publishing

THE GAME CHANGER

Dedication

To all the friends you make in college, who get to see the ups and downs of life, the good times and the bad and, despite it all, love you anyway.

Chapter One

Greta

Action movies are full of shit, feeding us fake information our entire lives. For instance, when a fight breaks out in a bar, there's no Mark Wahlberg look-a-like to rescue the damsel in distress. Second the sound of flesh hitting flesh is repulsive and meaty. There are no wooshes or bangs or ka-pows. Nope. It's just disgusting.

I cringed at the smack and crashing of a fist meeting the face of my date. That's right. I always picked the *best* of the best when it came to dating and tonight was no different. Todd, who had blood dripping down his eye, chin and nose, had made the bold decision to ask me out. I'd accepted, like a fool, and would live to regret this night for all eternity.

"Where is my money, Todd?" The broad-shouldered man with a beard longer than my hair pummeled his meaty fists into my date's face. "Where the feck you keepin' it?"

No response. Burly Guy didn't like that. He grunted, swung his arm back past the table and hit Todd square in the nose. *What happened in my past life for me to witness this?*

No one got up to help. No one moved. They all watched with half-smiles on their faces and I knew in the pit of my stomach I needed to get the hell out. Like, ten minutes ago. I slowly slid my trembling hand into my purse to find my phone, but Mr. Burly heard me. He whipped his face toward mine, the terrifying glint to his eyes making me gasp. I gulped, the fear suddenly *very* real.

"You know this fecking asshole?" he barked at me. Countless gazes followed his voice and now stared at me. They wanted a show and I was *so* not the person for the role. My chin trembled as I shook my head.

"N-n-no. I j-just met him tonight." I clutched my phone to my chest. I would use it as a weapon if necessary, although I had no fucking clue what damage I could do on this beast of a man.

He ran his fat tongue over his lips and studied me. I stood stock-still, my spine straight as a rod. "I think it's time for you to go, doll. My boss ain't gunna like me lettin' ya leave, but your blonde hair don't fit in here. Get the feck out and don't come back."

I nodded, glancing one more time at Todd. My gut screamed to get out, but I had been raised Catholic. *Do I leave my epic failure of a date to get killed? Do I call the cops?*

Mr. Burly thought I took too long and put his grimy fingers around my wrist. I squealed, yanking it out of his touch.

"Get gone, girl." He kicked open the door and threw me outside. I stood on a rundown street with one streetlight working correctly. The others flashed and made a high-pitched buzzing sound that sent chills down my spine. "Fuck. Fucking. Fuck."

I called my best friend with shaking fingers and snot running down my face. Oh, did I mention I had blood on me that wasn't my own? I gagged, looking at the splatters. The phone rang and rang again. I loved Callie to death, but if that bitch didn't answer right then, I would get her for it. Big-time. Because what the fuck? It appeared the downward spiral my life had begun a month ago still had a way to go before hitting pure rock bottom. Nothing topped this story, as long as I got home alive.

"*Give me my fecking money!*" A booming voice traveled through the closed door. My longtime sixth sense had sent warning after warning all day and I'd chosen to ignore it. *This is my own damn fault.*

I gripped my phone tighter and took a deep breath. *Count to eight. Make a box with your breathing.* It did me no good and my fingers still shook. After three failed calls to Callie, I called the other number I knew by heart. Aaron Hill answered after the first ring with his obnoxious and playful voice.

"G-spot, what's crackin'? Finally calling me for a booty call?" His voice had the power to make me smile and roll my eyes simultaneously. This was not that time.

"I need you to come get me." My voice shook as the shouting picked up. Why had I let Todd convince me this place was cool and a '*real biker bar*'? Standing alone on the dark country road made it feel more like a place where girls went missing than a legit biker hangout. *I fell for it. Dumbass.*

"Where the hell are you?" His good-natured tone shifted and I imagined his steel eyes going dark. "It's past midnight. Shit, G, are you alone?"

"Uh, pretty much." I sent him the address while still on the phone. "I texted you the place. I'm calling in my favor."

"Jesus, Greta." He let out a string of cuss words. "Why the *fuck* are you all the way out there?"

"A date gone bad." Shame filled my chest, regret chasing it. The feelings had my throat closing. Tears weren't far behind.

"Goddamn it. I'm on my way. Stay on the phone with me. I swear, I'm going to wring your neck. I hate this shit." A door slammed—he'd just gotten into his car. After a minute of silence, he sucked in a breath. "Are you at Dirty Matt's? Please say no. Tell me no, right now, Greta."

The neon signed mocked me, *Dirty Matt's*, blinking over and over. "I'm at Dirty Matt's."

"Jesus Christ." His deep voice got so low, so calm, I made a vow to end all my plans for dating. His anger and disappointment in me were well deserved.

I gulped. Ever since my childhood best friend Callie had found love the year before, I'd wanted to try it. She'd fought it, but seeing how damn happy she had been all year and how she'd grown into herself had motivated me. I was damn happy for her and in no way jealous. I just yearned to have the closeness she had with her boyfriend, Zade.

Okay, so all the longing and searching had led me to a series of bad, awful and miserable dates. Not one had clicked. Not one had ended with the promise for more. And, not one has ended with a guy acting like a gentleman. Apparently, I had a stamp on my head that read, *I tend to date losers.* And, now, I could add I dated felons. It was the *only* explanation I could muster why Todd had brought me here, and why they'd beaten the shit out of him.

"I'm twenty minutes out and I'm beyond pissed at you. You know the rep this place has? Do you?" His deep voice held nothing but rage and worry. I closed my eyes and leaned against the wall. I had known about the reputation, but I'd wanted an adventure. Todd rode a motorcycle. He had tattoos and looked as good as sin. I wanted, even an inkling if possible, of the happiness Callie felt. *Is that so bad?*

Yes. I shivered.

Aaron's shaking voice pulled me from my self-pitying thoughts. "Greta! Did you know and still go there?"

Shit. He was past mad. "Yeah."

"Why? Tell me why. I know shit hasn't been great for you recently, but stop with this self-destruction crap. I can't watch you do this."

The squealing tires informed me he was close. His dark SUV sped down the road on a mission, the headlights showcasing how wretched this place looked. He pulled up to the spot right in front of Dirty Matt's and threw open his door. He stormed out, his anger evident on his handsome face.

"Aaron, look —"

"You asshole," he said, yanking me into his arms. "You worried the hell out of me. I lost ten pounds on the drive here."

"Aaron," I managed to squeak out before he pressed my face into his chest. "I'm okay."

"Just, let me be."

So, we stood like that for at least three minutes. His ridiculously large frame towered over me, but not in the way Mr. Burly back there had. Aaron was different. His body was sculpted from hours and hours in the gym. My arms barely fit around his middle, but I tried anyway. He squeezed me one last time and broke our hug. His gray eyes still held on to some anger, but relief took over. "Thank you."

"You're welcome, G." His lips turned white while he glanced at the sign. "Now, get in the car."

I obeyed, not foolish enough to piss him off even more. He opened the passenger door and glared at me until I buckled myself in. Without a word, he shut it and pinched his nose walking to the driver's side. His cologne clouded the car, the pleasant aroma of wood and leather comforting my nerves.

My body shook, the adrenaline wearing off. Aaron must've seen, because he turned on the heat despite the high July temperatures. I understood him well enough to let him stew. We had been close for over two years, but last year things were different. His dad being diagnosed with cancer had made the Aaron we all knew and loved change and we had grown closer and closer. Callie was my girl for life, but I couldn't envision a future without knowing Aaron would be there. He understood me, respected me and pushed me to be better. He was allergic to feelings and emotions while I was forever giving up on men. Our friendship worked.

He drove the silent, dark path back to campus, one hand on the wheel and the other repeatedly making a fist. I blamed myself for his anger. He had enough to worry about and now picking me up… Remorse filled my chest and my eyes stung. "I'm *fucking* sorry. I'm an idiot. I don't know why I went there. I wanted to have an adventure or something."

He nibbled on his bottom lip, keeping his expression blank. *Shit.* Instead of remaining silent and letting him deal with it, I'd decided to ramble. Rambling was a favorite sport of mine and I couldn't stop.

"He had a motorcycle…"

"I thought he would be a winner…"

"I want what Callie and Zade have…"

"I didn't realize he was a felon or something and would get the shit beat out of him…"

"I had no fucking clue I would get manhandled…"

"Excuse me. What did you just say?" His jaw tightened.

"I didn't have a clue —"

"No. You said manhandled. Someone hurt you?" His grip on the wheel tightened and I swallowed, loudly.

"Not hurt, no." I tucked my arms further into myself. A bruise had already formed and Aaron was in no state to know that. "Forget I said anything."

"I swear to God, Greta." He pulled off the road and stopped the car. He shook, his large frame tight with pent-up rage. I wanted to crawl into a hole. Pissed-off Aaron could scare the boogeyman into retirement. "Don't fucking lie to me. Are you hurt?"

I shook my head, but kept my arms crossed. His gaze flicked to my arms, and without asking, he grabbed them. I closed my eyes and knew he'd seen the bruise when he sucked in a breath. My lip trembled.

"Take off your shirt. I might have another one in the back." He released my forearms and turned to grab something in the back of the car. He was too calm, too well-behaved. It freaked me the hell out. I expected him to lose his shit and break something. Calm Aaron was new.

"I-it's okay." My voice shook again.

"No," he growled at me. "You have blood on you. Take it off now. I'm getting rid of it."

He waited, staring daggers at me until I took my blood-soaked shirt off. He wasn't lying. He whipped it out of my hands and chucked it out of the window. "I can't find my gym bag. Take mine instead."

Aaron Hill taking off his shirt should be photographed and made into a calendar. Or, better yet, a promotion for a porn video. He had always been hot as hell, and this was so not the time to ogle my friend. But I was human and his muscles rippled as he tugged off his shirt. "Put this on, Greta. Don't argue."

I didn't. I took the warm black shirt and put it on. It was three sizes too big, but I felt loads better. It wrapped around me like my favorite childhood blanket. I sniffed it unabashedly and closed my eyes. Sleep took over, and it wasn't until we pulled into Aaron's driveway in the early hours of the morning when I woke up.

I yawned, not sure why he hadn't dropped me off at my apartment. He ran his hand down his face, getting out of the car without a word. *Okay then.* I followed suit and tried not to stare at his back. His beautiful, sculpted back. "Aaron, why didn't you drop me off?"

"We need to ice your bruise. I have stuff here." His clipped tone told me he still wasn't happy with me. I couldn't blame him, though. "Come on."

He put his hand on my shoulder, guiding me into his home without making a sound. I walked toward the kitchen, but he shook his head and pointed upstairs. The floor creaked with each step and I made a vow to myself then and there.

No more dating.

No more being a dumbass.

I am going to focus on school and my friends.

I needed to save as much money as I could, ensuring I could return my senior year, because one of the things that had triggered my spiral was my dad losing his job six years before retirement. My parents had had to sell our childhood home, retire three years before they'd planned, and most of their money had been spent helping my brother with his nasty divorce. Shame consumed me again at how selfish and foolish I had been. My eyes stung and I clenched my jaw, hoping to stop the waterworks.

I planned to delete my online dating apps and have someone change my password as soon as I woke up the next day. Tonight had crossed a line. Too fucked-up.

"Go ahead and sit on the bed. I'll get my kit." He held the door for me and disappeared down the hall. Aaron's room fit him well—baseball legends and pinup models plastered on the walls. Clothes scattered across the floor made it appear messy, but I knew the closet was organized by colors. The bed welcomed me, the exhaustion of the night taking me. I lay on it, just closing my eyes for a little. I would leave after I'd iced my bruised arm. Dreams began to take over when I felt the softest touch on my cheek, like a feather.

"Greta?"

A deep, hushed voice forced me to open my eyes and Aaron's gray ones were inches away from me. "Hm?"

"Sit up for a second. You can sleep right after." He nudged my leg with his arm and sat next to me. He was still shirtless, the handsome devil. He carefully put my forearm in his left hand and used his other to hold the ice against it. "It hurts me seeing this bruise on you."

I closed my eyes at his honesty. I leaned into his shoulder and sighed. "I'm so embarrassed. And sorry. And I hate myself a little right now."

"We all make mistakes. Hell, you knew me when I went on a bender. You stood by me when I drank every night, slept with countless women, and chewed my ass out the one time I tried drugs. I haven't forgotten that."

I groaned into his shoulder. "I would do it again if I had to."

"I know you would, G." He laughed softly, the first time that night. I'd missed that sound.

"There it is. I wondered if your laughing part broke."

"Okay, no need to be dramatic." He picked up the ice and hissed at my arm. "Promise me something."

"No need. I already made a vow to never online date again. No, to never date again. Or at least for five years. Don't worry. This will never happen again."

"It better fucking not." His hand came around my leg, squeezing my knee. "Promise me you'll call me if you need help. Any time. Any place. You're one of the most important people in my goddamn life."

"Okay." I met his gaze and winced at the intensity in his eyes. "I promise."

"Good." He yawned, taking the bag off my arm. "I'm going to sleep. I'm beat."

"Uh, should I call a cab?" I hesitated.

"Don't be a dumbass. Sleep here. You've crashed on the couch countless times." He leaned back, fluffing up the pillows and rolling over. *Damn those back muscles. I want to bite them.*

I pushed myself up to head downstairs when his arm wrapped around me. "Uh, Aaron?"

"Stay here. My bed is huge. Don't make it weird."

He pulled me back onto the bed but kept enough distance between us. He must've sensed my trepidation because he rolled over and mumbled, "You mean too much to me to try anything. Go to sleep."

Chapter Two

Aaron

"Tell us about your games, son. I miss watching you play." My dad wheezed into the phone, each breath a hand clenching around my lungs. He sounded weak. I squeezed the shit out of the can I held. It cracked in my hand, the crinkling of aluminum distracting me from the emotional prison I lived in. "Aaron" — he coughed, three excruciating times, before continuing — "how did you hit?"

"Overall, I went three for four with four RBIs. I found my swing. I'm timing the pitches well and I spent all summer working on avoiding the rise. You know how much I like to chase the high ones."

He chuckled softly, the sound paining me as much as it brought me joy. I scrunched my eyes shut, unable to accept the harsh reality of my dad's diagnosis. It had been almost ten months since doctors had told him he had an advanced form of cancer. Ten months of miserable chemo, ten months of hushed voices and ten months of endless tears from my mom, sister and me. He coughed again, his voice softening. "I remember you struggling with the rise ball in junior high. Do you remember all of us going to the park and throwing beer caps at you?"

The memory flashed in my mind. I smiled — the family outings we'd always had were so much fun. "I remember Kenzie liked to pick up dog poop and throw it at me."

"Good lord, your sister could be a handful." He laughed again. "She still is, honestly."

"Yeah? How's the end of her last summer?" I made a mental note to call my sister. It had been a couple of weeks and while we hadn't always been close, our dad's diagnosis had brought us together. Kenzie had dived into job after job, never stopping because the pain hurt too much. I'd retreated into myself after the diagnosis, but I'd recently felt like my old self and although I would never return to partying my issues away, I could stand being around people again.

"Kenzie is working at the burger place every night, so your mom and I visit her. I love those damn milkshakes."

"Yeah. They have the best." I checked my calendar and planned a trip home. I had to live on campus year-round — baseball never really stopped. I preferred it that way, but not seeing my parents as often as I'd like sucked. "Tell Mom I love her. I just got a text from my coach."

"Will do. Love you, son."

"You too, Pops." He hung up and I stared at the calendar for a full minute, trying not to do a countdown. *Live every day like it's the last.*

Bullshit.

I shook my melancholy mood away and reread my coach's text.

I need to speak to you today. Stop in.

Last year, I would've imagined worst-case scenarios and freaked the hell out. Now, I had more control of my emotions. We had the weekend off from summer ball after the last tournament and I planned on annoying Greta. I could stop by Coach's office on the way to the bar she worked at. They had cheap beer and good food for a college bar. No one bothered me there, and I preferred the solitude.

A half hour later, I knocked on my coach's door. He didn't smile or greet me. He motioned for me to sit in the red leather chair in the middle of the room. I sat, waiting to hear what he wanted to say. He twisted the end of his mustache, not saying a word. My nerves kicked in. Was it my scholarship? He knew my family couldn't afford it with everything going toward medical expenses. *Fuck.*

"Aaron," he began. I panicked. He hadn't called me Aaron in a year. It was always Hill or Hilly. I gripped the chair. "I don't know how to tell you this, son."

I waited.

I waited and prayed.

I held my breath when he sighed, his bushy obscure brows coming together. "Some girl created a fake Instagram account about athletes on campus and how they can do whatever they want. It started as an opinion piece for some righteous church group. You follow me?"

I didn't. Not at all, but I nodded, holding on to every word he said. He swirled his computer around to show me something. "The most recent one focused on you, Aaron. She gained enough followers the past year that, apparently, she reached out and people sent her pictures of you."

"Pictures?" I blinked. "Of me?"

"Yes. Look, it's better if I show you." He clicked the mouse and images of me popped up on screen. Keg stands, beer bongs, naked girls, naked girls on me, body shots, me skinny dipping, me standing next to a bong, a girl kneeling between some guy's legs that were supposed to be mine. "This isn't good, Aaron," he continued, but I wasn't capable of listening.

My future.

My everything.

I saw stars, the pictures swirling around in my head, each one worse than the others. I gripped the edge of the chair, the ringing in my ears growing louder and louder. *What if I lose everything?*

My stomach heaved, my instincts kicking in as I dove for the trash can. The small breakfast I'd had came up and I wiped the back of my hand over my mouth. "Would you like some water?"

"No. Tell me what this means." A pit formed in my gut. The anxiety, the desperation to do something crazy crept up my chest. It caused me to drink. To party. To sleep with anyone. I'd learned to tame it last year, but this...this triggered it. *Fuck. Fuck.*

"I'm not exactly sure. I'm meeting with the athletic director and chancellor soon." He turned the screen around, taking it out of view. "Two things before you freak out. None of these are time-stamped. You're twenty-one now. Technically, none of it is illegal. And the second thing, the last picture."

"That's not me."

He narrowed his eyes, his cheek twitching. "I know you don't believe me. I was a party animal my freshman year. Last year, I was in the beginning. But one thing I am always aware of is phones when I'm fooling around. That is not me."

"Do you have a birthmark or anything to prove it?"

"No." The sliver of hope I felt disappeared. "I don't."

"We'll figure it out, Hilly." His perceptive eyes watched me for a full minute before he tapped his pen against a pad of paper. "Now, let's break down what the post said about you and figure out what's slander, what's true and how we can have someone spin it in your favor."

I nodded, helpless and desperate. "Coach, I'll have nothing if I don't keep my scholarship. I'll do whatever it takes. Anything."

"Let's brainstorm then, son. I've seen you grow into someone I admire the past year. We all have our baggage and thank the lord the internet wasn't around for mine. Keep your head up. We need a plan first and foremost."

"Okay. I'm all ears. Please. Anything."

"Your reputation is a bit dicey." He twisted his lips and studied me in silence for about ten seconds. "Stability. Boring. Mundane activities. That's what you need. You've been all over the damn place with school, parties, the ladies, all that shit. We need to come up with something that shows the public — students and coaches alike — that you're not unstable or the party animal you used to be."

"How?" *God, I am unstable. Faking it seems impossible.* "What shows I'm not flailing about?"

"Not going to parties or hooking-up all the time. Not causing a scene."

"I won't attend another party for the rest of the year, I swear." I meant it, too. I'd do whatever the fuck he thought would help, even if I didn't drink for another two years.

He rubbed under his chin and gave me a quick smile. "Huh. Takes more than that to show you're off the market, son."

"Off the market?" Sure, repeat his words. *I sound like an idiot.* "What does that mean and how do I do it or get it?"

"Well, I might just have an idea…"

* * * *

Greta is not going to like this. Fuck. This won't work. I know it won't. I wiped my palms on the sides of my legs, thinking about the conversation I'd had with my coach and what he wanted me to do. It'd made sense when he'd said it, but now that I'd left his office, all my confidence in the plan disappeared.

I couldn't ask her to do it. How could I, after everything she'd done for me? It was insulting to assume she would stop her life.

I won't do it to her.

But what if I lose my scholarship? Or, worse, my future in the MLB? I couldn't ask my parents for money, not with my dad spending every penny to fight cancer. I gulped. The unsettled feeling that began in my gut hadn't left since that morning.

I hate myself.

Fuck.

The walk to the bar felt like two hours, instead of the normal twenty minutes, the severity of what I was about to do weighing me down. In all the years I had known her, I had never dreaded seeing her or coming to the Lion for a drink. But now, everything I did felt forced. Was some psycho bitch watching me, waiting for me to fuck up? Sweat dripped down my forehead and I wiped it away, searching around the block for someone holding a camera at my face. Instead of a hunched-over crazy person, it was just other college co-eds ready to have a drink.

My phone buzzed and I jumped. I wished I could disappear into the mountains for two weeks with nothing but a baseball field and some beer. I wanted to be off the grid. But I couldn't. It was part of the plan. The plan to get my life back on track and my future tangible.

Zade: Dude. What the hell is going on?

Tanner: Why are you all over Twitter?

Zade: DUDE. WHERE THE FUCK ARE YOU?

Aaron: I'll be back later. I talked to Coach. I'll fill you in.

I pocketed my phone and knew my teammates had to have found out. Social media was the worst and anything spread like wildfire. I used to enjoy gossip and reading about other people, so I guess this was a good dose of karma. My freshman year persona would have loved the attention—hell, I would've eaten it up. Now, rage took over. *I'm a fucking idiot.*

The weathered doors greeted me and a wave of revulsion took over—I couldn't do this to her. I shouldn't. But I had to and the notion almost had me throwing up again.

"Hilly! My main man!" Clyde greeted me when I entered the bar. It was situated on the busiest street on campus and had a chill, almost hipster vibe with the dark walls, constant smell of coffee and beer, and obscure art that was always for sale, but never bought. Her socially awkward boss tried a little too hard to fit in, but I waved regardless. "You here for Greta?"

"Yeah. She in the back?" I squinted, trying to find her bright blonde hair in the dark bar. It stood out like red in a snowstorm.

"No! Didn't she text you?" He frowned, but a grin broke out. "One of our bands had to leave. Well, I made them leave. They were garbage. She's playing on stage."

"All right. I'll check it out. Thanks." I nodded at him and went farther into the dive bar. I recognized her low, raspy voice the second I walked in. I headed straight toward it. She sat on the stool, holding an old guitar and singing with her eyes closed. She looked so goddamn peaceful and beautiful. I clenched my teeth thinking about last weekend and the shit she'd pulled. I still wasn't over it and the thought of what could've happened had me clenching my fists.

We had hung out since then, but she was my soft spot. Everyone knew she was my weakness. For the polyamorous athlete, no one compared to Greta. No one fucked with her, either. It wasn't because she was timid or weak. No. It was the opposite. She understood me. And very few did. *I can't ask her to ruin her life. I can't. Not for me.*

I found an empty chair at the bar and watched her. Sure, she'd had a rough couple of weeks, but her life was still on track. She needed to give up the fucking ridiculous notion of finding love. *Love.* Ugh. It came too close to jealousy and hate—two emotions I refused to feel.

She finished playing, the small crowd all clapping for her. "Thanks, guys. I'm going to take a break."

I whistled at her, her soft brown eyes finding mine. I waved, pathetically, at her and she bee-lined for me. "G-spot."

"A-a-ron." Her toothy grin eased some of the tension currently growing in my stomach. "You're rocking the troubled skater-boy look today."

I looked down, noticing I'd never changed. I wore dark fitted jeans and a thrasher shirt. I shrugged. "Your voice sounded amazing."

She avoided my eyes, a blush tinging her cheeks. "Thanks, man. It was weird. Clyde insisted on me playing once the band stunk it up. I mean, shit. It's a Saturday night. No one was here." She sucked her bottom lip, twirling the end of her long ponytail in her fingers. Two gestures I knew well. She felt uncomfortable. "I don't even know how long I played. It felt good. It felt really good being up there."

"Will you play again?"

"You know, I don't know." She glanced over at Clyde and frowned. "He said he wanted to discuss something with me before I leave for the night. Maybe I will. I'm not too worried. Want a pitcher of beer? It is our buy one, get one for a penny night. My brilliant idea, I might add."

I shook my head. "I came to talk to you."

"Ronnie, I've been on my best behavior since last weekend. I wasn't lying to you when I said I deleted everything." She rubbed her chest, her neck tensing. "Why do you look irritated?"

I sighed, double-checking no one stood too close to us. "Shit hit the fan today." I paused, the tightening in my chest returning. I bounced on my feet, unable to sit still. She glared at me, eyes wide.

"Well?"

"Uh, someone, some girl, wrote some shit about me on Instagram. She put up pictures of me. Drinking, nudes, sex. You name it." My throat clogged, my fingers clenching around the edge of the bar. "My coach called me in and…I could be fucked. He's meeting with people to find out what it means for me and my future."

Her head jerked back. Her mouth fell open, no sound coming out. "Aaron."

We shared a look. She blinked. Her bottom lip trembled and I saw how my pain hurt her. *How the fuck could I bring her into my mess?*

"I'm at a loss right now. Are the pictures real?"

"Some, yeah. Snapchat screen-shots. I'm positive it's not me in the sex ones. My face isn't in the pictures, but with all the other shit I did, it's not far off."

"Holy shit." She pinched the bridge of her nose and lifted her chin higher. "What can we do? Your coach is a genius. He had to think of something."

"We came up with a plan today. It sucks. But it's a start." I lowered my voice, hating myself for doing this. "I'm not sure it'll work. Maybe."

"What's the plan? Stop stalling." Red broke out on her neck. It was time. I could either ruin the best relationship I had in my life or risk losing my future. She'd end up hating me—there was no way around that—but she was my only option. Who else could I trust to do this? Who else cared enough about me to do this?

No one. It was her. Just her.

Family. Money. Baseball.

I said the words, loathing everything I had become. They came out choppy, unemotional and broken. "Will you be my girlfriend for six months?"

Chapter Three

Greta

What? What did he just say?

"Come again?" I blew out a long, shuddering breath.

He scrubbed his hand over his face. With a strained voice, he repeated the words I thought I'd heard incorrectly. "Will you be my fake girlfriend?"

I burst out laughing. I laughed so hard tears streamed down my face. It made no sense and I was being a total dick. He was going through a crisis and I couldn't control my giggles. *Way to win the asshole award again, Greta.*

"Greta." His tone sharpened, his gray eyes grounding me. "Chill."

"Give me a minute, please." I poured myself a glass of water and took my sweet-ass time drinking it. *Girlfriend. Fake girlfriend.* "Okay. I settled a little."

"Are you in?"

"Aaron. I need more information. We are really good friends. You know I'd do anything to help. But I don't see it. How would us pretending to be together make your situation better?"

He winced, a vein visible in his neck. "It would be a PR stunt. We would showcase everything on social media. Play up the good parts of your life, my backstory. I need to come across stable—unavailable and even boring. I would be using you," he said between clamped teeth. "I *despise* this plan. But it might help me and I'm clutching at straws here."

"Jesus." My heart raced. I thought about it for half a second before answering. It was Aaron. The guy who'd seen me cry countless times and patted my back. The guy who'd made me laugh more than anyone. The guy who'd picked me up thirty minutes outside of town without hesitation in the middle of the night. I had no choice. Not really. "Of course I'll do it. Anything to help you."

"No," he snapped at me. "I need you to genuinely think about it. About what it means and what I'm bringing you into." He tapped the bar with his fingers over and over, his gaze darting toward the exit. "I'm going to take a walk. I need one. What time will you be off?"

I got whiplash from his moods, but I answered. "In two hours."

"I'll walk you back. Don't leave without me." He then turned to go without a backward glance. The door slammed at his departure, and I felt like a truck had hit me.

Poor Aaron.

How much could one person handle before losing it? I fisted the rag in my hand and a rage so strong, so aggressive went through me that I wanted to hurt whoever had done this to him. I hated people sometimes. I really did.

"Greta." Clyde pointed at me from behind the register. "Now that the Hulk left, can you help Elisa out in the back? She's swamped."

"Sure thang, boss."

Two hours later, I waited twenty minutes without a sign of Aaron. I checked my phone at least ten times, expecting a text or a call after he'd *demanded* I leave with him. My feet hurt and a glass, no, a bottle, of wine sounded perfect. *So, screw Aaron.* I wanted to go home.

The walk from the Lion to the apartment I shared with Callie only took fifteen minutes. It was off the beaten path, but I had done the walk alone enough times to feel comfortable. I never listened to music or was on my phone. My mom always sent me those bullshit articles about how to protect yourself and one had stuck with me. It said attackers always went for girls in ponytails and those who were distracted. *Hello…phones are a distraction.*

The wet air clogged my lungs and I hoped for a storm soon. Midwestern storms had the best clouds. The mixture of cold and warm fronts produced wild wind and it was long overdue. Lost in thoughts of storms and rain, I avoided the topic of Aaron until I walked into the apartment. I desperately wanted to talk to Callie about it and I wept with joy when I found her sitting on the couch with a large bowl of popcorn.

"Hey, G. Want some?" She held out the bowl, her dark hair in a long braid down her back. I'd taught her how to braid last year and now she had it down. *Proud mama moment.*

"Yes. Did you make it?"

"Of course." She made a distorted face at me, knowing my obsession with her cooking. "Eat the rest. I already ate my bodyweight."

"F'anks," I said with my mouth full. I swallowed, attempting to be polite before bombarding her with what happened. "How was your day?"

"Pretty good," she replied with a cheery smile, but then her gaze went to my face and her lips curved down. "What's wrong?"

"Nothing," I responded too quickly. *Shit.*

"G, your cheeks are red and you have your crazy eyes going on. Did something happen at the bar?"

"I mean, I got to play on stage for a bit. That was cool." *Why am I not telling her? Just say it.*

"That's awesome! Oh my god!" she cheered before snatching the bowl out of my hands. "No more food until you tell me what the hell is going on."

I gulped, my pulse quickening when I thought about what Aaron had asked, his face when he'd said it, and how angry it had made me. "Aaron asked me to be his girlfriend."

Her eyes resembled two large saucers and her mouth hung open. "Why?"

"He got caught up in a scandal that has the potential to fuck up his future, so having a fake relationship with me for six months could help him out."

"Wait, what?"

"Pretty much what I said when he told me." I laughed at her expression. "I told him I would do it."

"Of course you did." She pursed her lips. "I would say yes if it would help him. That guy has gone through a lot more than anyone else I know. This sucks donkey balls. Big donkey balls."

"You can say that again." I closed my eyes and sank back onto the couch. "He was supposed to walk me home but never showed. I'm a little worried now."

"He might've headed back to the house. I don't know. Zade is having a bro night. He could be there."

"How do you feel about a bro night, Cal?" I teased her. He often attempted bro nights, but found his way back here.

"Perfectly content, actually." She laughed, pointing to the TV. "I can watch my baseball team and eat my own food. Plus, you're here. Win, win, win."

"You're a goon. But I love you." I squeezed the pillow to my chest, hoping to calm the ache. "What if this blows up in our faces, Cal? I'm scared."

She clicked her tongue, putting her hand on my arm where the faded bruise sat. "It's Aaron. Would you be able to forgive yourself if you didn't try to help him?"

I thought about the night he'd held ice on my injury, patiently dealing with my dumb ass. I knew my answer. I knew it without a doubt. "No."

"There ya go. You're a carefree, *livin' la vida loca* sort of girl. You said yourself you're done dating. This is an easy excuse to not date for six months. We'll hang out like normal. You and Aaron hang out almost every day, anyway. You add in a hand holding and cuddle once in a while in public and, *bam*. You help him, and you remain celibate."

I flinched. "Shit. I didn't think about that part. Celibate."

"It won't kill you, hoe bag." The insult was worthless, her goofy smile taking the sting out of it. "Do you still own the rabbit vibrator your cousin bought you in ninth grade?"

"How do you even remember that?" I shook with laughter. "I do, by the way."

"Problem solved. Help Aaron. Use the rabbit. Save the world."

I flipped her off and about jumped out of my shorts when a loud pounding started at the door. "Expecting Z-man?"

"Nah. He just texted me."

"Hm. I'll see who it is." I went to the door and checked through the peephole. "Shit. It's Aaron. He looks pissed."

"I can hear you, Greta. Open up," his voice boomed through the door.

I jumped back, sharing a guilty look with Callie. "Fine, come on in, Mr. Friendly."

He stepped into the small entryway and glared at me. "I told you not to leave without me."

"Uh, I waited a half an hour." I pointed my finger at his chest, pushing it slightly. "I called, a million times. You never showed up."

"I broke my phone. I got lost." His gray eyes turned to slits. "I hate when you walk home alone."

I stilled at his words, a sharp reminder of what had happened last week. "I felt exhausted. Everything is fine. Let's go talk, okay?"

He nodded at me and I led him to my room. Callie had made herself scarce, meaning the conversation between Aaron and me would be private. He didn't wait before plopping down on my lavender comforter. The bed creaked, the springs way too old. I sat on the opposite end, crossing my feet. He stared at my bare legs before relaxing. "Today has been hell, Greta. Hell."

"I'm sorry. I meant what I said earlier, Ronnie, I'll help you any way I can. Fake girlfriend, beating some ass, you name it." I scooted closer to him, grabbing his hand in mine. "What do we need to do? What details did you and your coach come up with?"

He clasped my hand, squeezing and releasing it. "Changing my public image. We need to be seen, in public, a lot and post a shit-ton on social media. The public need to see me as a changed man. Charity events. Tutoring. All do-gooder stuff. I need to stay out of trouble. All for show." His jaw tightened, the sound of his teeth grinding stopping me. "I have to put on a show or I could lose everything. I can't... I can't lose my scholarship. I need the money."

I sensed his breakdown. "We'll do it. We can pull this off."

"I can't have you hate me. I'm fucking terrified you're going to hate me after this." His gray eyes met mine, the dark irises swirling in warning. "I'm a mess, Greta. Promise me you won't hate me. No matter what happens."

I shivered. His words scared the shit out of me, but we had already been through so much. *Why does he think I could hate him?* I found myself nodding, ignoring the twinge in my gut. "I promise."

"I'll owe you, forever. If we pull this off, I will do anything for you for the rest of your life." He pulled me into his arms, his familiar woodsy scent enveloping me. "Think of something you want."

"Aaron." My face pressed into his shirt, which muffled my voice. "I want this bullshit to go away. That is what I want."

He hummed in response. His athletic body relaxed beneath me. It began in his shoulders, his grip on me lessening as relief spread through him. "Were you afraid I was going to say no?"

"Yes. No. Either way you answered killed a little part of me. You don't know what you're agreeing to, Gabs."

"Gabs?" I wrinkled my nose. "I haven't heard that one in a hot minute. Where did that name come from, anyway?"

"Freshman year. We took a Twitter poll to see who talked more. You insisted I did, but the results said otherwise. You're gabby. Gabs." One side of his mouth turned up, the first smile I had seen on his handsome face. I forgot what playboy, hot-as-hell Aaron used to look like. This Aaron? He frowned and glowered everywhere. I missed my playboy.

"Ah, shit. I forgot about that." I shrugged his arms off me. "I call bullshit, by the way. You had hella more followers than me."

"Everyone knows who you are. You were Twitter-famous for a while," he replied with a smug smirk.

"God, you have a great smile." I meant to compliment him, not do the opposite. His lips went flat, all humor erased from his face. "Stop looking so forlorn. Jesus. We always have fun together."

"We should talk about the six months." He straightened. He chose to look at my closet door rather than my face. "Let's go over some ground rules."

"Ground rules? Come on, man." I punched a pillow, annoyed at him. "I think it's self-explanatory. We act normal behind closed doors, but out there in the scary world, we hold hands and shit."

"Essentially, yes. Hand holding, staged kissing, events and pictures." He met my eyes, all serious and dark. "You can't go on any dates or hook-up with anyone. The entire time. If it got out, the whole thing could blow up."

"I get it." I gulped. *Six. Months. Thank God I have the rabbit.*

"You can't put the arrangement into words anywhere. Did you already tell Callie?"

"Yes. She said she would've agreed to it, too. We care about you. We want to help." His eyes softened when he flicked his gaze in the direction of Callie's room. I sighed, stuck between smacking him or hugging him again. He reminded me of a damn puppy. "Plus, Ronnie, this will be good for me. To clean up *my* act for six months."

"Okay. She'll keep it quiet." He completely ignored my *clean up* comment. "The guys, they won't say anything either." He ran his hand over the back of his neck for quite some time. "We have to go on dates."

"I love food. Shouldn't be a problem. Hell, I deleted my dating apps. I'm done with dating for a while anyway since last weekend." I twisted the end of my hair, refusing to look at him. "What are you so worried about?"

"It won't be real."

Each word felt like ice in my chest. I knew it wouldn't be real, but him solidifying it hurt. Like, I would forget it was an act. He didn't do feelings. I had my own shit to deal with. It would be a monumental disaster. I chewed on my lip again. I'd need to buy more Chapstick at this rate. "Yeah, I got that. It's a fake relationship. Don't worry, I won't forget the situation."

"Good. I don't want to hurt you. You're important to me." He slammed each syllable between his teeth. An unwelcome, unfamiliar emotion began in my chest at his words.

"You won't hurt me," I replied with as much confidence I could muster. "Stop worrying about me, Ronnie. Focus on keeping your scholarship. The rest is just details."

"I'll try." He sighed, squeezing my knee for a second. "Thank you."

"When do we start?" I meant it as a joke, but those dark eyes twitched.

"Tomorrow. I'm posting we are making it official. Everyone on the team can assume we've been seeing each other the whole time we've been friends. Tomorrow it'll be on my social media, hopefully yours, too."

"Yeah. I'll make it official." I held up my phone and added a heart emoji next to his name. "Look. We are legit as fuck."

He let out a small laugh, standing up. "You seem to be handling it better than I am."

35

"It's easy when it's for you," I replied, my words visibly comforting him. He nodded, opening my door, but paused.

"I have one more condition for you." He grimaced, avoiding my eyes.

"I'm listening," I replied, my nerves on edge. We had already discussed a hell of a lot of rules and stipulations.

"My family *cannot* know about the ruse, no matter what happens." Those steely eyes bored into me, daring me to look away. I didn't. "It would destroy them."

"Okay."

"I mean it. I don't care what happens on campus, but they must never know. Coach and I figured out a way to prevent them from finding out about the pictures. They'll remain clueless."

"If that's what you want, I won't say a word." I motioned a key and lock on the side of my mouth. Then, I pretended to throw the key in the garbage. Yes, I knew I was acting like a five-year-old, but it made him give me a half-smile.

"I'm going to head out. I haven't talked to the guys yet. I need to." His hand twitched in my direction but fell to his side. "I'll stop by soon. I shattered my phone, so I'll get another one tomorrow."

"Be safe, Ronnie." I bit down on my bottom lip, feeling helpless. "We can do this."

"I hope so. My future is on the line." He looked at the ground, dragging one of his large feet back and forth over the doormat. "I owe you forever."

"Knock it off. I already agreed to it. Don't keep saying shit like that. It's happening." I patted his face. "Go home, boy-toy."

His lip twitched ever so slightly and he turned to leave. I watched him disappear into the night and wondered what the hell I'd signed up for. I'd wanted an adventure the week before, and I knew deep down this was going to be a hell of a ride.

Chapter Four

Aaron

"You're going to fucking *pretend* to date Greta for six months? And she agreed to it?" Tanner spat out his drink when I told him. "Have you lost your goddamn mind?"

"Most likely," I replied without emotion. Jeff and Zade exchanged a look, probably worried about what would happen. "I trust none of you will tell a soul. If you do, the entire thing blows up."

"We won't ruin it. That goes without saying, man." Jeff put his hand on my shoulder and gave me a brisk nod. "There is nothing else Coach can do? He came up with this idea?"

I scratched the back of my neck, preparing myself for their questions. Only Greta would have agreed to something without knowing all the facts. "His cousin worked for a PR firm in Hollywood and he called him before I came in. I guess faking relationships and creating staged promotions are normal. Professional athletes have to do publicity stunts all the time to appear boring or tied-down."

"You're telling me you won't sleep with anyone for six months? *Six* months, Aaron." Tanner slammed his fist on the table. "You won't be able to."

Zade jumped in, defending me. "He doesn't have a damn choice and we'll support him. He can use his goddamn hand every day and we'll buy him some spank magazines. Shit."

"Thanks, man." I raised a fist to Zade. He had my back and it felt good.

"I know your concern is for Greta, but we need to be supportive." Zade gave Tanner a scathing look. "I want to look into this bitch more. Who is she?"

"She doesn't use her own name. It's an alias." I'd already spent hours trying to find out who she was and had come up empty. "The pictures were taken over the past two years. Different dates. Times. All screen-shotted from Snapchat."

"Has she gotten any other athletes in trouble?" Jeff asked, already pulling out his laptop and typing away. "Is Coach overreacting to this?"

"No. She has local media attention. The last one was a football player, Antonio something. He got suspended for half a season because he was photographed doing cocaine."

"At least you didn't do that." Jeff gave a half-assed laugh. "I don't think any of us will argue, but can we vote no more parties here for a while?"

"Agreed."

"Same." Tanner eyed me, an odd expression crossing his face. "I want to add that no strangers or one-night stands here, either. I know that cramps on your style, Jeff, but I don't want anyone taking pictures of him. Or us. We could be next."

"Dude, I'm with ya." Jeff held up his hands. "I'm good with that. We'll take a semester off from partying. Hell, Coach will be happy as hell."

"Hah. Yeah. It's true." I took a swig of beer and felt a wave of emotion bubble up. These guys were my family. They'd helped raise money for my dad all last year, had my back when I went off the deep end, and now they were standing with me. *Fuck.* It was too much. "Thank you all. You've all been a hell of a friend the last couple of years."

"Anyone would do the same. It's part of being a team." Zade raised his beer. "We'll get through this. We'll find out who this girl is and destroy these pictures."

"Like, breaking and entering? No way. I can't have a scandal or I'm out." I tightened my grip on the bottle.

"I'm not beneath that. I'm not fucking joking," Zade added and scooted over to look at Jeff's laptop. "I know a computer hacker. I'll reach out to her."

"What? How?" Jeff turned to look incredulously at him. "You and computers? No way."

"Yeah. My sister's roommate wants to write code for video games. She's awesome. But with coding, she once told my sister and me she hacked into her school's grading system to change her grade in art class. This chick knows her shit and maybe she can find something out."

"Ah, I feel like I shouldn't be a witness." I slowly got to my feet, a small bubble of laughter escaping. "But, let me know what she finds out."

"I take that as approval. I'll call her first thing tomorrow."

I left them in the kitchen and proceeded to lock myself in my room. The silence calmed me. It was about the only damn thing I could control in my life at the moment and I latched on to it. *My dad. The pictures. Greta.*

My head spun, making a priority list. First thing up, making the fake girlfriend thing real. I logged into my computer and pulled up an old picture of Greta and me. We had been playing flag football at a tailgate and she'd jumped on my back, with her hands making a Hercules pose. If I didn't know us, we would look like a couple. I sent her direct message, knowing I couldn't text her.

Aaron: I'm posting us as a couple. What should I say so it's not suspicious? Everything I came up with sucks.

Greta: Hmm, you could say, 'the potion worked. I fell in looove.'

Greta: No. Maybe…'I finally manned up.'

Aaron: Yours are worse than mine. Lol.

Greta: Did you really laugh out loud, or did you snort?

Aaron: I released a bit of air. So, Sol.

Greta: Snort out loud. Classy, Ronnie.

Aaron: Gabs. Help me. How do we become a couple? I've never had a girlfriend, real or fake, before.

Greta: You depress me. Tag us in a relationship and post a picture. You don't need words.

Aaron: Okay. It's happening. I'm doing it.

Greta: Okay, I'm waiting. I'll accept it real quick. Be prepared for boob pics. Girls will be heartbroken.

Aaron: No phone, remember? I could do without the boob pics for a while.

Greta: Here's to help you through the night. (.) (.)

Aaron: ...did you just send me boob emojis?

Greta: Sure did, boo thang.

I stared at them, torn between laughing and retaliating with a dick emoji.

Aaron: SOL

Greta: You're welcome. Now, I accepted your tag. We are an item, hot stuff. I expect breakfast in the morning. I'll be ready at nine.

Aaron: I'll be there.

I waited, wanting to say something else, something more meaningful to her, but nothing came to mind. She had no idea how much she'd changed my life the year before. She had been my rock, refusing to treat me any differently after my dad's diagnosis. Even now, my life was in shambles and I was smiling at my computer. *Only Greta.*

Notifications were already popping up and I made a mistake and read two of them.

He actually committed to another human being? Is the world ending?

Damn. Hope this bitch doesn't mess with his game.

I shut the computer, the short-lived happiness gone. I succumbed to my thoughts and fell asleep thinking about blonde hair and baseball.

* * * *

I managed to make it to the phone store right when it opened and replaced the shattered iPhone. *Fuck the cloud and pictures.* I would never be able to relax around a camera for the rest of my life. I cringed, the anticipation of hearing from my coach stifling me. He wouldn't meet them until noon. In three long, excruciating hours.

I texted Greta that I was on my way and nerves zinged through me. *What the fuck? Why am I nervous?* It was breakfast. We got breakfast all the damn time. I parked, the walk up the stairs slow and torturous. I knocked, putting my hands in my jean pockets after.

Greta opened the door, smiling widely. "Hey, boy-toy. Where are you taking me for our lavish breakfast date?"

"IHOP." I took her hand, her vanilla lotion subtle. It smelled amazing.

"Hmm. Am I too overdressed? You're rocking the skater look again." She motioned at my jeans and black v-neck. I checked out her outfit and admired her long, never-ending legs. She always wore dresses, so I wouldn't have considered it overdressed.

"You look great." I pulled her down the stairs and opened the passenger door for her. "You always look good, G."

"Aw, thanks, pookie."

"Pookie?" I paused, giving her an irritated glare. "Hell, no."

"I'm trying out nicknames. I would have a nickname if you were my boyfriend." She raised her eyebrows, making me feel like a dumbass.

"You already call me A-a-ron and Ronnie. Those are nicknames."

"No shit, Sherlock." She chuckled. "Friend nicknames. I wouldn't be calling my sex toy Ronnie. It is the least sexy name alive."

I frowned. It was unsexy. "Fair enough. But Pookie isn't it."

"Then back to the drawing board. Stop stalling. Mama needs some pancakes." She patted her belly and pushed me out of the way. She then shut the door in my face. I laughed. God, it felt good.

I slid into the driver seat and saw her studying me with one lip sucked into her mouth. "What?"

"Just being honest here, but it literally looks like you have a stick shoved up your ass. No one is going to believe this is real." She pursed her lips and shook her head. "Nope. Major stick in the ass face going on."

"That isn't a thing." I started the car, but she put her hand on my leg. I looked at it, taking my time turning toward her again.

"Ronnie, you need some fun in your life. Do you trust me?"

"Yes," I said without question. "Why?"

"Let me drive. I have an idea." She stuck out her lip, pouting. Those damn brown eyes didn't help either. I was pretty much ruining her life for six months so, sure, I could let her do whatever the fuck she wanted.

"Okay." I undid my buckle and traded spots with her. "What's your idea?"

"Um, first. What the hell? You've never agreed to let me drive your car in over two years. You must have a big stick up there, messing with your brain." She clapped her hands. "Second, I'm fucking pumped to drive your SUV. I love it."

"Don't crash it. I'll kill you."

"Nah. You won't. You need me alive for six months."

"And not a day longer," I joked, earning a huge smile from her. "What? I can joke around."

"I've missed your dumbass jokes and sarcasm. Do you have anywhere you need to be today?"

"Nope. Off weekend. Coach meets with the director at noon. He'll call when he has news."

"Perfect. I know how to distract you." She put the car into drive and took off down one of the country roads. If she headed back to the biker bar, I didn't know what the hell I would do. She turned on the radio, an old rap song coming on. She rapped with the beat. Every. Single. Word.

I watched, amused at how her hands made aggressive motions while she sang. She held up an imaginary microphone to me at one of the more famous parts and her 'stick up the ass' comment caused me to join her. I rapped with Snoop Dog at nine in the morning in the middle of the country.

If that didn't describe Greta, nothing did. I chuckled, and the car jerked to the left a little. "Use two hands, Gabs."

"Well, forgive me. I heard you laugh and it startled me. I forgot how it sounded."

"God, you're a pain in the ass." I found myself smiling. It felt weird at first, but it became easier the longer we were in the car. We played the 'would you rather' game, and her questions got weird, real fast.

Would you rather eat your hand, or never play baseball again?
Would you rather go back in time, or see the future?
Would you rather fart forever, or continually pee?
Would you rather walk in on your parents doing it, or have them walk in on you?
Would you rather use sand paper as toilet paper, or vinegar as eye drops?

"Where are you taking us? We are miles away from campus and, well, civilization." We passed a sign that said we were in a village.

"Almost there. Trust me, pooks, you'll have fun." She hummed to herself and finally turned into a parking lot. Hundreds of cars were already there. Lines of people ran into the entrance. Balloons, rides, horses and cotton candy filled the air with sound and noise. She'd taken me to a fair.

"Greta?"

"I don't care what you think. You're my fake boyfriend and a fake boyfriend goes to the fair. He buys his girlfriend cotton candy and holds her hand on rides." She turned off the engine and crossed her arms, studying me. "You love rides, Ronnie. Don't get shy on me."

"No. I'm not shy. I'm surprised, that's all." I grinned, her excitement getting me eager. "I haven't been to a fair this big since I was a kid."

"Well, let's get the hell in there!" She cheered, jumping out of the car. I followed her crazy ass into the line and laughed when she pointed out all the actors on stilts. "Look, Aaron. Ah! The clown is creepy as hell."

We got to the stand and I graciously declined her offer to pay. "Gabs, I'm buying."

"It's my treat. You buy the food, big guy." She patted my chest and shoved her credit card at the young guy. "Let me treat you, hot stuff."

I tried again to pay, but the schmuck had already run her card. The gesture meant a lot to me. I knew how tight money was for her. She handed me my ticket and I pulled her in for a quick hug. "You didn't need to do that. Thank you."

"You're welcome." She then smacked my ass with a wild grin. "I wanted to check to see if the stick came out yet. It's almost there."

"God." I laughed, grabbing hold of her hand to slow her down and to get used to the act. "Let me take a picture of us before we get high on sugar."

"Our first selfie." She pressed her cheek to the side of mine, and I snapped a picture of us. "Here's to day one of one hundred and eighty."

Chapter Five

Greta

We wandered around the fairground for an hour without getting on a ride. I was desperate to ride the tilt-a-whirl. We passed it three times, Aaron ignoring it each time. He still held on to my hand, and I couldn't say it wasn't pleasant. His hand engulfed mine, his callouses feeling good against my soft skin. Neither one of us were a hand holder, but it wasn't for my lack of trying. I cringed, a flash of Todd's face intruding. *No, thank you. Goodbye, Todd.*

"Ronnie, we are going on that ride." I hit his hip with mine. "It'll be fun."

"I'm having plenty of fun without the metal of doom ride." He shaded his eyes and looked all the way to the top of it. "I prefer to live. How about we do a different one?"

"I'm doing you a favor. You do *this* one for me." I jutted my chin out at him, challenging him to deny the fact. He clearly didn't care. He just shook his head.

"Chickenshit." I released his hand and was about to head to a different one, but his arms come around my neck. My back pressed to his chest, his head resting on the spot between my neck and shoulder. I shivered and broke out in goosebumps. He'd never had any problem getting in my personal space. Ever. But the fake-girlfriend shit made me nervous. Jumpy. Paranoid. *Ugh, pull yourself together.*

His strong, tight body tensed against me. He could break me with one squeeze if he wanted. He was that strong. And those massive biceps trapped me, preventing me from taking another step toward. I gulped, wiggling against him to try to escape. It was a pathetic attempt.

"Nice try, shrimp."

"Let me go, you barbarian!" I swung my legs up, but a low chuckle began in his belly. "Are you laughing at me right now?"

"Yes. You're all arms and legs. No muscle."

"Thanks, asshole," I said to his forearm. The forearm that was close enough to bite. An idea came to me. He lowered his mouth to my ear and I forgot my thought.

"Did you or did you not call me a chickenshit?" he whispered, his breath tingling my ear.

"Uh-huh." I gulped. I knew exactly what I'd said and what his reaction would be. Aaron had two weaknesses—well, just one now. They used to be competition and women. But, women were off-limits for six months, so his competitive streak had to be on high alert, desperate for anything. It worked. *Yes!*

49

"Oh. Hell. No." He then pulled on my earlobe with his fingers and kept his arm around me. "We are going on that *fucking* ride. But I pick the next activity."

"Deal. Perfect, actually." I grinned a little too wide.

He ignored my smile, his sole focus on surviving the ride. "And, if I puke all over you, I will laugh."

"You're doing it?" I yelled in excitement. "Yes!"

"You used my weakness on me. I never should've told you that story with that nickname." He tickled my side, making me jump into the air. I swatted his hand away as we approached the entrance.

"Guess you shouldn't have." I giggled, my heart hammering. The ride looked wicked. The guy motioned for us to enter once it stopped and we did. We went into a carriage, the only protection a small metal bar over our legs. Aaron's leg bounced, and he tapped the bar over and over. "You good, big guy?"

"Scared as fuck." He kept his eyes closed. I put my hand over his in a reassuring squeeze. It didn't work. "If we die, I'm going to haunt your dumb ass."

"I expect nothing less." I screamed when the carriage was lifted upward. We spun, over and over, each one picking up speed. *"Oh my god!"*

"Ah!" Aaron screeched, releasing a string of cuss words I didn't know he knew. He screamed again, his pitch almost higher than mine. It went on and on, the swooping sensation in my gut repeating. My adrenaline kicked in and when we stopped, I had tears in my eyes.

"Fuck. Fuck. No." Aaron mumbled over and over. He fidgeted with the metal bar. I hurried with mine, trying to get out as fast as I could. It wasn't fast enough, because Aaron picked me up from the waist and dragged my ass outside. "You're crazy. Fucking nuts. No. No more."

He set me down on a bench and paced aggressively in front of me. "Greta."

"You are cracking me up right now." I shook with laughter, his face killing me. "Do you need a pill or something?"

"Do I need a pill? Oh my god. That was... Torture. Prison. Hell. All the above. My heart went through my asshole, G. *Through my asshole!*"

His yelling stirred the families around us and I got up to drag him away. "Come on, you need a soda."

"I need something more than that. I almost died." He held his stomach in his hands and followed me toward the food court.

"Always so dramatic. At least you're pretty." I found a stand with soda and ordered him one. He sat at a table far away from everyone with his head in his hands. If I was a total asshole, I would've laughed. I had never seen anyone act like that from a ride. "I brought you a soda, princess."

He looked up with a pale face and took it immediately. "Thank you."

"My bad. I guess we won't do any more rides. And I won't use your safe word." I pursed my lips at him and waited for color to come back to his face. Slowly, it returned to its normal shade and he looked like himself again.

"Fun fact. I hate upside-down rides."

"Uh, yeah. I noticed. Thank you." I swatted away a bee that landed on the table. "Maybe I should apologize for making you go on it."

"I don't forgive you. I'll get you back. I just need my equilibrium restored first." He narrowed his eyes in a threat and I flinched. He *would* seek revenge.

"Did I make today worse?"

"Nah." He managed a tight smile. "I definitely lost the stick up my ass in there. It fell out during a flip."

"Funny guy."

He cleared his throat and took another sip. "How am I doing so far?"

"In what context? The rides are kicking your ass."

"No shit. Asshole." He shook his head. "I meant, boyfriend-wise. Am I doing okay?"

"Uh, A-a-ron, you haven't done anything boyfriend-y besides the hand holding. Everything else is normal you." I frowned, trying to figure out what was fake or real. *Shit. Is the whole six months going to be like this? Me questioning everything?*

"Hmm." He shifted in his chair, his shoulders stiffening. "I might need some help as this moves forward."

"Help with the act?"

"I don't know what I'm doing." He refused to meet my eyes, instead focusing on a cornfield. *Cool, glad the cornfield is more interesting.*

"You don't know how to be a boyfriend. That's what you're saying." I clarified.

"Yeah. I know the premise of one. But the rules are shaky." He ran his tongue over his bottom lip and checked out the group of girls three tables over. I chuckled, although a flash of irritation went through me.

"Ronnie, you can't blatantly stare at other girls if you are in a relationship. Well, if you are with the girl, you don't eyeball someone else. Men are pigs sometimes."

He frowned, bringing his gaze back to me with a focused look. "Okay. What else?"

"God, I'm not the best person for this." I took a much-needed swig of drink. It went down real smooth. The temperature had risen quite a bit since we arrived. "You have the hand holding and pictures down. Thank god, we get along well enough it shouldn't be too weird when we hang out in public."

"Should I be affectionate?" His dark brows came together, a cute line forming right in the center. "Do I need a pet name for you, too?"

"Hmm. Pet name, uh, not really. Affection, you are a touchy person as it is. We might have to stage a kiss. Are you prepared for that?"

His gray gaze went back and forth between my eyes, slowly dragging down my face. It landed on my mouth, his nostrils flaring for just a second. "I'll be fine. Will you?"

"Oh, pookie." I shook off the butterflies in my belly and found my inner badass. "I will handle you just fine. I know how to kiss."

"Is that so?" He bit down on his bottom lip, a smirk forming. "I'm curious now."

"I'm sure you are." I stood and pointed toward the petting zoo. "Are you going to lose your shit over baby animals, too?"

"Fuck off, Pita." He joined me and conjoined our hands, but a way-too-smug look formed on his face.

"Pita?"

"Yeah. I figured out your nickname. Pain In The Ass." He cackled at his own joke, the sound echoing around us. "Pita."

* * * *

I walked into work later that night and wished I owned ear plugs. The garage band duo that took the stage sucked. They weren't bad to look at, but their talent was lacking. They'd clearly left it at home. I shook my head, watched them for a song or two, and went to wipe down the bar. We had a steady stream of customers come in, order two pitchers, because, hell, one was a damn penny, and leave. My boss and manager, Claude — which was his *legit* name — waved me over.

"What's up, Sir Claude?" I teased him every chance I got. To make things worse, he was an art major. An art major named Claude who managed a bar and taught painting classes. He needed a mustache and to speak French and he would fit the entire stereotype.

"Whiskey and women suck," he said, without emotion.

"I don't know if you're coming out to me right now, giving up whiskey for life or just making a casual observation." I had my hands on my hips, lips pursed. Claude was special and often lacked social skills or the ability to read a mood. I had zero clue how he'd become a manager at a bar, in a college town, filled with young co-eds. But it wasn't my place to judge.

"You and your charming wit," he said, again without showing emotion. His large lips pressed in a flat line. "I need your help. Again."

"Name it, Claude with a hot bod." I tried out new nicknames on him every shift I had He vehemently refused C-Man because it sounded like semen, and he scoffed at Mod-Claude. There was also Clotty the Hotty, Claude-Wad and C-Nut. I might not have been the best at coming up with nicknames. This one, though, Claude with the hot bod, got one of his firm lips to quirk up. That was like scoring a touchdown the last minute of the game on a Hail Mary pass.

"I need you to play again." He glanced at the stage and back to me. "You are great and people are leaving. This is the fourth time a band has driven people out!"

"True. For a Saturday night in summer, a lot of people came in." I ran my fingers over my bottom lip, thinking about playing. *Can I do it? Do I want to?*

"Sure. But you have a great voice. We need talented people. Damn!" His eyes grew wide and his voice lowered like he was telling me the dirtiest secret of all time. "We're competing against the bar down the road, Geo's."

I bit back a smile. His face told me this was not the time to laugh at him. I nodded, hoping my enthusiasm seemed real. "Competing in what?"

"Numbers, Greta, numbers." He scoffed, quite a burst of emotion from Claude the Robot. I liked that one.

"Do you have a guitar I can play or something? I can't just sing. Last time I borrowed one of the musicians'." I could, but I never felt comfortable enough to. I wished Callie had magically appeared with me. We'd sung in a band together in high school and having someone else on stage boosted my confidence. I had no qualms about how I looked. I knew what assets I had and could play up. But my voice…it crossed the overexposed line where all my vulnerabilities came to light. I thrived on the adrenaline, but choked on the nerves.

"I don't know." He raised his hands in the air. "Get on stage. Sing. Tell jokes. I don't care, but go up there." He walked with his awkward gait to the gentlemen on the stage, pointed to me a couple of times and they all three looked at me. *Aw, hell.*

I poured myself a whiskey sour and resigned myself to an uncomfortable open-mic night. I never minded attention and sometimes I even enjoyed it. I had no doubt I wouldn't enjoy it tonight, though. Since the news about Aaron and I dating had broken, students I'd never met said hello to me. Girls were torn between high-fiving me or punching me in the cooter. Aaron had been a celebrity here, still was, and I'd 'taken him' from the other girls. *Fuck that. He belongs to no one. Goddamn cleat chasers.*

There were still a handful of patrons in the normally booming bar. Maybe twenty people sat in the various dimly lit booths. The dark would help. I could sing if I knew a crowd wasn't gawking at me.

One of the band guys, this one with a long dark beard, nodded at me when I got on stage. The shorter one with Clark Kent glasses held out his hand. "Hi. I didn't know you played, too."

I shook it with an amused expression. "Yup. Surprise."

"Claude said he messed up scheduling and hoped we could split the night with you. We got paid and are heading out now. Sorry if we angered ya," Clark Kent said with a wide smile. He was cute—a little dorky, but still cute. I grinned like it was no big deal and I wasn't playing into my manipulative boss.

"Don't even worry about it. Not a big crowd tonight anyway. Get out now before it gets super quiet and weird." I took a sip of my drink and fanned my lashes at them. Call it cocky or just self-aware, but I knew they were affected by my looks. They blushed, the bearded one looking at the ground before meeting my eyes. I put my hand on the shorter one's forearm. "Would either of you mind if I borrowed your guitar for a song or two? I'm chickening out. I thought—" I paused for effect. "I thought I could handle just singing, but now I'm flustered."

"Of course. It'll take us a bit to load up our stuff. Have at it." Clark Kent handed me his acoustic. I took it and thanked him with promises for free drinks. He blushed, his hand now resting on my arm. They left me with smiles and I had no choice but to take the seat on stage. I tuned the guitar to a key I liked and began with an old acoustic version of one of my favorite Rolling Stones songs. I closed my eyes and strummed and sang. When I performed, or sang, I got lost in my thoughts. It was pure bliss where nothing could touch me. I escaped from worrying about my future, Aaron, my lack of love life, my failures, my parents' finances, and I just played.

Chapter Six

Aaron

My thighs burned. Sweat poured down my back. Heat seemed to rise from the ground and someone was cutting grass. This was my favorite thing in the entire world. The smell. The air. The motions. It calmed me when the world seemed to spin faster.

"Get your head out of your ass. Take more. Move faster. Let's go!" Coach barked at me. I didn't have time to react before I heard the spin of the ball coming at me. I didn't think. I reacted.

I dove to the right, trapping the ball in my glove and whipping it to first from my knees. He nodded in approval and I ate it up. A nod was enough from him — it was practically a standing ovation.

"Nice one," Jeff yelled from behind home plate, adorned in his catching gear. "Keep that shit up next game, eh?"

"Ten dollars I will," I shouted back, the guys around me laughing. They all knew Jeff and I were friends, but they also knew we gave each other shit any chance we got. "Let's amp it up. For every pass ball you get, you have to call me Captain."

"Fuck that."

"Gentlemen! Unless you want to run the rest of practice, focus," Coach hollered, bringing us back to the present. Jeff and I shared a look, though. The bet was on. We took hundreds of grounders and ran through plays I had dreamed about since I was six. Sweat poured out of us as the Midwestern sun and humidity did its damage. By the time we'd finished practice, I'd passed exhaustion hours ago.

"I'm so fucking thankful we got the weekend free. I needed those three days." Jeff put his hand on my shoulder and patted me in his motherly way. He took the team captain role to heart and, although I would never tell him, I admired the hell out of him. His upbeat attitude kept our team together. "You did good, Hilly."

"Thanks. I felt fucking good." I chugged a water and saw Tanner walking up to us. "How's your arm doing, Tan?"

"No pinching. No pain. I'm all good, baby!" His grin took up his entire face and he looked way too damn chipper after the killer of a practice we'd just had. "I'm ready to party and start my junior year with a bang."

"Yeah? What you thinking?" Jeff looked on, a smile forming. "It's been a while since we went to one. That okay, Hilly?"

I knew he was asking because he cared. I shrugged. "Ain't no thang."

"Hell, yeah." Jeff and Tanner fist-bumped and hollered over to Zade. He was getting his arm stretched by our trainer, Nicole. I saw Callie walk by a couple of times, but she had her hands full every time. If anyone would've pinned down Zade, it was Callie. "Z!"

He looked up and shook his head, pointing to Nicole. We all laughed. She was a little, strong woman with short hair. She loved her family more than anything in the world and we were terrified of her. If she said no eating potatoes and one of us did, she would know. And when a player lied to her... I cringed. She would make him pay majorly for it. I heard a rumor one time that a freshman snuck soda into the dugout. She laughed while she made him run five minutes on the highest speed. She was wicked.

"You sure you're okay with us going to a party?" Jeff asked, a little while later after we'd all showered. "I know we talked about not throwing them. But I'm itching for a drink and bad decisions."

"Bro, don't worry about it. My head is in a different place now. I'm good with it." I hit his back this time. "I appreciate it, though, you asking me."

"Any word from Coach about your scholarship?"

I clutched the water bottle tighter. "He confirmed I won't be losing it yet. We aren't in season. I'm twenty-one. The one picture, you know which one, can't prove it's me. If I have a slap on the wrist, I'll be suspended for a third of the season."

His eyebrows came together tight, as if he was in pain, and I felt a sense of loyalty that couldn't be faked. "God. I still can't believe this is happening."

"I've accepted what it is." I lied. I still slept like shit and thought about saying *fuck it* every second. "I'll hang with Greta tonight. You guys go out."

"Okay, well, catch ya later, man." He took off and I laughed. His attempt at finding a girlfriend had blown up and it was funny as hell. He didn't realize a guy had to be monogamous *and* truthful during the process. I shook my head. *What a dumbass.*

"How's Greta doing? I haven't seen her in a while." Tanner snuck up behind me as I took off walking. He was always such a quiet guy, despite his size.

"She's the same." I turned to him with an eyebrow raised. Greta, Tanner and I had been inseparable freshman year and now it seemed it was just Greta and me. Tanner was a brother from another mother, but he'd distanced himself and I had no idea why or how to ask about it. My drama made everything worse, and a tinge of regret filled me.

"I meant, how is she doing with *everything*?"

I nodded, understanding his words. *The fake arrangement.* The third day of being in a fake relationship with Greta, our spunky third musketeer. "I haven't seen her since Saturday, actually. I'm stopping by the bar tonight. I think she's handling it well."

He didn't reply, instead twisting his mouth into a grimace. Then his expression changed and a smug smile appeared. "You used to fuck with the Kappas, right? Should I head to their summer bash or Thetas?"

"Tough call." I thought about the last two years, how I'd acted and how I'd used my baseball status to hook up. *God, I suck.* "Kappas were clingy but easy on the eyes. Real easy. Thetas know how to drink, man. What kind of night you wanting?" Our normal banter came back like nothing had changed. I went with it. I had enough shit going on in my mind that I couldn't afford to worry about friendships.

"Like I need to say it? No promises, no relationships. I have all this energy and I want to release it." He clapped his hands with a whistle and his gaze followed the girls who walked by us. "Damn. They were... Damn."

"Must be getting close to move-in day." I, too, had an energy I couldn't explain even though my body had nothing left to give. It was a different type of energy. The kind I used to get the year before that caused me to party my ass off and sleep with anyone. I needed to get some control. I barely grasped it now.

"Hell, yeah it is. New girls, new meat. I can't wait to explore the options. Man, I'm realizing that I didn't take enough advantage of my baseball status the past two years, like you."

"Pretty sure we have. Multiple times. Remember those girls who flashed us for no reason? That was great." I closed my eyes, picturing it. "They were fucking hot."

"Didn't you sleep with two of them that night?" He laughed when I nodded. "Damn, you're a dog, Aaron." *Yeah, I used to be.*

Tanner and I played videogames for a good three hours before they began prepping to head to the party. I chose to run some errands but thought about Greta. I called her, even though I knew she hated phone calls.

"This better be good, pookie," she answered, her annoyance clear as day.

"Hey to you, too, Pita." I smiled, picturing her flipping me off. "I was actually calling to see if you wanted to run to the store with me. I'm running to get some food and shit. I know you don't have a car." I stayed in Park, waiting to see what direction I needed to head.

"Damn it. I hate it when you're nice and I'm the asshole." She covered the phone and said something to whoever she was with. "Sure. I could use some things."

"Where you at? Home?"

"I'll text you the address. Bye."

I waited for a text to pop up and seconds later it did. *Odd.* I had never been to that area of town before and couldn't wait to bombard her with questions. If she was somewhere dangerous again, I swore I'd lose it. My fingers hurt, I pressed so hard on the wheel. *I'll kill her. I mean it, too.*

I followed the directions to an old music shop and nodded in understanding. She was here for the guitar parts and what not. I knew she had been wanting one for a while and I felt bad I hadn't thought to get her one.

I texted her to come out, but I saw her through the window. She stood, confident as hell, her blonde locks hanging in loose curls down her back. I always thought hers was beautiful. I loved hair on women, the longer and curlier the better. It was a weakness of mine and about the only thing that differentiated girls for me. I was seconds away from honking when I saw a tall figure approach her. She smiled up at him and he bent in for a hug. His hands went around her to stay right above her ass.

Two things flew through my mind. The first was *who the fuck is this guy?* The second, *why do I want to punch his face?* My grip tightened on the wheel and I took a deep breath, envisioning how good it would feel to sock him. This made zero fucking sense. I didn't have time to react before she burst through the door with a wide smile. My eyes stayed on the guy, though.

"Hey, Hilly." Her voice was a little breathless and her cheeks a little red. "Thanks for inviting me along. You know I always put off groceries until the last minute."

"Sure." I had no fucking reason to be mad at her. It was a hug. A fucking hug. I cleared my throat, forcing the irritation out of it. "What were you up to?"

"Ah, yes. The reasonable question. Let's see… remember me saying a mutual friend owned a music shop?" She pulled her legs up so her arms were around them. She could fit about anywhere with her tiny build and I guess I'd never noticed before how small she was.

"Sure." I racked my brain, not sure what she was talking about, when it hit me. "Wait. Yes. I recall that conversation. You found a nice guitar?"

"Yes." She bit back a laugh and I looked over at her quickly. "I can come get it in two days. My fingers are dying to play. Did I tell you I played again Saturday?"

"Yeah?" I kept my eyes on the road, but glanced at her at the lights. Whenever she talked about music, her voice rose and got all giddy. It was cute. She gabbed and gabbed about playing and how Clyde wanted her to perform every week and he would pay her. I nodded, enjoying her company more than she knew.

"So, you'll come?"

"Remind me what I'm agreeing to again." My muscles clenched at how obvious my daydreaming had been. She knew me, though. She just hit my shoulder and scoffed. "Gabs, you talk a lot. I got lost."

"You can be such a fuckstick." She crossed her arms and chose to look out of the window rather than at my face.

"Regardless of what you invited me to, I'll be there," I admitted. It didn't matter what it was.

"Okay." She paused, dragging her finger over her sandals in such an innocent way. "Maybe you're not a complete fuckstick."

I laughed at that, hard enough to hit the steering wheel. "Your use of colorful vocabulary is entertaining. But you insult me a lot."

"It's good for your ego." She shrugged. "But I'm going to play once a week at the bar, not sure if it's a weekend or weeknight. I'm starting in two weeks and they are going to promote it on social media and everything."

We came to another light and I shifted to look at her. She nibbled her lip, pulling on the ends of her nails. *Nervous.* "G, that's impressive."

"I don't know," she mumbled and cracked her neck a couple of times. "What if I suck?"

"What if you don't?" I put my hand on her thigh, its creamy color contrasting with my tan hand. I squeezed for five seconds then gently released it. "My fake girlfriend and *real* best friend kicks ass. I'll be at every show."

"Damn it, Aaron. Sometimes you suck and sometimes you say the sweetest things." She sniffed.

"I'm not sweet."

She bit her cheek and let out a small laugh. "I know *that.* You're quite barbaric, most of the time. Childish other times. Annoying. Whore-y. I can keep going."

"Settle down." I pulled into the parking lot and waited for her to get out before continuing. "I'm awesome. Don't forget that."

She scrunched her nose and let out an exasperated sigh. "And sure, you're awesome and all that jazz."

I held the door for her entering the store. "I'll grab a cart."

"Cool. But fake or real, relationships are not your thing." She shoved my arm. "I would compare it to you asking me how to swing a bat."

"Am I that awful?" I stuck my lip out and pouted. "You're hurtful."

"Your ego can handle it, champ." She smacked my ass and walked ahead of the cart. "You're allergic to relationships. Plain and simple."

"I might be slightly allergic to them. I hear there are good allergy medicines, though. Should we take a detour to the medicine aisle?" I pointed in the direction and felt mollified when she laughed.

"Good one." She threw in some cereal boxes and girlie shit I had no business to figure out. I watched her take stuff, grabbing things from my own list when we walked by them. "You're lucky we are such good friends, actually. I get asked about ten times a day about you, dude. I don't know how you handle the attention."

I paused, my hand inches away from snatching a jar of protein powder. She leaned on the cart with an apprehensive look on her face. My core tightened. *Is she already regretting this? Am I the biggest asshole on the planet?*

"I *am* lucky. Please know I think about it every day. I'm not sleeping," I admitted, avoiding her stare. I vowed to do anything for her. Anything.

"Hmm." She eyed me for a second and a small smile broke out. "Do you know what helps me sleep?"

"Porn?" I tried, a sliver of our old banter sneaking out. It was easy to be myself with her. "Nah, never mind. You don't look the type."

"Jesus." She widened her eyes at me, aggressively telling me something without words. It didn't work and she caved. "Try wearing socks to bed."

"Uh, what?" There was no way she said that. No fucking way. "Socks won't help."

"Trust me. My mom always made me grab a huge pair of fuzzy socks when I couldn't sleep. I remember these obnoxious blue polka dot ones that looked ridiculous. I wore them and bam, I slept like a little bitch."

"Do you still wear these monstrosities?" I fought a smile. Young Greta, all legs and arms and wearing those socks, was a fun picture. "Please say you *just* wear socks to bed."

"Aaron Hill. Do I detect flirting?" With a hand on her hip, she stopped the cart.

"Maybe." I winked at her, and she barreled at me. Her hands went around my waist and she about knocked the wind out of me. "G, what the hell?"

"I've missed the shit out of your stupid flirting and perverted jokes. I missed them so much."

I wrapped my arms around her small body and enjoyed her sweet scent. I had always loved women. All types. Curvy. Athletic. Willowy. What I'd never had before was complete trust and admiration for them — until Greta. I ran my hand down her back, pulling the ends of her long blonde hair. An uncomfortable pit formed and, like I had done countless times before, I needed to ruin the moment. I was a self-sabotager. "Are you PMSing? You've hugged me quite a lot the past week."

She broke the hug, pushing me away. "And you're back to being a fuckstick."

Chapter Seven

Greta

Why am I searching for fuzzy socks online at two in the morning? That's right. I chose to drink way too much coffee and my heart started racing in circles. If I stopped breathing for a second, I could literally hear each beat slam into my chest. I clicked through picture after picture, searching for the perfect pair. It was the best distraction instead of reading my parents' email. They were downsizing their house, moving to a cheaper side of town. Everything was fine, they said. They'd just made some tough decisions. They wanted me to create an Excel sheet of monthly expenses to see how they could contribute.

No. I would not have them lose any more money. My brother Corbin deserved it more. His wretched ex-wife had dragged the divorce out for so long I'd forgotten what it was like to not have to ask about it. My head pounded, my poor speeding heart going into overdrive.

Socks it was. Socks were happy. Socks were fluffy.

I clicked past hot pink ones with capes, purple ones with zippers and clapped when I saw the perfect pair. They were dark and light brown, the shape of bear paws. They'd even added little claws on the front. I ordered them without a second thought and couldn't wait to see his face. I wondered if he still couldn't sleep from our conversation earlier that week and took a chance texting him.

Greta: Are you up?

Aaron: Yes. Why are you up? Don't you tutor in the morning?

Greta: Ugh. Yes. My dumb ass drank a little too much coffee. Anyway. I bought you a present. I did one-day delivery. You should get it tomorrow.

Aaron: I don't need a gift.

Greta: Don't worry. It's nothing big. It might be a bit em-bear-assing.

Aaron: You're so odd.

Greta: Yeah, you love me though.

Aaron: Yes. Go to sleep, Pita.

Greta: I can't. I tried, trust me. I've reorganized my entire room, the kitchen, planned out my meals for the next month and created a fifteen-year plan.

Aaron: Jesus.

I laughed, picturing him pinching his nose at me. Whenever he made that face, he transformed into a curmudgeon and I got a picture of what he would look like in fifty years' time. My phone rang in my hand, making me jump. "Hello?"

"What's your fifteen-year plan?" His gruff voice sounded bogged down with exhaustion.

"Hello to you, too." I laughed, sinking farther into my bed. I was not a stranger to Aaron's late-night calls. They'd happened a bit the year before after his dad's diagnosis. But this time, he sounded different. "You actually want to hear this?"

"Yes. I'm curious," he replied, the deep timbre of his voice affecting me. *What the hell?*

"Well." I cleared my throat. "I'll be in my thirties. I want at least two kids, maybe three. I hope to be working in an awesome district that supports teachers. I've always wanted dogs and a house with toys everywhere. Not messy, but lived in. Location isn't that important. My hunk of a husband will have abs of gold and will cook for me. We both know I can't cook for shit. Hmm."

He didn't reply, but I heard him breathing. So, I kept gabbing. I talked about the names of kids I wanted. I told him my wish to maybe be a principal, a goal I'd never told my parents. I loved the concept of having a huge impact on the young lives of students. I spoke about picnics and vacations, grilling out on the weekends, and plants. Ever since Sims had come out, I'd spent hours as a kid designing the most badass houses with impeccable landscaping. Thinking I'd gone a little too far, I stopped. "You haven't said a word. You must think I'm batshit crazy."

I heard a snore. The asshole had fallen asleep listening to me talk. I hung up, not mad although not any calmer than before the call. Hopefully he didn't hear about the last part. Not many people admitted to playing Sims for hours on end. *Oh, well.*

Although I felt a little more tired, sleep was hours away. I tried counting backward from one hundred. Didn't work at all. *I guess socks it is.* I found my oldest, comfiest pair and succumbed to the fact that I would feel like hell and look like death the following morning. I hoped the kids didn't judge me too much.

The blaring sound of my alarm woke me way too soon. I hated that sound. I wanted to murder it. But I had responsibilities and shit. I could do this adult thing. *Yeah right. You avoided making a budget and bought socks. You suck ass.*

Cool. I was so sleep deprived I was holding full conversations in my head. I needed coffee. *Shit, do I have a coffee addiction?*

Today would be the first of a semester-long partnership with a local elementary school where I would come in every Monday morning to tutor some fifth graders. I'd volunteered there twice a month the year before, this year expanding to actual lessons. *Eek!* I was so excited. I just hoped the dark circles under my eyes didn't make me look like a vampire.

I chose a red polka-dot dress that fell to my knees. It was extremely comfortable to bend down and work with the kids but also didn't show too much skin. I called it one of my professional yet perky outfits. Yes, I named sections of my closet.

"Callie, you still there?" I shouted into the living room that connected our bedrooms. "Did you make coffee?"

No reply. I prayed, wished, hoped she'd started the coffee. I needed to leave now and although my addiction was part of the problem, nothing else would get me through the next four hours. "Shit."

The pot sat empty, the depressing sight almost making me cry. Almost. I poured a cold glass of water and surrendered to the fact my eyelids would feel like weights. My teacher bag said *Ms. Aske* in bold letters, a gift my brother had bought me last year when I declared my major. I picked it up and mapped out the quickest way to walk there. It would take a good twenty minutes.

I locked the door, putting on my favorite playlist. Two-thousands R and B. Nothing was better. I would fight whoever thought differently. The most perfect wave of coffee hit my nose, and I sniffed the air. Maybe the neighbors had brewed some.

"Greta?"

Aaron sat at the end of the stairs, holding not one, but four cups of coffee in one of those cup holders. Bless his heart. He was my hero. "You brought me coffee? Please say I can have some."

"I brought you coffee. Yeah." He grinned sheepishly. "I've seen you order about ten different things. I never know what your actual favorite is."

"It depends on my mood," I whispered, but I had a tunnel vision thing going on. The dark, rich smell drew me in like a wizard. "I don't know why you're here right now. I don't care. All I know is I could literally kiss you for bringing me coffee."

He chuckled, pointing to the first one. "This one's black. I think this is a latte or something. This is a chai tea and the last one is a gingerbread one."

My hands wrapped around the latte and I took a large, full sip. "Fuck. This is perfect."

He watched me drink my coffee, his gray eyes softening at me. "This is my way of saying thank you."

"For what?" I managed to get out, but I went back for more. Coffee was the light and I was the moth.

"Talking to me last night. I had a hell of a day. I'm real sorry about falling asleep." He cringed and ran his hand over his face. "Your voice calmed me. You started gabbing about all these things and I don't know... I relaxed."

"I'm glad my fifteen-year plan bored you." I wasn't mad. Not when he said things like that and brought me coffee. "I never got to mention how you fit into my plan."

"Oh?" One eyebrow rose, his half-smile distracting me. "Am I there?"

"Obviously." I bugged out my eyes. "You, along with Callie and Zade and the gang come over on weekends. And holidays. You'll bring your hot Brazilian wife, a different one each year, and we'll all reminisce about our crazy college days."

"Interesting." He fought a grin. "Now, how hot are my wives?"

"Smokin' hot," I joked. "Shit! I need to go. I'm going to have to run to make it on time." I took a step toward the trail, but he caught my wrist in his large hand.

"I'll take you. Hop in." He dragged me to the car and opened the door. "It's the least I can do. You helped me sleep and gave me hot wives."

"I won't turn down a ride. I'm tired as hell. Do you see these huge-ass bags under my eyes?" I pointed at them. "They're worse than when I have a huge zit. A zit goes away. These will take days."

He sighed, shutting the door and entering the other side. "I told you coffee is a drug. What made you drink it so late, anyway?"

"I figured I'm young and could handle it," I replied, rather than say the truth. Then I changed my mind. It was

Aaron. "No, I lied. My family. The money issues. I need to figure out how to make enough to pay for rent and tuition, apply for scholarships and student loans for next semester, all while convincing my parents to not give me a dime."

"Ah, hell." He grabbed my hand, holding it in his. The nerves in my belly danced the Macarena at his touch and I had no idea why. "I'm sorry, G. I can help you if you want."

"We'll see. My plan is to have a stern talking-to with myself and do it this afternoon. I have tonight off." I twisted my hand away from his, but he tightened his grip. Interesting.

"What time are you done tutoring?"

"Noon. Why?"

He finally let go of my hand and signaled left into the school parking lot. He parked and twisted to me. His intense stare contrasted with his tan skin, but this time, his eyes looked warmer. *Softer. Happier.* "How about I pick you up at noon and we head to that used book store on campus? I know you love that place."

"Um, hell yeah." I clapped, but then tilted my head at him. "What's in it for you? You hate reading."

"I want to treat you. Let me, Gabs. Now get out. I have shit to do." He grinned, motioning at the door with his head. "I'll see you at noon."

I had no choice but to accept the ride and wonder why he wanted to treat me. I wondered about the coffee and the ride the entire morning. Aaron had been known for doing random, nice things before. That wasn't new. One time he'd bought Callie and me a cake for acing our finals.

Another time he'd stocked our fridge because he ate a lot of our food.

Just last summer, he'd bought us a vintage poster of my favorite movie, *The Count of Monte Cristo*.

So why did it feel different now? *Maybe you're sleep deprived.* I compartmentalized my entire life and I shoved all my Aaron emotions to one side of my brain. I locked it up and focused on working with the summer school program.

* * * *

Aaron: I'm outside when you're done.

I didn't reply and shook Ms. Scott's hand. "Thank you again for allowing me this opportunity. I adore your kids. They're amazing."

"Of course." She smiled warmly at me, holding on to the clipboard like a boss. "We're lucky you got paired with us for your observation hours. You're so good with the kids. You said you'd be able to come every morning, even when school starts?"

"Yes." I cheered with a little too much oomph and drew some stares. I didn't care, though. My excitement was pure. "It replaces one of my classes. Instead, we write reflections and keep a journal of everything we learned. It's an experimental class — the first time they're forgoing the lecture."

"How exciting. Honestly, I wish I'd had that option. The real part of education is the doing, not those riveting lectures." Her sarcasm was not lost on me. "Thank you again, Greta. We'll see you next week."

"Bye!" I waved to her, feeling high as a kite, and walked out of the old brick building. Aaron's SUV stood out and I threw the door open. "Best day *ever*."

He shook with laughter and made the mistake of asking why. He should've known better, because Gabs was coming out.

"I love the kids and how they learn…"

"The teachers. They are so nice and dedicated. I want to be like that…"

"The school is so beautiful. It's old and perfect…"

"I could spend a month in that library…"

"Three kids hugged me. Hugged me, Aaron…"

"I can't wait to have my own class someday…"

I talked the entire ride to the used book store, which, by the way, sold the best coffee on campus, and I felt embarrassed when I realized it. "I should wear a muzzle."

His gaze slid to mine across the car and he shook his head. "Nah, I loved hearing about your day. You have so much joy in your voice. It makes me happy."

"So, you actually listened?" My mouth fell open. I didn't believe it.

He blushed, just a little. "Yes. I did *this* time. Now, let's get you coffee. I heard this place makes the best coldbrew in all the land."

"I don't appreciate you mocking me, Ronnie, but you said my favorite word on the planet, so I'll forgive you." I opened the door and took off at a quick pace to enter the quaint shop. It was my favorite place. It smelled like books. Old and antique books with the dusty pages and stories that stretched from ages ago. It was magical. I found an old copy of *Wuthering Heights* and held it to my chest. It was perfect. I loved old, used and ratty books that had been read thousands of times. It pleased me to see proof of someone else's joy. It was poetic and that was how Aaron found me, hugging a book like a psycho.

I expected him to make fun of me or something. But, no. He ran his teeth over his bottom lip for a second, reaching out and taking the book from my hands. "I'm buying this for you."

"You don't have to." I tried to keep hold. But he was a star athlete and outweighed me by one hundred pounds. My fight was pathetic. "Aaron—"

"I want to. Give up, Gabs." He won. The book now sat in his hands. "Consider this a thank you for my socks."

I squealed, pulling up the ends of his pants. Yes, it was weird and I'd crossed a line. No, I didn't care. I'd hoped he was wearing them and was thoroughly upset when I saw regular black socks under his skin-tight jeans. "Damn it."

"They're—what was your expression?—mostrosities." Humor laced each word and he grinned ear to ear. "I can't wait to try them. Even though they are em-bear-assing as hell."

"Ah! You did get my *punny* joke." I laughed and a couple of girls at the other end of the store looked over at us. The air left my lungs. They were part of the cleat chasin' crew who loved going after the baseball team. *Why the hell are they here?*

Aaron saw me tense and turned his gaze toward the back of the shop. His shoulders stiffened, making him taller than his already six-foot height. Something settled over his face—determination, fear… I wasn't sure. But I knew something was going to happen. My gut churned. "Greta. Follow my lead."

I gave a slight nod and he cupped my face. Those heated charcoal eyes danced with…what, I had no idea. But they danced and twinkled at me. *Humor. That's it.* He was laughing at me with his eyes. It had to be it. His gaze dropped to my mouth and his tongue came out to wet the bottom of his lip. *Why did I never notice how nice his lips looked?*

I held my breath. *Aaron.* My goofy best friend lowered his lips closer and closer to mine. He rubbed his thumbs over my bottom lip, the sensation sending a tremble through my body. All this attention, fake or not, had me instantly horny. I would've jumped him then and there with how turned-on I was. *But it's Aaron. It's fake.*

Then those perfect lips met mine and my toes curled so hard and my eyes rolled back into my head. There was no tongue. Nothing too romantic, besides the perfect combination of my coffee and the mint in his mouth. I could never have peppermint coffee again without thinking of him. Those soft lips left a trail of tingles all over my face when he ended the contact.

He kept his hands on my face and slowly opened his eyes. They still swirled, all emotions I couldn't recognize because my head was spinning out of control. My heart slammed and I cleared my throat. Pure self-defense kicked in and word vomit masked the inner turmoil I had. I patted his chest. "Not bad, big guy."

His lip quirked up. "Not bad yourself. Your lip stuff tastes nice."

"Dr. Pepper flavored. I don't drink soda and it's the closest thing I have to it." I ran my fingers over my lips, the sensation of his leaving a permanent mark. "You can borrow it sometime if ya want."

"Thanks, asshole. I'll keep that in mind." He chuckled and put his arm around me. "I had to kiss you, just so you know."

My stomach dropped at his words. But then he added, "It was the perfect opportunity. One of those girls is a huge Twitter troll and I hope she got a picture." He ran his other hand down the back of his neck, sighing in discontent. "Let's buy your book and get out of here."

I nodded, still dumbstruck by that kiss. His words hit like cold water. Ice-cold water waking my damn senses. *It was staged, asshole. It was just a kiss. Get over yourself.*

"We good, G?" He paused and put his hand on my shoulder. His eyes narrowed and I swallowed down the emotions. Compartmentalizing could be my future career. I nodded and plastered on a fake smile.

"Always, Ronnie."

Chapter Eight

Aaron

Kenzie wanted to kill me. I could feel it through the phone. She ground her teeth and I winced. I *hated* lying to her. I despised liars. And yet, here I was, surprised my pants weren't bursting into flames. "Yeah, Kenz. We're a couple. It's official."

"Why did I have to find out from my friends, asshole? You couldn't tell me!" she shrieked, a loud bang echoing over the phone. I imagined she'd hit her locker. Kenzie liked to be dramatic. *Are all the women in my life dramatic? God.*

"It just happened." I tried to think of a way to appease her. *But nada.* "Look, I would never intentionally keep something from you," I lied again. My stomach soured, the familiar feeling of self-loathing. "You've met Greta a bunch of times."

"I love Greta. I'm surprised she agreed to this. You were kind of a dog, bro." She laughed, the anger evaporating. "I really am happy for you. She's awesome. She cusses just as much as you and doesn't think you walk on water. I don't know how you pulled this off, now that I think about it."

"Hey, now."

"What? I remember seeing her last year and you did something douche-y, like high-fiving yourself—"

"I did *not* high-five myself," I scoffed. I was a showboat for a while but *that* crossed the line. "I know I didn't."

"I don't know, man, you were a douche-nozzle for a good year." Her voice dropped an octave and the uncomfortable feeling returned to my core, the guilt and shame causing all sorts of turmoil in my chest. She cleared her throat, both of us remembering what had changed me. *Our dad.* "Are you coming home for a visit soon?"

"I plan to. We have a tournament this next week, then a week off. I'll plan for the week off."

"Good. I miss your dumb face."

"I miss yours, too." I smiled. I did miss my sister and her crazy nail colors and stupid insults. "I heard you're working a lot now. Are you saving up a lot?"

"Ha! No. I now have a shopping addiction."

I frowned, unsure if she was joking or not. "Really?"

"Yeah. I make hella tips waitressing and I have no willpower to save it. I put, like, twenty bucks into a drawer and don't touch it, but the rest goes toward clothes and shoes. *Sooo* many shoes."

"Kenzie. Save some money." The older sibling side of me came out. Our parents were in no condition to worry about her cash flow, but I was. She wouldn't get a full-ride scholarship and who knew how much our parents could help us out next year. They didn't talk about money and we didn't ask. "Don't be a dumbass."

"You partied your face off. I spend money. We all cope in different ways," she snapped at me. The rude tone of her voice caught me off-guard. She never talked like that. "I need to go. I leave soon for my night shift."

"Kenz," I sighed into the phone, knowing damn well I'd pissed her off.

"No. It's fine. I get it. You're looking out for me."

"I'm sorry."

"I know. I am, too. But we're fucked-up, Aaron." She laughed, but I found no humor. "Glad you found a way to pin Greta down. She's the yin to your yang."

Then she hung up. I stared at the phone in my hand for a solid minute before the guilt went away. I was fucked up. So fucked up.

"Ay, want breakfast burritos?" Tanner's booming voice distracted me. He approached me in the living room with half a burrito hanging from his mouth. I took one from his hand and bit into it. It was good shit. "I knew you'd want one. Sammi's has the best ones in the state."

I nodded, enjoying the combination of chorizo and cheese. We had an hour before we needed to go to the field for a double header. It was against some small school a state away and my blood pumped for a game. *Competition.* The field was one of the few places I felt safe and comfortable. "You look rested, Hilly."

"Yeah. Slept like a baby last night."

"Guess you didn't hear me come in around three, then. I ran into the fucking corner table I hate." He glared at the table Jeff insisted we keep. I didn't mind it, but for whatever reason Tanner despised it. "I finally convinced Angelica to sleep with me."

I stilled. Angelica. I knew her. *Slept with her roommate, a handful of times. Kellie or Kylie or something with a K.*

"Krystal still loves you, by the way." He laughed.

I guess her name was Krystal. I scrunched my nose, trying to remember her. All I got was red hair. Boobs the size of pillows. And that was it. Tanner waited with an expectant expression for my reply, so I nodded. "She was an animal in bed."

"So was Angelica. Damn." He grinned. "I can't wait to hit that again."

"Are you trying the monogamy thing for a second time?" I wondered. Zade made it look easy. I had no choice with Greta now, even though it wasn't real, just a way to save my future. Last time he'd attempted it, he'd slept with someone else within a week.

"I don't know. She was a lunatic. A lovely lunatic." He paused with a finger to his chin. "You'd be shocked to know she didn't want to define it. She's my kinda woman."

"Good for you, man." I meant it. Tanner liked the ones he couldn't have. He always had. "Want to play a round of Madden before we leave?"

"Bro." He scoffed and threw his phone to the couch. "I beat you every time."

"Bullshit." I laughed. "I kicked your ass a month ago."

"I was drunk. Not a fair match," he fired back, the competition riling us both. "But I see you're all cocky and shit. Game on, fucker."

"One game. Loser wears a onesie to breakfast tomorrow." I'd come up with the idea after watching Greta shop for them the week before. She was obsessed with finding one for the winter months. She may have had the best mouth I'd ever tasted, but she was an odd duck.

"Dude? Do you want people to feel bad for you?" He tossed me a controller and fell back onto the couch. "I can't wait to see your dumb ass wear a Batman onesie. You're gunna look like such a tool."

"Watch it, Johnson. I got hella sleep last night." I'd given in to Greta's ludicrous idea and tried the socks. They'd worked, goddamn it. And they helped me kick Tanner's ass.

"Bitch," he mumbled at me as we headed toward my car an hour later. Zade and Jeff had left earlier for pitching warm-ups and we were forced to leave together. I felt amazing. I loved winning at anything and knowing this shit was going to wear a onesie tomorrow made me smile. I smiled a lot. "Knock that shit off your face."

"Hell no. You talked so much shit." I blasted underground rap and tuned him out. It was our pregame warm-up and I knew both of us would play out of our asses that day. "Want to do double or nothing who gets on base more?"

"Sure thing, ass face."

* * * *

"Hill. See me before you leave," Coach said to me right before we all headed to the showers. I nodded, but dread filled me from head to toe. I never knew what he had to say anymore. Tanner overheard him and clapped my shoulder.

"I'll wait for ya."

"Thanks, man." I showered within minutes and had my bag packed to head out for the night. I walked the short path to his office and strode in. His weathered face showed no emotion. *Fucking awesome.*

"Your focus lately is something to be reckoned with."

"Thank you."

"How are you holding up?" He leaned forward onto his elbows, the first sign of worry coming into his eyes. "How's the relationship going?"

I sighed, pinching my nose. "I'm fine. Greta's been a hell of a sport with it all. We were photographed a week ago. I haven't checked anything on social media. I just post shit, like we discussed, and exit out."

"Good. You have no business reading anything of that. This is a lesson when you're famous one day, too, kid. You must be wary of everyone. Keep your circle small."

I knew *that* now. I would never again trust anyone outside my friends or family. I was scorned. *Having my life flash before my eyes fucked with me enough to change my path.* "I know, sir."

"Now, this is awkward. But hell, I've seen it all in my career. I need to know. Are there any more naked pictures of you going around?"

"No," I replied with full confidence. "My high school coach scared the shit out of me. He told me, no dick pics ever. He specifically told me dick pics were for gross lonely men. Not for athletes."

He clapped his hands, his body shaking with laughter. "Good. I like that."

"I don't know if I should tell you this or not—" I began, but he held up his hand.

"You can tell me anything, Hilly. However, if you're doing something illegal, I don't want to know." His sparkling eyes winked at me. *What the fuck does that mean?*

"Coach," I tried again, wanting to get his take on having a hacker take down the picture. Zade and I were heading to his sister's place the next weekend to see what Naomi could do. I prayed she could hack it.

"Nope. I trust you. You do what you need to do." He pointed to the door. "Now get out of here. Our week-long tourney starts in two days. Enjoy the time off."

"Yes, sir." I walked out, feeling more confused than before. Tanner was waiting for me against the white wall, an expectant look on his face. "It wasn't anything. He wanted to check on me."

"He's turning into a softie." He chuckled. "Want to hit up the Lion? Jeff and Zade are heading there, too."

"Sure." Seeing Greta sounded nice. Plus, I never turned down a pitcher for a penny. "I can drive us."

"I was counting on it." He rambled on about the teams we were going to face in two days. I listened, his voice not as entertaining as Greta's. The drive to the bar didn't take long and soon enough, we headed into the seedy local favorite to find Zade and Jeff in a back booth.

I waved at Clyde, his shiny bald head practically glowing in the dark. Greta wasn't on stage or behind the bar. I scanned the room for her blonde hair and spied her leaning against a booth opposite where our friends sat. She threw her head back, laughing at something a customer said. The sound hit me in my chest. She always complained her cackle sounded like a goose. I loved it. Being the creeper I was, I watched her. Her expressive brown eyes widened, her hand covering up her mouth when she laughed again. The guy sitting at the booth put his hand on her shoulder and she leaned into it. She lifted her long arm and gave the guy a side hug.

My eye twitched.

A wave of protectiveness hit me. My jaw tensed. My back stood straighter.

"Aaron, I got you a pitcher. You're welcome." Tanner reappeared next to me and forced me to stop watching her. I thanked him and reluctantly followed him to the other side. "Dude, look at the sign!"

I followed the direction of his finger and saw a sign advertising Greta. Her official debut was the Saturday before school started. Pride filled my chest, my heart rate picking up as I glanced back over at her. She waltzed back to the bar with such ease and happiness my chest tightened.

"We gotta go. Fuck yeah, Greta!" Tanner yelled. Greta turned, flashed a huge, bright smile flashed in our direction and Tanner hopped onto the bar. He gripped her around the shoulders and held her against him. "You're going to be famous."

"Get off me, you goon." She pushed him away, but not with real force. Her cheeks tinged red while Tanner kept his grip on her. Suddenly, an entire pitcher of beer sounded awesome.

"I'm proud of you, G," he said, planting a kiss on her head. She closed her eyes for the second it lasted, and my throat hurt. I took a large swig of beer instead of punching a table.

"Thanks, Johnson. Now get off the bar before Clyde fires me." Her gaze went to Clyde and she shrugged. "Sorry, C-Man, I can't control these barbarians."

"I know," he said in resignation. "At least they bring a crowd."

And we did. Once one of us posted a picture or status, girls followed. When girls came, guys came. And within an hour, the bar would be filled. Tanner continued to smile at Greta even after she pushed him off and only then shifted her gaze to mine. Her light brown eyes looked nervous.

I approached the bar, setting my pitcher down on the counter. "Tanner stole the show."

"Johnson does that sometimes." She bit her lip, glancing around the bar every other second. "Should we kiss again? There are lots of people here."

I gulped, remembering her taste. *Will she taste like heaven again? Do I want her to?* "Maybe later. I wanted to congratulate you."

"Well, I like cake and coffee and chocolate." She crossed her arms, the motion pushing up her boobs. I glanced down, an odd feeling sweeping through my body. Her uniform consisted of skintight jeans that hung low on her trim hips. Her shirt, or half of her shirt, read *LION* in big red letters and left her bellybutton on display. *Shit.* I liked it. She cleared her throat and I met her eyes again. They crinkled on the sides, sign of a smartass reply soon to come. "Well, congratulate me, pookie."

I ran a hand down my face, then held out my hand for a high-five. "Nice job, Pita."

She shook her head with a half-smile. "Thanks, big guy."

She put her hand against mine, the smallness of it pinching my heart. I clasped my fingers around hers and yanked her closer to me. She gasped, and I didn't know if I did it for show or because I wanted to, but I kissed her on the cheek. I chose the spot right where her lips spread to the rest of her beautiful face. A hint of sweetness teased me, but I kept my mouth away from temptation. Then, I bent close enough so only she could hear me. "I'm so happy for you."

"Will you be here?" Her shaky voice told me everything. My bold, ball-bustin' Greta was edgy.

"I wouldn't miss it."

She released a breath and her body relaxed. "I need you there."

Those words... The thickness in my throat came back. I couldn't respond to that, so I pointed to the booth the guys were at. "I'll be over there. I'll hang out until you're off."

"You don't have to do that. It could be a late night." Her normal swagger came back and the insecurity in her eyes disappeared. "Go drink. Have fun. Be a dumb boy. But not too dumb."

I chuckled and carried my pitcher back to the table. Silly Greta didn't realize that I had more fun with her than anyone else. Waiting a couple of hours for her was no big deal. I'd done it before and often. She was making it weird.

"Yo! You fucking killed it today." Zade cheered at me, a little tipsy already. I grinned and fist-bumped him. "I don't know what you were on, man, but shit. Play like that every day and you're going first."

"I beat Tanner at Madden before we left," I admitted, Tanner snarling at me. "Don't be a bitch about it. Have you told them our deal?"

"Actually, we need a tie-breaker."

"No, we don't. I hit better than you today," I fired back. Jeff watched us as if we were a tennis match, his expression amused. We got that a lot — people watching our verbal banter like a sport. "I went seven for ten."

"I went six for ten with a walk. We were on base the same amount of times. That was the deal."

"No, it...ah fuck." I closed my eyes. "It was."

"Hell titties! We tied, mofo. We are both wearing onesies. I'll order yours right now, ass clown."

"Excuse me, what?" Zade joined in with laughter bubbling up. "Why?"

"It was our bet. We have to wear onesies to the next team breakfast." I sighed and found myself enjoying the bet. I needed more reasons to laugh and, hell, onesies were a good reason.

"Jesus." He cackled and pulled out his phone. "Have you ordered them yet?"

"I haven't, no. I expected to win."

"Dude, let's order them right now. This shit is awesome. I might want one, too." Zade was having a little too much fun right then and I bit back a grin. I guess we were starting a new wave on the team. We ordered four different ones, each one ridiculous in its own way, and an hour or two passed as the four of us enjoyed our pitchers of cheap beer. Greta stopped by once or twice to chat and each time it took all my willpower to not look at her toned body.

Zade and Jeff headed out earlier than normal, both to go see their women. I had no idea who Jeff was seeing, but it couldn't have been serious. He'd gotten the numbers of three girls within the two hours he was at the bar. I remembered those days. *Don't miss them.* I was about to go sit at the bar and ask Greta something when a body blocked my view. A body that was too tan, too plastered in spandex and too much in my damn space. "Excuse me?"

"Aaron," the girl purred, stretching my two-syllable name into four or five. I gagged. This chick smelled like strippers on spring break. Her manicured fingers touched my face without permission. I scooted back farther, but she didn't give up. "Why are you playing hard to get? Last year you loved my body. You told me over and over."

Now, I had two options. Deny it entirely and embarrass her, or go along with it and dismiss her. I couldn't tell if I'd slept with her or not. I'd had a lot of drunken nights that turned into regrets before the scandal. Tanner tensed up across the booth and would have my back if needed. "Listen, my friend and I here are having a nice conversation. I'm going to ask you to leave."

"You don't dismiss me," she gasped, putting her orange hand against her chest. "You loved how I rode you last year. Why are you pushing me away?"

I groaned and a mean, nasty side of me bubbled up. *Is she the one writing the shit about me? Did she try to ruin my life?* But, before I could say anything else, Greta marched over in her black outfit and plopped right onto my lap.

"Hey, pookie," she purred into my ear, my arms automatically going around her waist. She smelled like candy. "I'm almost done. Were you waiting for me, lover?"

"Yes." I buried my face in her neck so the aggressive girl didn't see me laughing. I nipped at her skin on impulse and she jumped.

"Don't get frisky here. There are patrons." She giggled—real or fake, I had no idea. She ran her hand through my disheveled hair and pushed my face back. "I missed your face."

Then she kissed me. It was quick, entirely for show, and I fucking loved it. Her mouth had as much personality as she did. She kissed passionately, loudly and without hesitation. My dick sprang alive, despite the show we were putting on. She slid off me with glazed eyes. She tilted her head at Orange Barbie and frowned. "Oh, hi. Did you need something?"

"Uh." The girl was speechless, a sick expression on her face. "No. No. I'm good."

Greta laughed and blew her a kiss. The girl ran out of our section without a glance. "Thata girl."

"Being a girlfriend has perks. I would've fought her," Greta said.

"My money's on you, G-spot." Tanner added with a cheeky smile. She ate it up and raised both her arms in the air.

"First girl fight—well, almost girl fight—is accomplished. You should tweet about it, Ronnie."

"Yeah. I will." I would as soon as my dick calmed down. She was still sitting on me. Still wiggled on my lap and if she didn't get up soon, I would have to explain the major boner I had going on. *I'd rather shit doesn't get more confusing than it already is.*

"Good." She pushed herself up and cleaned up our empty glasses. "I'm almost off but I saw her itching to get her hands on ya, so I thought I'd save your pretty ass."

"Always so thoughtful," I teased, finally able to breathe since she wasn't on top of me with her sweet smell. "I'll walk you back still."

"Whatever. No need, but I think ice cream sounds good." She glanced at Tanner with an arched eyebrow. "You can tag along if you want, TJ."

"I'll think about it. I have plans later."

"And by plans, you mean an ass to plow," she said. Tanner spat out his drink. She chuckled and patted his back. "Too far?"

"You never cease to amaze me," he replied after coughing up the beer. "But I'm going to be here for your show, no matter what."

"Good to know. Okay, see you later." She took off.

Tanner watched her walk away and tapped his fingers against the table. We small-talked for a bit and he began to pull at his collar. He avoided my eyes for a minute before he rubbed his chin. Dread filled me at his expression.

"I gotta tell you something, man."

I'd assumed as much, but all I did was nod at him.

"You know Greta and I had a thing last year, right?" Tanner said, the words slowly making their way into my brain. *Greta and I.*

The glass in my hand shattered and spots flashed in my vision.

Chapter Nine

Greta

I made over two hundred dollars in tips that night. Elation didn't begin to cover it—I could put a lot away. I'd buckled down to create a budget each week a couple of days ago and, based on that plan, I knew I was over my goal for the week. *Hell. Yeah.* "I'm heading out, Clyde. I'll see ya later."

"Goodbye, Greta. Keep promoting the show on your social media accounts. There has already been a lot of buzz. This might help us beat Geo's." His somber face broke into a weak grin and I rolled my eyes. He was such a worrier. He needed a chill pill.

I waved over my head and heard the shattering of a glass. It came from Aaron's table and I ran over there. "Ah! What happened?"

"Nothing," Tanner said a little too quickly. "I'll get the broom." He took off and Aaron avoided my gaze. *What the hell?*

"Are you okay?"

"Fine," he barked. His hand was bleeding, his throwing hand, and I panicked.

"Let me help." I frowned, hoping the bar still had a first aid kit. I climbed onto the bench but he used his other arm to push me back.

"I'm good." His jaw looked like marble, it was so damn tense. I reached out to touch it, but changed my mind. The vibes he was putting out were not good. "I'm going to go clean this up."

I hadn't moved out of the way yet so he stood and nudged me with his hip. I had no choice but to move to the side and I felt slapped in the face. He looked livid. My fingers shook and I fought the urge to cry. *What happened?* Clyde appeared a second later with a rag and a disappointed face.

"Another one bites the dust," he said as he picked up the large pieces of glass. "I hate when glasses break."

"Are you emotionally attached to them?"

"No. I made the mistake of ordering nice ones. Bad move. Each time one breaks, I cry inside."

I would've laughed at him if my heart wasn't pounding with worry. Aaron had retreated into the bathroom and Tanner had never come back with a broom. Something had happened and I needed to know. They were my two *amigos* and now they had gotten all weird. *Fuck that noise.* "I'm going to head into the bathroom to see if Aaron's okay."

"Knock first. I can't have anyone call you a perv."

"No one is going to call me a damn perv, Clyde the Ride." I made the short walk to the men's bathroom and pushed open the door. Aaron stood at the sink, his back toward me. He met my eyes in the mirror but remained silent.

The muscles in his back tensed with each step I took. "Aaron."

"What, Greta?"

Oh, it was Greta now. Okay. Cool. I masked my hurt expression and continued toward him. The blood flowed from his hand into the drain and I felt the tension coming off him, like waves of heat and hurt. Why, I had no idea. "How's your hand?"

"Cut up."

He wanted to play it that way, fine. I sighed, pinching my brow where a light pounding had begun minutes ago. "I'll get the first aid kit."

"No. I have one in my car."

"Then let's go. I'll help you." I went to grab his forearm but he pulled it out of my reach.

"I don't need your help," he snapped, his jaw tensing. His steel eyes narrowed in my direction. I bit the inside of my cheek and crossed my arms.

"Too fucking bad, Aaron." My anger crept up my throat and came out full force. "I don't know why you're being a dick right now. I don't care. I want to help you. You hurt yourself. Friends help each other."

"Friends," he sneered, looking back into the mirror. His stiff shoulders slumped and he turned off the water. "Fine."

I took that as my cue and I grabbed his arm. I knew I couldn't possibly drag him due to his being a sasquatch in size, but he let me lead him. We left the bar without a backward glance and I marched right up to his SUV. "Where's the kit?"

"Under the passenger seat." He unlocked the car and I gently shoved him into the trunk once the hatch went up. He obliged and I gave him a look that said, *don't fucking move.*

I found the red box and rifled through the shit in it. He needed tweezers, anti-bacterial stuff and bandages. I sent a quick prayer he could still throw. He had a major tournament in two days.

"Let me see it," I demanded before straddling his leg. I had to. It was the only way I could get a good look at his hand. "Hold up your phone flashlight, please."

He did and became stiff as a board again. I wanted to punch him for being a dick, but I didn't. He could be panicking about not being able to throw and I felt like a schmuck. *That* was why he was in such a foul mood. That made sense. "Okay, big guy. I'm going to grab the piece of glass stuck in your palm."

He grunted and I bent low. My hair fell onto his chest and I took my time, pinching the little clear piece wedged in his skin. I pulled and he sucked in a quick breath. I waited about five seconds and repeated the action. This time, it budged. "Almost done."

His response was something like a grunt. I tried one more time, removed the piece of glass and threw it to the ground. "Finished."

I sprayed all the wounds and wrapped them in a bandage. He blinked rapidly at me while I finished taping him up. It wasn't the best, but it would do. He ran his clear hand down his pant leg and grazed my thigh in the process. I jumped, my pulse pounding into every limb I had. He caught me before I fell and I made the mistake of looking into his soulful eyes. *Fuck me.*

"Thank you." He pushed a strand of my hair behind my ear, slowly moving his fingers down my neck.

"You're welcome," I whispered. The air seemed to crackle between us. Real or fake, I cared about him. I cared about his well-being and his *stupid* hand. I wanted to ease his hurt and make him laugh. "I, uh," I stuttered when his hand rested on my waist. His grip was firm but not painful. It was possessive. It was predatory and my heart skipped a beat. Then someone giggled behind us and Aaron's gaze moved from me to over my shoulder. Then he pressed a light kiss on my forehead, confirming it was for show. My lungs constricted with unease until I remembered my place — helping him and his reputation. That was the goal. I cleared my throat, hoping to get my bearings, and said, "I heard you played well today."

"Sure did." His teeth grazed over his bottom lip and he pressed his fingers into my skin. I scooted closer, wrapping my arms around his neck. His eyes heated, his nostrils flared and I forgot everything.

He brought his lips to my ear and my head fell back. He took the small lobe between his teeth and pressed down. I didn't give a flying fuck and I moaned, "Fucking hell."

He did it again, bringing his fingers dangerously close to my ass. He used his tongue to tease my neck but then he stopped without warning. His eyes became like ice and he let go of me. "They're gone."

They who? Oh. The girls. That's right. Fake. Fake. Fake.

"Nice thinking," I said with a dry throat. "Well, I'm ready to head back. Can you drive?"

"Yeah. I'll take you home."

Aaron drove in silence, the only sound him moving around uncomfortably in the seat. It was ten minutes of hell. The silence built, each second without talking like a stab in the heart. I was restless. I had no nails left to bite and they began to hurt.

"Stop biting your fingers."

"Stop making me squirm. Did I piss you off?" I blurted out.

He parked the car and slid his gaze over to me. He remained silent and that made me talk more. "I don't understand what happened. I mean, I played the girlfriend role at the bar as part of our plan. Then you break a glass, which happens a lot. Clyde's just a ding-dong who gets worried over stupid things. Did he say something to you?"

"No, he didn't."

"Oh, so you *can* talk. You just chose to make me sit here the entire drive home like I did something wrong."

"Shit." He closed his eyes, sucking air into his lungs. "You didn't do anything wrong. I'm sorry I made you feel that way."

Well, damn. His apology seemed sincere. "Thank you." I unbuckled my belt and opened the door. But I paused. "Do you want to come on up? You know a good marathon of *Bob's Burgers* helps."

His thought about it for a second, then nodded. "To be honest, that sounds like a damn good idea. Yeah. Let's watch for a bit. The guys are all out tonight and I like hanging out with you."

My stomach did the weird swooping thing again as we headed up the stairs. Nothing about what he'd said stood out, but I became anxious. We entered the apartment and I called out for Callie. There was no response and, for the first time in my life, being alone with Aaron in the apartment worried me. "Guess it's just us."

"Why don't you make us a drink? I'll get the show started." He walked past me and the combination of his sweat and cologne was intoxicating. I searched the fridge for some beers and was thankful that we had a six-pack in the back. *I'm going to need a drink or five.*

An hour later, I lay on my couch with Aaron's head a foot away. The L-shaped sofa was perfect for a bunch of friends to hang out, but it also provided close interaction if two people chose to lay their heads together. We always had. Today was no different, beside the rate of my heart and the questions in my head. We always talked throughout shows or movies, making fun of storylines or talking shit. This seemed normal. But now... *Is this fake? Is this a photo op? I have no idea.*

"Dude. You never explained how well you played today." I flicked his ear, getting a grunt in return. Whatever had bothered him before was gone and the regular Aaron was back. "How did you play?"

"Seven for ten," he said without an ounce of cockiness. "I had about six put-outs at shortstop and stole two bases. I played well."

"Hell yeah, Hilly." I held out a hand for a high-five and he obliged. I considered it a win when he gave me a small smile. Something had been bugging him and it had worked itself out, thank god. "You've really found your groove, huh?"

"I don't know about that, but I feel confident out there. My life is a hot-ass mess and I channel all my frustration and energy into the game. I'm a huge believer that when you love something and put the time and effort into it, it'll reward you. Maybe that's just happening."

I grinned, tilting my body onto my side so my elbow sat inches away from his. "I like that. You can be wise at times, A-a-ron."

"It can happen." He chuckled and shifted so he faced me. "I posted another picture of us today."

"Yeah? Which one?"

He showed me his phone and I saw an older picture of us from freshman year. I wore his hat backward, my hair in braids as I hung on his back. His smile was as big as a banana, mine annoyingly happy as we kicked ass at a ping-pong game. "I remember that day. It was fucking awesome."

"Yeah, I do too. Do you remember how pissed Zade got at us?" He laughed, slowly blinking at the memory.

"Oh, my god. He totally got pissed. He broke the paddle."

"I loved making him mad. He's such an over-reacter." He moved the phone, but I stopped him when I saw a little number in the corner. I snatched it from him.

"Jesus, Aaron. Our selfie's received a thousand likes. Ridiculous. Only you would get that many."

"You aren't bad on the eyes, G. Lots of people like your stuff, too." Sleep clogged his voice.

I took the pillow by my feet and hit him in the face. "Wow. You're so charming. *Not bad on the eyes.*"

"You know how you look. You don't need any affirmation from me." He smirked, pulling the pillow from my hands without effort. "Now shut up. I want to watch the next episode."

"It's *Bob's Burgers*. You've seen every episode. You *quote* every episode." I rolled my eyes. My phone pinged, and I opened a message from Tanner. *Tanner.* I blew out a long breath and pushed my hair behind my ears. He'd upped and disappeared after the glass-breaking incident and I wanted to know why.

Tanner: We need to talk. Can we grab coffee tomorrow before your shift?

I typed out various responses, the previous year coming back to me. I'd crushed on Tanner, with his bronzed skin, perfect arms and contagious laugh.

Crushed hard. We'd played a game all year, him pretending to ignore my signals and me pretending he was into me. It had been ugly. Nothing had happened, nothing remotely physical, but it'd still hurt for a while. He saw me as a sister. That was what he'd told me with a straight face. He wasn't attracted to me that way. *Nope.* To say shit wasn't awkward would be a big fucking lie. We used to text inappropriate things all the time. Now, they were few and far between.

Greta: Sure. I think you owe me. Plus, what the fuck happened tonight?

Tanner: I'll explain tomorrow. And, what do I owe you for, not that I mind ;)

The winky face. The epitome of flirting over text. *Why?* I gawped at it. *Why is he sending that now? He knows about me and Aaron.*

Greta: Two weeks ago you farted in the car. While it was raining. Low blow, man.

I typed it out, shutting down the winking asap.

Tanner: I'm an asshole. I'm sorry. Want to meet at the Bean? Does noon work?

I sighed, rubbing my temples before responding. Aaron noticed, nudging my arm. "Are you okay?"

"I'm good." I sent a quick thumbs-up and set my phone upside down. "Tanner and I are getting coffee tomorrow."

His entire body tensed, his gaze snapping to me. "Oh. Why?"

"No idea." I gave him a bemused expression. *What an odd thing, to ask why I would get coffee with Tanner.* "He said he wants to talk. Plus, you know I love my caffeine."

"Greta. Caffeine is a drug. It stunts your growth." He flicked his gaze to my legs for a second. He met my eyes again and one side of his mouth turned down. "Drink milk. Water. Protein shakes. They're so much better for you."

"For starts, Hilly, my bones are doing fine. Look at these legs. Do they need to grow anymore? No. I'm already tall enough for a girl." I raised my pale leg in the air. His gaze followed, sending a small shiver through me. I had long legs. They were skinny white legs that had barely learned how to function like a normal person. I fell more than the average person and running wasn't even in my vocabulary. Me...running... The only thing to get me to run would be a bad guy chasing me. Or a tornado. Or if I was running to cake. I was a selective runner.

"You aren't freakishly tall."

"Uh, I never said freakishly. Thanks for adding that in there." I pushed him so his head hit the back of the couch. I mumbled under my breath, "Dick hole."

I did not expect him to burst out laughing. His shaking body made the entire couch move and I smiled at him. This was *my* Aaron. The way-too-loud, boisterous, borderline-inappropriate baseball boy. He wiped his eyes and shook his head. "You said dick hole."

"Yeah, I did." I grinned again. "I insulted you."

"But you said dick hole." He chuckled again and the wariness present seconds before was gone. "Tomorrow is my last free day for a week. Hang out with me."

"Was that a question or a statement?" I loved his smile. It made me want to pinch his cheeks and squeeze him. I didn't appreciate his demanding tone, but he could get me to agree to just about anything with that grin.

"Don't be a Pita." He laughed at his clever nickname again. "Please hang out with me. We can go get your guitar and get cake. Chocolate cake."

"Hmm. You run a hard bargain." I pretended to think about it. "I guess."

"I'll pick you up at noon."

"Uh, I'm meeting with Tanner then." I rolled my eyes. Boys were annoying. "Were you tuning me out *again*?"

"No, I heard you. I'll pick you up at noon." He stood, stretching his arms over his head. "I can't wait to hear you play your show."

"Are you leaving?" I saw it was midnight. "You can crash here."

"Nah, I should head back. I have something I need to do." He patted my leg a couple of times, lingering just long enough for me to suck in a breath. "I'll see you tomorrow."

"Bye," I attempted to say, but it came out in a throaty whisper. He opened the door but stopped. I waited. Three seconds, then more.

He didn't do anything. He just walked out of the door. *Puzzled.* I felt puzzled and sad and giddy and tired. Too many emotions for this girl, so I locked the door. It wasn't until I was lying in bed an hour later that I saw I had a text.

Aaron: The socks worked. I just ordered you a present.

Greta: Me? A present?! I love presents.

Aaron: I know you do.

Aaron: You're good at this fake girlfriend thing.

Greta: Thanks, I think. Not sure how to respond to that.

Aaron: Whoever wins your heart is a lucky son of a bitch.

Chapter Ten

Aaron

As much as I hated the internet because of my current situation, I loved the instant gratification of it. I held in my hands the most ridiculous mug I had ever seen. It said *Pot Head* and had a graphic of a coffee pot. It screamed Greta. An unnamed emotion had hit me last night after Tanner had dropped that bombshell. Him and Greta had been involved? My stomach tightened at the mere concept of them together. The thought was ridiculous. Unbelievable. I refused to accept it. Greta would have told me, I was sure.

So, instead of acting like a dick to her again, I'd bought her a coffee mug. It was the least I could do, seeing as my fuzzy bear socks had helped me sleep the past couple of nights. I sighed, checking my watch.

It was eleven-thirty and Tanner hadn't returned yet from his coffee date with Greta. She'd moved their meet-up to nine-thirty in deference to me and, while I was glad she was getting cake with me, I was desperate to know what they had to chat about. I'd seen him leave two hours earlier and had sat in the living room watching episodes of *The Sopranos.* Call me old-fashioned, but a good mob show was a weakness of mine. It was the perfect distraction from why, all of a sudden, I questioned Greta and Tanner grabbing coffee.

Greta would have coffee with the devil if it fed her obsession with it. Yet the uncomfortable feeling wouldn't go away whenever I thought about it. I needed to knock that shit off. My phone pinged, capturing my attention. It was my sister.

Kenzie: I know you're coming home next weekend, but can you come home for the third week in September?

Aaron: Probably. Why?

Kenzie: It's homecoming. Mom wants us to get some family pictures done.

The lump in my throat grew eight sizes. I read between the lines. Family pictures...homecoming... Mom wanted to get pictures of the four of us because who knew if we would again? *Goddamn it.*

Kenzie: Well?

Aaron: I'll be there.

She never responded after that, not that I blamed her. We were both dealing with the same emotions and most of the time it was easier to ignore them. Taking pictures would be hard as shit, and the idea of asking Greta to come back with me popped into my head. That would help. I'd convince her to visit with me as part of our ploy. Girlfriends went back to meet their families and, at that point, it would be almost three months into the plan. A car door slammed and Tanner walked in seconds later. He had the same stupid look on his face he always had, and the urge to smash it surprised me.

He stopped when he saw me and raised a hand. "Hey, Hilly."

"Hey, man." *He's my teammate. Calm the fuck down.*

"You watching *The Sopranos*? Hell, yeah!" He sat on the couch without hesitation and joined me. "Look, we good about yesterday?"

I thought about it. Was I good? I had no idea. "Sure."

"I thought you knew, man." He sighed. "It's nothing to worry about for your six-month deal. It was months ago."

My patience dwindled. I wanted clarification and details, but I wanted to hear them from Greta. Not Tanner. I chose not to respond, which made him more fidgety.

"It won't blow your cover or anything. Just ask her."

"Sure."

"Were you why she changed our original plans, though?"

"Yup. I gotta go." I stood, hitting him on the back of the head. "That's for taking off last night. You worried Greta."

"Shit, I know." He rubbed the spot where I hit him. "I cleared it up with her. I bought her coffee."

"That'll solve almost anything." My mouth curved into a smile and I picked up the gift I had for her. "I'll catch you later."

"See ya, man. Oh, we might be going mini-golfing later. She found a glow in the dark place and you know how she gets. I'm asking Zade and Jeff if they wanna go, too."

"I'll be there."

I hated mini-golf. I preferred the real thing where I could channel my frustration into long drives and pure focus. It was impossible to just swing a golf club hard to hit it far. It took precision. Mini-golf was the drunk brother of golf. But my fake girlfriend wanted to go. That made my decision easy.

According to the plan, I needed to post at least five times a week on all my accounts. I had to vary the posts, pictures of Greta and me, things we were doing, posts about my family, posts about the team and playing up the good things Greta does. It felt gross typing out some bullshit post about my sister. I wanted to remain private. I wanted to go off the grid and not have anybody find me on the web. But that would make me look guilty.

I hit the Post button and pocketed my phone so I wouldn't have to look at it for the rest of the day. The only shining light in the already dark morning was Greta. She somehow managed to pull me out of my hole when my thoughts went dark. I walked, rather than drove, to her apartment because the weather had cooled off. The temperature made me want to play baseball.

I arrived at her door but wasn't able to knock because Greta swung it open. She wore denim shorts that left little to the imagination. Her long legs seemed to go on for miles and a sliver of her petite waist showed. My heart fluttered.

"Hey, pooks. I wondered if you'd stood me up." She snatched a plaid shirt off a hook and put it on over her tank top. Good. She didn't need that much skin showing. It was brisk out.

"I wouldn't do that."

"I'd kick ya in the nards if you did." She smiled at me, really smiled. The slight curve of her lips drew me in and I wouldn't have minded a photo opportunity right then. Just to taste her. "Okay, let me lock up real quick."

"Wait, I brought you a present." I held out the mug for her. She took it in her small hands and blinked. My heart shrank. She didn't like it. "It isn't much, I know, but the socks helped me. I love the stupid socks. I wanted to get—"

"Shut up, Aaron!" She held the mug to her chest, smile widening. "I fucking love it."

"You do?" A small ray of hope hit me. Maybe she didn't hate it after all.

"You baboon." She rolled her eyes and threw her arms around my neck. Her sweet scent felt like home. "It's perfect. Coffee and inappropriate things are my favorite."

"I'm happy you like it," I said into her hair. She was wearing it down today. I liked it when she did that. I fisted her blonde locks in my hands and instantly thought of what it would look like spread out around a pillow. *Fuck. No. Stop.*

I released her. My voice cracked and I took a step back. "Go put the mug inside, then we can go get cake."

"Okay." My abrupt and harsh tone caused her to frown. Great. I was a moody bitch and she received the brunt of it. Her teeth bit on her bottom lip when she came back outside. I put my hand on the small of her back, a gesture I had always made.

Why does my heart pick up?

Why does her hair blow in the wind like that?

Why do I want to smell her hair?

"Where are we going, big guy?"

"Insomniac's. They have the best cake and ice cream. I think they might have a coffee-flavored one."

"Ronnie, don't be foolish. I love cake and coffee but never mixed. One time, it was my dad's birthday and we all snuck out to buy him this amazing, perfect-looking chocolate ice-cream cake, right? Wrong. We all cut it into these huge pieces because our eyes were bigger than our stomachs and we took that first bite and gagged. It was coffee ice-cream cake and that moment ruined it for me."

I chuckled at her story. "Duly noted."

"This shit is important. What if we have to do one of those interviews to prove we really are dating?" She stopped and turned her head to face me. Her eyes were wide and her hand went to her heart. "Oh, my god. Do we know everything couples should know?"

"We aren't dating to get anyone citizenship, Greta. It's not like a movie."

"It sort of is." She frowned, running her thumb and pointer finger over her chin. "What's your favorite color? Movie? Food? Oh my god. I don't know your middle name."

"Greta. Take a breath, babe." I said the word without meaning to. Her brown eyes widened, but she gave nothing away. "I'm a bit offended you don't know that already. Think about it."

"Hm. Well, do you know mine?" She scrunched her button nose and goddamn it was cute.

"Purple. *Count of Monte Cristo*. Coffee, but that's technically not a food, so anything Callie makes. And your middle name is Michelle."

"Fuck me. You're good." She laughed and put her arm around my waist. The contact went straight to my groin.

Hearing her say *fuck me* didn't help me. "Okay. Let me think, lover boy... Black. You own way too much black."

"I look good in black."

"Yeah. You really do." She pinched my side and I tightened my hold on her shoulder. It felt so natural. And easy. And she fit right into me. "Okay, your favorite movie. I know you like mobsters. Should I be worried about that?"

"About mobsters? I think this area is pretty clean of them."

"Ha ha. I meant about you. You're super into them and you're half-Italian. Are you related to one?"

I chuckled, remembering a story my dad had told me years ago. "When my parents got married, twenty years ago or so, my dad said a tall, Italian-looking guy came up to them. He introduced himself as a friend of his aunt and presented a one-time offer of taking care of someone."

"No fucking way." She stopped walking and I had to pick her up to get her to keep moving. We were by a crosswalk and traffic had increased with classes starting in almost a week. A car honked and she flipped them the bird. *My little lunatic.*

"Don't get into a fight with anyone today. My hand still hurts from last night and I can't afford to punch anyone." It stung like a bitch but her taking care of me would be one of my favorite memories of all time. She'd had no idea what she was doing in the back of my SUV, but her straddling my leg and bandaging me had been worth it.

"Are we going to talk about what happened?" She looked up at me and, for the second time that day, I wished people were around so I had to kiss her. "Hmm?"

"No need."

"Yes, need." I opened the door to the dessert place and ushered her in. She thanked me, her pulse going haywire in her neck. She was a nutbag for desserts. "Don't think I forgot about what happened. But right now, dessert takes priority. Never ask me to pick between a dessert and a person if you don't want your feelings hurt."

"I'll remember that for our interview." I flicked her ear and stood behind her, hands on her shoulders. She shook with a laugh and pointed to three different types of cake. "Get whatever you want. It's my treat."

"I'm all about equality, but I told you, my brain gets wonky around sweet things. I might get all three. Want to share, lover boy?" She turned to me, all pink cheeks and rosy lips, and I had to touch her. I had to.

I put my hand on her neck, cupping her face. I ran my thumb over her bottom lip and her breath faltered. *Good.* So did mine. "Yeah. Let's get all three."

She let out a shaky breath and ordered. The doe-eyed hostess checked me out, a normal occurrence for me. But I felt nothing. I straightened. "We'll take all three."

"Of course." The hostess glared at Greta, then slowly took three different slices of cake. Red velvet, double fudge and peanut butter chocolate. Greta had great taste. Without thinking, I kept my hand on her hip and slid it across so it sat just above her bellybutton. I patted it.

"You better have room in there for all of these. I sure as hell can't eat it all. I'll pass out tomorrow with all this damn sugar."

She laughed, the sound hitting me in the chest. "Don't you worry about that, pretty boy. I'll pound the shit out of the cake."

I snorted when the hostess gave us a weird look. *Perfect.* I used my other hand to tilt her head back, exposing her neck. I pressed a soft kiss right under her

113

ear. She gasped. The hostess saw, sneering at me, but I kept my hands on Greta.

"Your total is twenty," she informed us with an annoyed expression. I handed her the bill while Greta held three different plates. She strode over to a table with her long legs and she didn't wait for me to sit down before taking a bite.

"Oh god," she moaned. "Heaven."

"Yeah?" I grinned. I took a small bite of the red velvet and nodded. "It is good."

"No. Good is too soft. Heaven." She crossed her eyes. God, I wanted to be the cake. She twirled the fork in her mouth, taking her time licking off each crumb of cake and *shit*. "Thank you for the cake."

"You're welcome." I thought about gardens. And buying cereal. Lifting weights. Anything to not think about her mouth on that damn fork. "So, did you and Tanner have a nice coffee date earlier?"

She looked down, pushing her hair behind her ears. "Yeah. He bought me coffee."

I waited. I wanted her to bring up her past with him. Suddenly, it mattered a whole fucking lot to me. Inexplicably mattered. "What did ya guys talk about?"

"You know, mundane things. The show coming up. And his big debate this year. Accepting if he's drafted or staying another year." She took another forkful of cake and moaned.

"Anything else?" I grasped for straws. She had to know what I meant, right?

"Uh, not that I can think of. Oh, I want to go mini-golfing tonight." She smiled and took another bite of the cake. "Here. Eat more."

"I'm fine." Anger crept up my throat. How could she be so nonchalant about it?

"Okay, psycho." She gave me a weird look and frowned at something on her phone.

"Are you having second thoughts about this?" I asked the question, not sure where the hell it came from. It blurted out. Maybe it was my insecurity or the fact that she was keeping something from me.

She flinched. "No. Not at all."

Worry remained in her eyes and before I could stop myself, I had to know. *Tanner*. "Is it because of Tanner?"

She threw her head back and laughed. "Uh, what?"

"Are you second guessing this because you still have feelings for Tanner?"

Her mouth dropped open, her kind eyes hardening. She blinked at me. Then she blinked again. Seconds turned to minutes and an anxiety I'd never experienced before hit me. *Can I handle if she has feelings for someone else? Even if this is fake?*

"Why would you ask that?" she said, after minutes of silence that stifled me. She was never quiet. Ever. She was my Gabs. Her eyes were not soft now.

"Tanner told me you had a thing last year. You were involved. I thought you would've told me, but since you didn't, I'm assuming you still have feelings for him." My voice sounded foreign to me. It was hard, angry and rough.

She crossed her arms and her entire face hardened. It hurt. I couldn't blame her, though. I was verbally attacking her and I couldn't stop. "If you do, I don't care. But don't do anything about it until the six months is over. You know what's on the line for me."

Liar, liar. I fucking care. I can't fucking stand the thought of her and Tanner.

She sucked in her bottom lip, nostrils flaring out to a dangerous degree. Her hand twitched and I prepared for a slap to the face. I deserved it. But she closed the distance between us and kissed me. *What the fuck?*

It was rough. Passionate. And angry? Her teeth clamped down on my bottom lip so hard it hurt. When she released her grip on me, she lifted her mouth close to my ear to whisper, "You're a fucking idiot. We have an audience and *that* is the only reason I am not smacking you in the face."

She clenched her fists at her sides, but her eyes gave everything away. Sadness, regret and disappointment. Then she walked out and left the cake. Warning sign. Greta *never* left a dessert behind.

Chapter Eleven

Greta

I slammed my forehead onto the table once, twice and a third time. Maybe, just maybe, if I hit it hard enough, the overwhelming doom would go away. I hit it again but remained in the same place. *Too damn bad we aren't wizards.*

"G?" Callie bounced around the apartment in her running clothes and smelled like outside. "Was someone knocking?"

"Nah, that was me." I did it again. "I'm having a pity party. Want an invitation?"

"Are there free drinks?" She chuckled and sat across from me. "What's wrong?"

"All these scholarships for future teachers. I need to win some. Then, there is financial aid and the applications suck. My parents make enough right now so I won't get help. They won't have this much after the forced retirement and after my brother's divorce is finalized. I'm stressing."

"Shit. That sounds like a lot." She rubbed my back. "God, your back feels like rocks are in it."

"It's my tension. I carry it around with me all day like your damn fanny pack." I cracked my neck and she worked on the knots. Bless her little athletic training hands. "Am I having a quarter-life crisis?"

"No." She stopped massaging and smacked my neck. "You get ten more minutes of feeling sorry for yourself. Then I'm going to force you to run with me."

"No. Not the R word." I pushed myself up and scanned all the documents on the table. "Fine. You win. I suck."

She ran her finger over her chin and studied me. "Does this have anything to do with Aaron?"

"Oh. Him." I grunted. I hadn't seen him in six days. Six days. Because of baseball. He was expected to get back tomorrow, the day of my official performance. I was anxious and nervous and desperate to see him. We hadn't ended on good terms. Not at all.

I commented on all his posts like we'd planned. I posted my own pictures of us and everything. But he'd been playing baseball out of town all week and hadn't had time to text. Not that I was waiting for texts. That would be needy. I still hadn't received an apology from him and I needed one. *Like I have feelings for Tanner when my world revolves around Aaron? Psh.* "I'm still upset with him."

"Girl, I would be too!" She sighed. "Zade's called me each night, but it's for minutes. I feel pathetic. Missing him so much. It freaks me out. What the hell am I going to do when he's off pitching in the majors some day? Will he forget about me?"

My heart folded. Callie was feeling insecure and that took priority. I preferred to focus on the problems of everyone else because I was a mess. "Cal, you and Zade are going to do whatever it takes. He loves you. You know this."

"Yeah, but he seems so sure about our future, like it's no question we'll make it. How can he be so damn sure?"

"You're going to do whatever you need to. My parents always said relationships, good ones, take work. It's not all rainbows and fairy dust and shit." I patted her hand. "Him playing baseball is a part of who he is. You'll adapt to it, just like you adapted to school here. And look how well you're doing here."

"God. You win the best friend award." Her eyes didn't hold the same amount of worry. "I'm an asshole. You were stressing and I made it about me. Talk to me, Goose."

"Uh, it's stupid." I stretched my arms, procrastinating. Callie was relentless. "Aaron and I have always been close. When we're talking or hanging out…it's never weird. I mean, the couple of staged kisses we had were a little shocking."

"Is he a good kisser?" She wiggled her eyebrows at me. "I bet he is."

"Yeah. He is." I laughed. "He'd better be. He had enough practice."

"True. So, you guys are close, kissing isn't repulsive. What's the deal then?"

"I don't know. He accused me of having feelings for Tanner. Which I don't. Not anymore. Plus, it was more of a crush last year. Not real feelings. Anyway, he accused me of it almost a week ago and we've barely talked since. Just bullshit small-talk texts."

"Hmm. Yeah. Aaron can be over the top with texting. Have you guys talked about last week?"

"No. I don't want him to worry about it when he's playing. It's not fair."

"Once again, Greta puts others above herself." Callie shook her head at me. "We need a girls' night. Our real and fake men are gone. We're wallowing. "

"You know what? You're right." I stood, nodding a little too hard. "We haven't hit the town for a while. Drinks, dancing and bingeing on burgers sounds amazeballs."

"I'm going to finish stretching, then get ready. Wanna leave in two hours?"

"Hells yeah, girlfriend."

She walked out and I felt better. Sure, my worries were still there, but I had been focused on the bad all week. I hadn't focused on how many tips I'd made. Or how my brother had called and we'd laughed for the first time in months. Or how my parents had found a nice, cozy home to put a bid on.

My mother's words came back to me. *Happiness is a mindset. Force yourself to think of the good. Not the bad. Choose to be happy in every situation.* "I'm happy," I said to myself. I tended to talk to myself from time to time. It wasn't entirely strange.

My phone pinged and Aaron's name popped up. My stomach did the awkward dance again. I must have been excited for a night out. That was all.

Aaron: We ended up getting second.

Greta: Nice job.

Aaron: Second is the first loser.

Greta: Change your mindset. I rolled my eyes at myself.

Greta: It's not even the real season. It's summer ball. You're there to get reps in.

Aaron: How have you been? We come home tonight.

Okay…hello, mood swings. I contemplated my response. I hated playing games. We'd texted casually all week, him needing to focus on baseball and not any drama with me. But now, should I respond honestly or lie?

Greta: I've sort of missed having you around.

Aaron: I assumed you were still pissed.

Greta: I am. But that doesn't mean I didn't miss your annoying ass.

Aaron: Did you post a photo today?

Greta: Yes, sir.

Aaron: Thank you.

Aaron: I left you alone this week because I thought you wouldn't want to talk.

Greta: Ronnie, being upset or angry with someone doesn't cease all conversation. You talk it out.

Aaron: Can we talk then?

I intended to say yes. I really did. But Callie waltzed in at that moment and blasted music from her speakers.

"G, get some tequila and Latina music. Mama wants to dance."

"Atta girl."

And I became distracted. It felt like old times, when Callie and I would spend hours getting ready and listening to shitty music in high school. We shared her bathroom mirror, curling our hair and applying makeup a little too heavily. We did shots of tequila, both of us gagging.

I helped do her hair into braids. She wanted me to pick out her outfit, which I did without hesitation. She had a killer body but chose to wear athletic gear every day. Good for her, but I forbade it tonight.

"Wear the black dress, Cal." I giggled, the two shots already getting me warm.

"It's short." Her red cheeks gave her away. "Maybe it'll be fun. Yeah. I'll wear it."

I left her closet to find my outfit, an ivory laced romper that brought out my weak summer tan. It was short enough to be risqué, but had a high neckline. It was the perfect flirtatious outfit. "Boom."

"Looks good, G." Callie joined me ready in her outfit. "Want to Uber there?"

"Yes, please."

I picked up my phone to call for an Uber and saw I had multiple texts from Aaron. Multiple. I gasped, reading them.

Aaron: Greta? I owe you an apology. I'd like to see you tonight.

Aaron: I'm pissed you didn't tell me about Tanner. He told me. I handled it poorly and I took out my frustration on you. I'm sorry.

Aaron: Can I make it up to you? I missed you more than I thought I would.

Aaron: Okay. I'm getting annoyed. You don't play games. REPLY TO ME.

Greta: I was getting ready. Cal and I are going out tonight. Not my intention to ignore you.

Aaron: Does Zade know?

Greta: Why does that matter? I did wonder if Callie had told him. Not that that would change anything.

Aaron: Because he likes to know where she is. Where are you heading?

Greta: I'm not sure yet. We're seeing where the night takes us. You know how it is.

Aaron: Be careful. Don't do anything stupid.

Greta: Ronnie, I'm safe.

Aaron: Hello, remember Todd? I had to fucking get you before you got hurt.

Greta: We aren't going anywhere off campus. I promise. Calm down, mom.

His name popped up, calling me. "Yes, dear?"
"Don't forget you're in a fake relationship, Greta. I've seen you dance. You're wild," he barked at me. *Hello to you, too.*

"I'm not going to whore it up, dick face." My mood soured. "Have some trust."

"Promise me."

"Promise you what, exactly?" Anger laced my tone. We were off. I felt it, and he did, too. Our easy banter was gone.

"You don't do anything fucking stupid. You're known for it." His words felt like a knife to my chest. *Why is he so angry at me?*

"Message received."

"I'm just looking out for you," he growled.

"Whatever, Aaron." I sighed, desperate to get off the phone. "I need to go. We're leaving soon."

"Let me know where you go."

"I don't know yet. We'll see."

"I want to know," he demanded, a little stronger this time. "I deserve to know."

"Uh, no, you don't. You aren't in town and it's none of your business. You aren't being nice right now."

"You're my girlfriend, Greta. I can know where you're going."

"Or how about you trust me?" I left the words hanging, my heart clenching again. "I gotta go, Aaron."

I hung up. Angry. Annoyed. *Ugh.* My phone pinged at the alert I'd set on his accounts and I scrolled at the notification. He'd posted a picture of me, one I'd sent him on Snapchat months ago. I'd used a dumbass filter to give myself dog ears. My heart shrank at his post.

Hilly_A: Look at my girl, have fun tonight xo

I shook my head in disgust. It was fake, fake, fake. "Let's go, Cal. I need more tequila."

"Girrrl. You and me both. I feel so loose. Like loose as a noodle. I want to sway to shitty music and have fun with my bestie." She slurred her words. She didn't drink as often as I did. But I did work in a bar. It made more sense. "What if some cute boys hit on us tonight?"

"Then we send them on their merry way, chica." I put my arm around her. "Don't worry your little head about that, Callie. I'll take care of you."

"I love you, G."

"Love ya, too, Callie girl."

* * * *

Music. Lights. Dancing. Hands. Repeat. That was how I found myself hours later, dancing to some house music with Callie grinding her little booty against me. I felt great. Free. Happy. And not at all worried about my life.

I took charge, being the more responsible between the two of us. I had more to lose. Well, she had Zade and I wasn't worried about her messing that up. I didn't trust myself. I was in a fake relationship with a guy who was a dick and had no feelings beyond friendship. I was horny, lonely and looking for a distraction.

I couldn't afford to be drunk—I would do something stupid. So, I took the responsible friend role and watched after Callie.

"Grrrettaaaaaaaa, I love dancing. I feel like I'm on *Dancing with the Stars*. Am I awesome?" she yelled with a dumbass grin.

"Yeah. You are awesome." I laughed and danced with her. I didn't need alcohol to wiggle my jiggle. I could dance sober or drunk, in the rain or sunshine. I loved a good rhythm. "Did you answer Zade's text?"

"Yup. Yup. Yup. An hour ago. Or ten minutes. I don't remember when I told him. But I did. I think I did." Her eyes widened, a whole lot of drunk. "I assured him I was dancing with you. That's it. He's the man for me."

"Of course. He knows that," I reassured her and pulled her off the floor. "Want a drink, or water?"

"Nahhh," she slurred again and my neck tingled. It was midnight, from my guess, and I knew we should head back. "Let's dance, Greta Michelle."

"Okay, Callie girl." I laughed and continued dancing. We danced again, for two more songs, then I made the big-girl decision to leave. It was almost one, and I wanted to not feel like total shit the next day. My gut told me it was time to go. And it was right.

Todd walked into the bar a minute later, bruising around his eye and everything. I gasped. *What. The fuck.*

"What is it, G?" Callie swung her arm around me. It was mainly for her support, but I appreciated the gesture. "Why are you as stiff as a board?"

"Todd's here."

"Biker bar dick Todd?" Her scary eyes narrowed. "I'll kick his little ass. I swear it."

"Calm down, boo boo." I petted her head. "He won't see us. Let's head out."

"I need to pee now. Now," she begged and I obliged. I had been on that end of the line before. She had always waited for me. So, I would do it for her. "Gretaaaaa. I need to pee."

"You got it. Let's go then." I tugged her to the back of the bar. We were at Geo's, the rival to where I worked. Clyde would probably cry if he knew, but hell. I was a college kid. I could live a little. We passed a group of girls I recognized, but not by name. I nodded to them.

"Fake-ass bitch," one mumbled under her breath. My blood boiled but I swallowed down the urge to fight. Callie, on the other hand, did not.

"Excuse me?" she replied. "What did you say?"

"You heard me." The tall, tan girl sneered at us. "I know you two. You're fake as fuck. Acting like one of the *boys*. You're not. You can't hold our guys."

"Why would you think that, huh?" Callie argued, getting right in the girl's face. "You think you're the right one? As if!" She laughed. A little nuts, a little scary.

The girl's face blanched. "Uh —"

"That's right. You think you are. You're not. These guys aren't property. They don't date cleat chasers like you. You're just a place for a dick to sleep over."

The place fell silent.

Awkwardly silent.

A glass fell. My heart raced. Someone sneezed. And this bitch chose to hit Callie in the face. *Oh. Hell. No.*

Callie roared, slapping the girl's hand away while I pulled her back. Callie was persistent, throwing blind punches and kicks, but most of them hit me. I managed to get her to the main dance floor when all hell broke loose. Suddenly, my life was a movie, yet again.

People yelled.

Callie's fist hit the girl in the mouth and she gasped. "Oh."

The girl screamed. She charged at Callie, who stood off-balance to my left. Callie somehow dodged to the side and the girl fell to the ground. Callie and I shared a look before I grabbed her hand. "Let's get the hell out."

"Yeahhhhh," she slurred and tripped as we headed toward the entrance. It suddenly felt packed — I couldn't see more than two feet ahead of me at a time. Being tall had some advantages so I pushed through the crowd and found myself face-to-face with Todd.

His eyes widened, the bruising a sick reminder of what happened all those weeks ago. "Greta?"

"Hi, Todd," I said without emotion. My focus was getting Callie out of there. "We're on our way out."

"Come on, looks like you need a back way out." He took the tip of my elbow, gently, and helped push a way to a side door. "Your friend there is a little spitfire."

"Yes. Callie is." I smiled at my best friend, who was minutes away from crashing. "Thank you for the help, Todd."

Callie chose *that* moment to pay attention. She jerked out of my hands. "This is the Todd?"

Todd's face blanched, damn well knowing she couldn't mean anything good by it. He ran a hand over the back of his neck and cringed. "I've been meaning to call you, Greta."

"Trust me, no need," I scoffed. "I'm glad to see you're alive at least."

He let out a string of curse words and frowned at me. "I didn't realize… Look…I'm not a bad guy."

"Not saying you are." I checked my phone. It was one now. We needed to head out and walking wasn't an option. I opened the Uber app and saw it was fifteen minutes away. *Jesus.*

"I owe you an explanation." He stepped closer toward me, his handsome face showing regret. My stomach tightened. This passed *awkward*. "My brother is in their gang. He stole money from them. I had no idea."

Callie gasped and looked at me with wide eyes. "Is this real life?"

"Yeah." Todd smiled at her. "Sadly, yes. Anyway, they decided to send a message to him through me. I never would have taken you there if I'd thought you could've gotten hurt."

My gut told me he meant it. It was the truth. But it didn't change anything. I sighed, hearing angry voices farther down the alley. "I appreciate knowing you're not a criminal. Which I assumed."

"Naturally." He put his hands in his pockets and kicked a rock on the road. "Can I at least give you both a ride back?"

"Nah, we'll wait for an Uber. Thank you, though." I smiled and heard the voices get louder. I glanced down the alley and saw two massive shadows coming our way. My neck tingled.

"I'll wait with you then." He didn't look alarmed or in a hurry. "How did you get home that night anyway?"

"My friend came to get me." My chest hurt at the reminder of my stupidity. Callie sank to the ground and I joined her. Our outfits would be ruined, but fuck it. I was exhausted. The night had been fun until an hour ago. *I knew we should've left at midnight.*

"I know this is a long shot," Todd said, "but I really liked you. I assumed you would never talk to me again after that night. But would you want to try again?"

I didn't get a chance to answer before someone punched him in the face. A large, swift body came out of nowhere and it took me thirty seconds to realize it was Aaron.

Aaron punched Todd in the face.

"What the fuck, man?" Todd spat out, wiping blood from his mouth. His eyes were wild and afraid.

"That's for the shit you pulled at Dirty Matt's." He pulled back his fist and hit him again. "That's for pathetically asking my girlfriend out."

129

"Aaron!" I jumped into action, confused as hell about how and when he'd got there. "Stop. Let it go."

"I'm good. I got my two shots in." He twisted so he faced me and Oh. My. God. His eyes were lethal. Steel gray, calm and predatory. "I'll never forgive him for scaring the shit out of you that night."

I stood, dumbfounded. "How... Why are you here?"

"Zade came for Callie. I came for you."

Ugh, my goddamn heart. His words could kill me or light me on fire.

Zade already had Callie on his back, him carefully looking at her fingers. I assumed he'd found out about the fight and was whispering sweet nothings to her. I glanced back at Aaron and he was still studying me. His chest heaved, the tight gray fabric leaving nothing to the imagination. My mouth dried up.

"I think Zade's taking Callie home." He bit his lip, a grimace coming over his face when he noticed his hand. "I'll walk you home."

"I have an Uber on the way." I checked my phone and saw it would arrive in two minutes. "I can't cancel."

"I'll go with you. Come on, let's leave this asshole alone." He put his arm around me, his familiar scent intoxicating me. Being around Aaron was like a ride on a roller coaster without a seatbelt. I had no choice but to follow him toward the main road. His fingers teased my skin, up and down my bare arm. I shivered. "Are you cold?"

"Slightly. My adrenaline wore off." My teeth clattered, the car pulling up that second. I sighed. "Good."

We got into the car, but Aaron wrapped his arm around my waist. He prevented me from scooting all the way over. Instead, he pulled me onto his lap. He wrapped his strong arms around me. "Wh—what are you doing?"

"Warming you up." He chuckled, his laugh hitting me in the chest. *What the fuck is happening?*

"Oh." I welcomed his heat and soon enough, we were dropped off outside my apartment. Aaron kept his arm around me while we headed up the stairs and my nerves took off. He turned me on. I didn't know when that had started. He messed with my head and emotions. We needed to talk, but it was already super fucking late. Did I invite him in? I had no idea.

"I'm coming in. I'm beat." He shut the door and locked it behind him. He winked and added, "Remember I have an extra key?"

"I should probably take that back." I fumbled with my words.

"Not a chance in hell. Do you need to sleep right now? Can we talk first?" His tone changed, confidence replaced with insecurity. "Please?"

I eyed him. He looked broken. "Sure. I can stay awake."

He plopped onto the couch and patted the cushion next to him. "Come on."

I obeyed and crossed my legs. I re-crossed them at least three times before he started talking. "Greta, I'm a shitty friend and an even worse fake boyfriend. I assumed you didn't want to talk all week because I pissed you off."

"I—"

"Don't interrupt, G." He put his long finger on my lips. He smirked. "Thank you. I know you're the gabby one, but it's my turn."

I nodded, the first sign of relief flowing through me.

"You're not like how I envisioned a girlfriend. You don't fit the stereotype. Certainly not to me. I won't do that again." He held my stare and I gulped. "I hated not talking to you every day. I don't know when you did this, but I blame you."

"Blame me for what?" I blurted out.

"You got into my head. My day sucks when you're not in it." He shrugged, grabbing one of my bare feet. I gasped when he massaged it in his hands. I had no idea what the fuck was happening but I closed my eyes. It felt like heaven. "I'm not done."

I nodded, but he let go of my foot. He grinned. "I'm listening, Chatty Cathy."

"Ha ha." He dramatically rolled his eyes. "I was jealous as hell when I heard you and Tanner had a relationship."

"What?" I sat up straight, our faces a foot apart. "What did you say?"

"I was jealous." His gaze flicked to my mouth for a second. "I liked thinking we were closer. That you and I were best friends. I don't know why. It didn't make sense, but thinking you had anything with Tanner annoyed me. I'm not used to feeling jealous, Greta. Ever. It's new and gross and I hate it."

"You were jealous?" I grinned.

"Yes, Pita." He crossed his eyes at me and my heart warmed. Playful Aaron was back. My world felt right again. "I assumed, which I now know to never do. But I assumed all this shit instead of asking you."

I nodded and he tipped my chin up with his fingers. "So, Greta, will you tell me what happened and put me out of my misery?"

Misery? "Nothing happened, truly. I had a crush. You know, well, maybe you don't, but if you're around people a lot and they're off-limits…it was like a high school crush of sorts. I attempted, once, to hit on him. I had a couple of drinks and I used some asinine pick-up line. He shook his head and told me very firmly no."

"Why didn't you tell me?" His brows pinched together.

"Uh, embarrassing as hell." I shook the memory away. "Enough about it. Are we good?"

"Yes, Pita. We're good." He smiled his *Aaron* smile and I felt it in my toes. "Now, lie back down. I'll massage your feet again, just to make sure I'm not in the dog house."

"You punched Todd," I mumbled minutes later on the verge of sleep. "Why?"

"He put my girl in danger. Ain't gunna get away with that."

Then I fell asleep.

Chapter Twelve

Aaron

My dick woke me up. *Seriously.* He throbbed, desperate for release. Christ, this was the mother of all morning woods and I decided to head into the shower to take care of it. It would be the millionth time doing just that as my thoughts drifted to Greta. I attempted to move my arm, but something held it down.

Greta lay, sound asleep, on top of me. Her blonde hair hung all around, tickling my skin. Her thin body had plastered itself to me — we must've fallen asleep on the couch. I tensed. If she were awake, she would feel —

"Happy to see me?" She grinned and lifted her head. Her eyes were filled with sleep, the sweet chocolate color beautiful. She twisted her hips, making no sudden movements to get off me.

"Morning, G." I lifted her slim hips and moved her to sit next to me. All thoughts focused around my dick and her tiny outfit from the night before didn't help. "Can't blame a guy. Morning wood is a real thing."

"I can see that." She flicked her gaze to my tented pants. She continued to stare at them, a slight flush creeping up on her neck.

"Greta. He knows if you're thinking about him. Stop ogling."

"I'm just curious." She wet the bottom of her lip. That piqued my interest a hell of a lot. I sat straighter as more blood rushed to my cock. "Never mind."

"No, say it," I demanded. Apparently, I was a glutton for punishment. "You blushed. What were you thinking about?"

"I think it's *ragingly* clear what I was thinking about, Aaron." Her gaze never left my crotch. "I've heard rumors about you."

"Are you imagining the size of it?" My voice strained. *God, if she wants to touch it, I won't stop her.*

"Yeah." Her breath hitched. Big bold Greta licked her lips and twitched her hand out. "Can I see it?"

"I'll show you mine, if you show me yours," I replied. She nodded, dragging her gaze to my face. Her pulse matched mine, the base of her neck pounding. "Do you want to see my cock, Greta?"

She nodded, getting bolder by the second. She moved closer so she could touch all of me if she wanted to. And boy, I fucking wanted her to. "Go ahead," I instructed. She sucked in a breath and fingered the edge of my waistband.

She snuck a finger in, my stomach tightening. My chest heaved, air getting heavier by the second. Bold Greta chose to straddle me and she slid the waistband of my boxers down, down, down until my raging hard cock sprang out. Her mouth widened.

"Christ Almighty." She gulped, her rosy cheeks giving her away. "I...uh."

Keys went into the front door at that moment. The knob turned just as I pulled my shorts up.

"Hey, guys!" Callie burst through the door and Greta flew off me like I'd caught fire. With a blazing red face, Greta tossed a blanket on me and ran to her room. *Coward.*

"Sup, Callie?" I hid my boner, going over math equations in my head. I needed something, *anything* to get my guy to calm the fuck down. Later, I could analyze what the fuck Greta and I had been doing. "What time is it?"

"Eleven, did I wake you guys?" Concern was etched on her face. "I'm the hungover one. I shouldn't have more energy than you."

I ignored her comment and focused on my phone instead. She slammed shit in the kitchen, drawers and cabinets. My head felt like deadweight, but it had nothing to do with drinking and everything to do with Greta. *Fucking Greta.*

Greta: Is she still out there?

Aaron: Oh, Jesus. Are you hiding?

Greta: Maybe.

I groaned, gathering the blanket into my hands to hide the evidence of whatever had happened. Callie could mind her own damn business at this point. I pushed open Greta's door to see her pacing her room, her body still clad in the skin-tight outfit, worry pouring out of her. "Greta."

"Gah, you." She pointed a finger at me. Her voice lowered. "You and your magic dong."

I snorted. My dick would've laughed if he could. "Uh, care to expand on that insult, G?"

She twisted the end of her hair for two minutes. Maybe three. "I'm sorry about my reaction."

"Sorry?" I walked up and put my hands on her shoulders. "Don't be sorry. I love how free-spirited you are. Feeling was mutual, Gabs."

"I got carried away." She frowned and pushed my hands off her. "I need to shower. You can hang out if you want. I'm going to practice for my show tonight."

Damn. She'd dismissed me plain and simple. I wanted to urge her for more. The desire was both ways—hell, I would've done anything she wanted. But she'd put those walls up so high right now I couldn't do anything about it. I tried regardless. "Okay. You need help in the shower?"

Her eyes heated over for a second before she smiled. "Nah, I'm real good with my own hands. See you later, Ronnie."

Great. She left me in her room with thoughts of her touching herself. I needed to run home to shower. *Goddamn it, Greta. What have you done to me?*

* * * *

Hours later, I stood with a bunch of other schmucks all having the same thought—how fucking awesome Greta was. Tanner hollered at her in between every song, Zade and Callie made ridiculous cheers and Jeff had brought his latest fling. Even some of the fucking sophomores on the team had showed up to cheer her on. It annoyed me. Selfish, I know.

"Get it, G!" Callie yelled and jumped up and down as Greta played her final song before a quick break. It was a two-hour show, the first half of it already amazing me. Her silky voice made my chest tighten.

"Damn it, Hilly. How did you get her? I swore I had a shot." Young Chris, as we called him, hit me on the back. The kid had swagger for someone who'd been a walk-on freshman the year before but hitting him in the face suddenly seemed like a great idea. "She's a dime piece, bro."

"Yeah. Yeah, she is," I said, watching her thank the crowd and say she'd be back in fifteen minutes. *Fuck manners.*

I made the gap between us close and she didn't have time to register who it was before I enveloped her in my arms. I kissed the hell out of her. I gripped the nape of her neck, loving how her long hair dangled down her back. But the best part? Her mouth welcomed me home. She tasted like an aged whiskey and, fuck me, I needed more. She moaned into my mouth and I deepened the kiss, marking her, wanting desperately for her to remember it for every other guy she would be with. People catcalled, clapped, and I slowly, delicately slid my hand down her spine, releasing her. "You're remarkable."

"Shit." She ran her fingers over her lips. "Hell of a kiss, pookie."

"Trust me, I had to stop myself from doing more." I tightened my grip on her lower back. "You're killing it up there. I'm proud of you."

Her eyes glistened for a second, a little bit of the vulnerable Greta I knew poking through. The quick blinking, the slight tremble of her lip… I had to kiss her again.

And I did.

"I'll let you go, but I'm walking you home." I released my hold on her, noticing the hard outlines of her nipples poking through her skin-tight black shirt. *Shit.* I did not like that at all. I didn't have a chance to say anything to her before other people surrounded her. Our friends, part of the team, even Clyde jumped in and hugged her. I choked on my beer when she mouthed *what the fuck* to me as Clyde put his gangly arms around her.

"When did it get real for you?"

I flinched at the smoky voice. Cindi Clementine. Former hook-up, semi-relationship my freshman year. I had been foolish. High on celebrity status. She'd wanted to tie me down. I'd refused. Her purple fingernail grazed my arm. "I see you with her."

"Cindi, what are you talking about?" The rock in my stomach doubled in size. The knowing guilt of the façade. The lie. The fake relationship.

"Don't play dumb, Aaron. That was never you." That damn purple fingernail collided with my hand, the gesture repulsing me. "I *know* you, baby."

"Look, you need to not grope me." I slid my hand out of her grasp. "I don't know what you're after. But today is about my girlfriend. You know, the one killing it on stage right now?"

"Hmm. Yes." She swiveled her head toward the stage with a menacing look on her face. My warning signs went off. "Greta Aske."

"Leave her out of whatever the hell you're thinking." I stepped closer to her. "I apologize a million times about freshman year. We're good, right?"

"Yup." She popped the damn *P* so hard I was surprised no one heard it. "Farewell, Aaron Hill."

I winced. She was trouble. I followed her as she left the bar and noticed her talking to Veronica. *Queen of cleat chasers. Walking STD.* Young Chris appeared next to her, those long purple nails going through his hair. He didn't know any better and someone needed to warn him. Before I could get Zade to go chat with the young kid, Greta got on stage and spoke directly to me.

"Hey, guys, I want to dedicate this next song to my *super* hunky boyfriend, Hilly."

The crowd cheered and parted, everyone looking at me. I had no choice but to smile at her. I blew her a kiss. She caught it with a wild look in her eyes. "See, I'm not sure if you all know this or not about our favorite shortstop, but he *loves* roller coasters."

I shook my head, a huge grin overtaking my face. I flipped her off. People who knew us laughed. Everyone else gasped. I cupped my hands around my mouth. "Careful, G."

She laughed, the sound like magic. "This song is for you, Ronnie."

The Ohio Players song *Love Rollercoaster* blasted throughout the bar with the help of Clyde. She dropped the guitar and sang the lyrics, not missing a beat. She danced. She clapped. She performed and, fucking shit, I was hooked. We all clapped as she sang the upbeat song, but then she pointed for me to come up on stage. I obliged and wiped tears from my eyes at how much I laughed.

It might've been the best moment in my life.

She twirled around me, rapping in her own way, and as soon as the song ended, I picked her up. "You're an asshole."

"I'm *your* asshole," she replied with a cheeky grin and I pressed a quick kiss on her cheek. "Did you like it?"

"Fuck yeah, Pita." I set her down and held our hands up in the air like we'd both won a huge award. I had to kiss her again and I did. I had an odd sense of joy as I left her on stage. Tanner stood at the table we'd reserved and looked pissed. Pissed as hell, to be honest. "TJ, what's up?

"Dude. What the fuck are you doing?" The laughter he'd had when I'd spoken with him an hour earlier was long gone.

"Uh, excuse me?" My jaw tensed at the second accusation I'd had for the night.

"I thought this shit was fake with Greta." He fisted the napkin in his hand and let it fall to the ground. "What are you doing?"

"It is fake," I scoffed, my heart flipping me off. It knew I was a lying piece of shit. "Most of our— Look." I checked around us to make sure no one could hear. "It's staged."

"Bullshit." He bit the inside of his cheek and glanced back at Greta. "I don't like whatever the fuck you're doing. You can't mess with her. Or hurt her."

His words hit me in the chest. I would rather die than hurt her. "Tanner. I'm a mess. Why would I hurt her?"

"You *are* a mess. Don't forget that and think with your dick," Tanner spat, shaking his head at me. I felt as small as a goddamn fly. The kicker, though? He was right.

What the fuck am I doing?

"I appreciate you looking out for her, but we both know what we signed up for," I said through clenched teeth. "So calm the fuck down."

His eyes widened at my tone and I waited to see if he had anything else to say. He opened his mouth twice but closed it. "Glad that's settled."

"Sure, man."

He left me alone for the rest of the show, and I didn't appreciate how he went up to Greta and hugged her a little too long after she'd finished. She grinned up at him, wild eyes and beautiful hair. It felt like a punch to the gut.

I remained in the back, watching her make the rounds and get all the congrats she deserved. She'd nailed the first night. Totally nailed it. Her path led to me, after what felt like an hour. Her eyes warmed and her arms opened for a hug.

Of course, I obliged. "Hey, G. Stellar job."

"Thanks. I feel high!" She lifted her legs and I spun her around. "I loved it. God. I'm amped up."

"You want to stay for a while?" I wanted to pick her up and keep her for myself, for no other reason than to appease my own sick indulgences. It was her night. If she wanted to stay out all night, then I would, too. "What does my star want to do?"

"I don't know! I feel like I could run five miles, get a tattoo, or dance until the sun comes up!" She laughed and threw her head back. "Do you ever get this feeling in your chest you don't know what to do with?"

I slid my hand down to rest on her hip and I gripped it. "Yes. After a major win, I get this itchy feeling in my chest. It's a mix of anxiety and blood-pumping adrenaline that makes my fingers twitch. The feeling starts in my chest and spreads through my body."

"Yes!" Her gaze bounced between my eyes and mouth. "That's exactly it. What do you do?"

"You want the truth?" I lowered my voice, my brain telling me to shut the fuck up. I ignored it.

"Yeah," she lowered her voice and leaned in. "What is it?"

"I fuck."

Chapter Thirteen

Greta

I fuck.

I gulped. His steel eyes heated over and the air shifted between us. The morning flashed back to me and my face paled. I could hear my heartbeat through my ears and I wondered…

"Greta, you okay?" His voice was low and deep. My legs clenched together. "Your eyes went all crazy on me."

I remained silent when he pushed some of my hair behind my ear. With that gesture, I realized how long it had been for me. Two months? *Shit. Way too long.* His thumb snuck up and pressed against my bottom lip, and I made up my mind. "Let's go."

"Wait, what?" His brows scrunched together. I yanked his hand in the direction the exit and he laughed, stopping me. "G, what are you doing?"

"I want to finish what we started this morning." I faced him. This time, his eyes widened. His breath hitched. *Score one for me.* "What? You not up for the challenge?"

"Oh, Greta." He slid his tongue over his bottom lip, drawing all my attention there. "Don't talk the talk unless you follow through. I take your word very seriously."

He pushed us into a nook right before the door, not quite outside but not in the main area. It was just the two of us. His stubbled jaw pressed against my neck, him playfully biting my earlobe. I groaned, fisting his shirt. "Cat got your tongue?"

"Why play games?" I pushed him off me. "Let's get the hell out of here."

He sighed, closing his eyes with a pinched expression. My stomach sank and humiliation took over. *Oh my god. Did I go too far?* I backtracked. "Never mind. Listen, I'm acting crazy. Let's just forget it, okay?"

I moved to leave the private spot we'd found but his arm stopped me. He gently grazed my side, his fingers tracing the side of my breast. I sucked in a breath, backing up so I hit his chest. "Oomph."

"You've been driving me fucking crazy, Greta. This shirt... God. I want to rip it off you and explore your tits." He traced the skin under my ribs, the sensation shaking me to my core. "Your nipples perk up when you get turned on. Did you know that?"

I moaned, and he pinched them. "Oh, my."

"Just as I thought." He slid his hands up my shirt and let out a long cuss word when he discovered I was braless. "Fucking hell. Greta. You're killing me. I can't wait to explore these with my mouth all night. I want to suck the hell out of your tits."

He pinched and pulled the pebbled tips, each touch building me up to the point I almost forgot where we were. He didn't stop, though, no. Not Aaron. "Are you wet for me, G?"

I whimpered, completely sucked into him. He kept one hand under my shirt, moving his other to the waistband of my shorts. My stomach tightened when he slipped one long finger into my panties. But he stilled. "Answer me. Are you wet for me?"

"Y-yes." I closed my eyes, desperate for the release. "Yes."

He slid two fingers into my shorts, gently exploring my folds. He slid inside me, the sensation almost too much. "Oh, Greta, my sweet girl. You're soaked. I can't wait to taste you. Do you want that?"

"Fuck yeah, Aaron." I bucked against him. Music pounded around us, the dark nook shielding us from everyone. I didn't give a shit at that point. All I wanted were his fingers to pick up the pace.

"You want to stay here and continue talking to everyone?" He increased the pressure of his fingers, going in and out. I rocked into it, forgetting everything. "Huh?"

"No. I need…"

"Tell me what you need," he demanded, his tongue dancing down my neck. "You always smell so fucking good. I can't wait to see how you taste."

I gasped at his language, but forgot why when he flicked my swollen nub. He used his thumb to twirl my clit while he continued to rock me with his fingers. I was so close. So fucking close. I moaned, jerking against his hand while he held me. "God, your pussy is so tight. Fuck my fingers, Greta."

And I did. I rocked harder, faster against his fingers and the orgasm hit me. No, it exploded inside me. The overwhelming burst of pleasure rushed from my core. I cried out his name, but his hand smothered the sound. It continued — my toes lost feeling and my body ached for more. "Next time, I'm watching your face as you come all over me."

I didn't have time to react before he slid his fingers out of me. "Aaron, what — "

"If you question this, I'm going to lose my shit." His eyes blazed at me. "I have to taste you now. Non-negotiable. Now, say goodbye and get in my car."

I grinned. Needy Aaron thrilled me. My body throbbed and I gave him a curt nod. "Okay."

He smacked my ass and I ran to say goodbye to Clyde. He hugged me again, which freaked me out because it was Clyde, and told me we would totally kick Geo's ass. I waved to the people I needed to and sprinted outside.

Aaron leaned against the hood of his SUV, and I felt his gaze all the way down my body. *Holy shit.* His eyes smoldered. Burned for me. My confidence skyrocketed and I walked as fast as I could to him. "Let's go."

"Read my mind." He opened the door for me, bending low to nip at my neck. "I'm pre-coming so hard right now, I'm surprised you can't tell."

I giggled and looked down. Sure enough, there was a little circle on the outside of his jeans. "Thank God you're wearing black."

"You won't be giggling like that when you're spread out in front of me." He shut the door and I clenched my legs together. God, my body pounded for more release. I had never been shy about sex. I loved it. The orgasms, though, I craved them. Some girls were one and done, but not me. I needed five or six before I felt satisfied. I turned to Aaron, his face pure determination while he drove.

"How's your cock doing?"

"Don't talk about him. Or say cock. Shit. Hearing you say it makes it worse. Just sit there and breathe," he barked.

I laughed at him, only getting another piercing look. "Greta. We have five minutes until your ass is mine. Enjoy it."

Fucking hell.

The drive felt like an hour but soon enough, he parked outside his house and faced me. His jaw could cut bread, it was so tight. "Two things. The guys won't be home tonight. If you were worried they'll hear you, they won't. Second, are you absolutely sure about this?"

"Yes, Aaron. After seeing your cock this morning, I need to ride it."

"Christ. You're gunna kill me." He ran a hand down his face and turned, wild eyes replacing the worried ones. I reached over and cupped the outside of his wood. It was massive, flashes of it this morning coming back to me. He groaned and snapped into action. "Bedroom. Now."

We ran inside. It took him two tries to get the door unlocked and I held back laughter. Once inside the privacy of his room, he did exactly as he'd intended. He ripped my shirt off, the sound piercing the quiet air.

"I want to look at your tits. God." He pushed me against his door, his fingers tracing the outsides of my nipples. "I knew you had nice ones, but, Christ. These pink nipples... I need to taste." He lowered his head and pressed his tongue against one. I bucked into the door, grabbing onto his hair. *Can I come from nipple play?*

He bit and sucked and looked some more. "I could spend hours on these. Hours. But I'm desperate." His gaze met mine and his eyes turned the darkest color I had ever seen. I gulped, my throat not working properly.

"Can I take these shorts off, Greta?" His voice now came out soft, sweet.

"Do it fast." I leaned further into the door as he slow, slow, slowly slid my shorts and panties off me. I stood butt-ass naked in front of Aaron Hill. And I didn't give a fuck. "Like what you see, Hilly?"

"You're hot as hell." His gaze roamed me, but his fingers twitched. Without warning, he picked me up and threw me on the bed. "Spread your legs."

I did as he'd said and arched my back as he ran his nose up my inner thigh. "You smell so fucking sweet. I wonder how you'll taste."

But he didn't dive in. He kissed and sucked and teased my inner thigh to the point I brought my hand down to my clit. I needed the release. It hurt. He stopped my hand with force. *Kinky.* "No. I want to taste your cum."

"Then do it. I'm dying," I screamed, sitting up on my elbows. I watched him study my pussy like a damn piece of art. "Use your tongue, Aaron."

"What do you want me to do?" His rough voice hit me right in the center. "Tell me."

"Lick me," I whined, release so close.

"Where? Tell me what you want, baby. I want to hear you say it." He kissed my stomach, dragging his tongue all the way down to my clit but stopping. "Say it."

I moaned. He inserted two fingers into me. "I want…"

He thrust the fingers in and out.

"I want you to use your tongue to flick my clit."

"Like this?" He added his tongue to the mix, the sensation of his fingers and mouth just what I needed. I bucked against him, the orgasm shattering my reality. It was the orgasm that put all others to shame. He licked and sucked up every drop before I came back to earth. "You are the hottest thing I've ever tasted."

I smiled, drunk from the high. "Wow."

He laughed, the sound of his shirt hitting the ground somewhere making me open my eyes. Suddenly, the idea of falling asleep post-orgasm wasn't the best option. His naked chest called my attention. "I hope you're not done, Greta. I like to go all night."

"I'm not done. No." I sat up and ran a finger down his firm pecs. "You jizz in your pants yet?"

"Almost. Why don't you help me take them off?" He grinned. I had to agree with him. I scooted closer to undo his belt buckle and pulled the tight trousers down to his ankles. The prettiest cock I had ever seen stood in front of me.

"God, I want to lick it." I leaned forward, but he stopped me. "Why?"

"Baby, after drinking up your pleasure, I'm two seconds from exploding. I want to be inside you." He pushed me back onto the bed so he was kneeling over me. "Tell me, how tight is your pussy right now? As tight as it was an hour ago?"

"Y-yes," I whimpered. Aaron was a sex god.

"Your cream tasted like heaven. Sweet. Like you. Want to try your taste, Greta?" He lowered his mouth to mine and I welcomed him. I could taste my musky scent, the combination of his tongue and the smell driving me wild. We made out, like two horny teenagers dry-humping on a couch. He kissed with such experience and passion. I was pumped and ready to go again when he reached over for a condom.

He slid it on and propped himself over me. Heat was still in his eyes, but so was a vulnerability. The hesitation. The worry about *me*. "You sure about this, baby?"

"Fuck me, Aaron."

My words sent him into the frenzy he needed. He pushed inside me, the sheer length of him stretching me to the max. I lifted my hips to make him fit. "Oh, fuck."

"You're tight as hell. Oh, my god, Greta," he moaned into my ear. He fisted both of my ass cheeks in his hands as he thrust into me over and over. He changed pace and grabbed my legs, bending my knees back farther. I moaned. "Does this feel good, Greta?"

"Yes." I could barely form words. He pounded into me, finding an angle with his fingers to swirl my clit and, seconds later, I saw stars. I screamed his name, his mouth capturing mine as I rode out the orgasm.

"I love hearing you scream my name. Shit, I'm close," he panted into my neck. His body tensed, his thrusts becoming harder and more aggressive as he held onto me tighter. I arched my hips up, his response nothing more than a deep groan. Then he bucked one, two, three times before releasing a guttural sound that had my stomach swoop. With a final kiss on my mouth, he pulled out of me and collapsed on the bed.

My ears rang. My toes tingled. My body hummed. I felt spent. Totally, blissfully happy and spent. He got up and went to the bathroom, leaving me in the darkness of his room. *Do I regret this?*

Does this change everything?

Is it real?

I shut my mind off. I enjoyed sex and trusted Aaron. That was all. I knew countless friends who fucked around and it changed nothing in their relationship. It could be done. Plus, my legs and clit were incredibly happy at the moment.

He snuck back into the bed and let out a deep sigh. "Wow."

"Yeah. Ditto."

He reached out, smacking me on the ass before turning me to face him. He had a hesitant grin. "How you doing?"

"Aaron. Don't be a fuckstick." I laughed and shoved him away from me. "I'm doing fucking great. I'm an orgasm whore so I'm not quite satisfied."

"Wait, what?" He arched a brow, his mouth widening. "You're not satisfied?"

"Oh, I'm satisfied, but my problem is once I get going, I need a lot to settle down the burn." I used my fingers to touch myself, the familiar buildup of an orgasm blossoming. "See, I've thought about you while touching myself before."

"What?'" His voice disappeared. His shocked expression turned me on, like I could hustle the sex god. I quickened my pace on my clit. "What are you... What?"

"I'm getting off." I closed my eyes. "Oh, I'm close."

Then, he flicked my hand out of the way and took over. He bent down to suck at my nipples again and I instantly came all over his hand. I moaned his name and bit down on his lip as trembles went through me. "Holy fuck."

He sat there, dumbfounded. I chose that as my cue to head to the restroom and take care of business. I walked back out and saw he was still in the same position. "Aaron?"

"Who are you?" His gaze slid to mine. Awe, lust, something else were in those eyes. "I just—"

"I like sex." I crawled back onto the bed and paused. "Oh, can I not stay? I know you like to send your little cleat chasers on their way."

"Fuck off, G." He laughed, pulling me into his chest. "You're not a cleat chaser."

"But we just had sex."

"My dick is still tingling from it, by the way." He chuckled and turned the lamp off. "You're my fake girlfriend. And best friend. You sleep here."

"Thanks for the royal treatment," I mumbled into the pillow, exhaustion hitting me. "Thank you for tonight. I needed the release."

"Any time, babe." He laughed and smacked my ass. "You sure you're still okay?"

"Aaron, it was sex. Honestly, I think we should do it as often as possible until the whole shtick is done." *Wait, did I just say that? Did I just propose friends with benefits?*

He sucked in a breath, kneading the spot on my lower back with his fingers. "You're so casual about this."

"Are you not okay with it?" I turned and faced him. I couldn't see his face in the dark, but I leaned over and pressed a small kiss on his cheek. "We are in a fake, monogamous relationship until January. We cannot see other people and we both really like sex. I can get myself off ten times a day if needed, but after what we just did? You want to walk away from that?"

"Hell no, G." He tucked my head in his shoulder. "I'm so into this plan. I'm just worried about you. I don't want to hurt you in the end. When this is over, you promised you wouldn't hate me."

My gut churned, his words hitting a weak spot that I buried deep. I refused to listen to him. I wanted this. My body did. *So screw you, brain.* "I won't." I pinched his side. "Now sleep."

Chapter Fourteen

Aaron

"Where the hell is it?" A frantic voice woke me.

I craned my neck—Greta ran around the room cussing up a storm. "G, what time is it?"

"My guitar, Aaron." She turned, hands on her hips. She ignored my question. "I'm freaking out. Did I leave it at the bar?"

I stretched, pulling my arms way above my head. Her eyes narrowed, her foot tapping. "It's in my car. I put it in there."

"Are you sure?" She bit her lip, deep frown lines crossing her face.

But she didn't wait for me to answer before sprinting out of the door. My keys rested on my nightstand. I chuckled and threw on a pair of loose shorts before grabbing them. She ran smack into my chest on the stairs. "Where are your keys?"

"Calm down, crazy." I rubbed her arms, her body squished against me in the narrow hallway. "Let's go look."

"I swear if it's not in the car I'm going to freak the hell out," she whined and yanked the keys from my hand. She skipped the porch steps altogether and yelled, "Thank sweet baby Jesus."

"I told you." I scratched my head and wiped sleep from my face. The sun had yet to rise. It had to be six…too damn early to be up. "Are you good now?"

"Yes." She clutched the guitar to her chest. "I woke up freaking the fuck out that I left it at the bar. I can't lose it."

"Yeah. You woke me up, too." I fought a smile. She held on to the damn instrument like it had all the answers. Hell, maybe it did. "I'm heading back to bed. You coming?"

She glanced away from me for a second. Her tongue came out and wet her lip, and my blood pumped faster. Flashes of last night hit me hard. "I'm up already. I should go."

I sighed, running my fingers through my hair. *Shit. I don't want her to go.* "It's up to you. The invitation is always open."

She clutched the guitar tighter and stared at me. I would've given anything to know what ran through her mind at that moment. "I should go."

"Yeah, you said that." I clenched my jaw in annoyance. "Let me drive you back."

"Oh, you don't have to. I can walk." She eyed her outfit of the night before. "Hmm. On second thought, I could use a ride."

I gave her a tight smile and drove the short distance to her apartment. I couldn't fucking believe we weren't talking about what happened. She hadn't said a word about it, yet she commented on the breakfast she wanted and how excited she was for quad-day. Nothing about last night. *When did I become the one wanting to talk?*

"You look like you're holding in a fart, Ronnie. What's wrong?" she asked as soon as I pulled into her lot. She laughed at her dumb joke. "You're going to get wrinkles with that frown you got going on."

I gave her a fake smile. "Better?"

"Nah, you look goofy." She sighed and undid her seatbelt. "Want to head to quad-day with me? It's a perfect opportunity for pictures and public displays of affection."

"Sure." I ignored my chest tightening. "Sounds good."

She studied me, those brown eyes not blinking. "Aaron. Do we need to talk?"

"Hell, I don't know," I admitted, feeling like a goddamn idiot. "Maybe?"

She chuckled and put her hand on my thigh. My entire leg tensed. "Ronnie, I'll force you on another roller coaster if you don't knock it off. Seriously, how far is that stick up your ass?"

That snapped me out of my funk and I glared at her. Her face flushed and she just grinned at me. "Jesus. You're such a pain in my ass."

"Eh, I can live with that. Now, let's talk about sex. Clearly, you need to." She removed her hand from my leg and ran it over the guitar. Her mood shifted and my back tightened. "Do you...do you regret last night? Is that why you're upset?"

"Fuck no." I turned to face her, feeling like a huge asshole. "No. No. Not it at all. Last night fucking rocked."

Her lips curved into a small smile, a slight blush appearing on her neck. "Okay, good."

I hated feelings. They complicated everything and caused pain. Having all these thoughts and concerns going through me was confusing. I hated myself for worrying her but also hated how relaxed she was. I couldn't win. "Sorry I'm being weird. I assumed you'd want to talk about it. And when you didn't, I didn't know what to do."

"Ah, I see." Her plump lips toyed with me. Desire shot through my body, the urge to kiss the shit out of her scaring me. "I'll reiterate what I said last night. I was high from orgasms and there is a high chance I mumbled it. But we both like sex. We are in a fake, committed relationship until January. I see no problem."

Yes. Fuck yes! My dick twitched, but the unwelcome pinching in my core made no sense. My voice came out rough, almost a bark. "It'll still be fake."

"Yes, Aaron." She stuck her tongue out at me. "I know. I do prefer we keep this secret."

"Secret?" I repeated the word, tasting poison. *Why does she want it secret?*

"I think it'd be best if our friends didn't know we're hooking up. They'll pester us and tell us it's wrong. I prefer not to deal with that. You cool?"

Her brown eyes showed no hidden emotions. No warning signs. It soothed me. I nodded. "I'm good with it."

"Sweet." She patted my face with a high-pitched laugh. "We sneak around to help our addiction to sex, do our planned public displays of affection and still be best friends. Easy enough, yeah?"

"Yeah." I grunted. It was the *perfect* scenario. I shouldn't have complaints. Yet something bothered me about it. I had no idea what, though.

"Try not to look happy about it. Please. It's great for my self-esteem." She flicked my nipple and held on to her guitar. "Wear the gray shirt today. It makes you look dreamy."

"Dreamy?" I scoffed. "Get out."

"Bye, boy-toy." She flipped me off as she walked to her door. My nerves calmed down at her gesture. My spitfire best friend had never left, she just enjoyed the hell out of sex. *Huh, this could turn out to work better than I thought.*

* * * *

"What would it take for you to join the Quidditch Club?" Greta pointed to a table of people all decked out in Harry Potter gear. She laughed, dragging me toward the booth with way too much excitement. "Seriously, Ronnie. They have T-shirts. Brooms. I need to join this group. You should too."

"Ah, I'll take a hard pass." I nodded at the kid wearing a Pott Head shirt, not unlike the mug I'd bought Greta, but this time Harry's face stared at me. I had to admit, they had a nice setup with free shirts and lots of swag.

Greta wrote her name on the clipboard and grinned like a doofus as we went to the next booth. She had already signed up for a teacher fraternity, squirrel watching, Breaking Chad, a fan club for the show created by some kid named Chad, and now Quidditch.

I signed up for absolutely nothing. I had more fun watching Greta explore each booth with such precision, as if signing up for some club could affect her entire future. She reached for my hand, as we'd planned on the walk here, and her laugh worried me. It sounded too suspicious. I glanced at her face and knew she'd done *something*. "What did you do?"

"Nothing. Nothing at all." She giggled. I did not trust that sound. Not one bit. I almost went to kiss her to get the truth, but she pointed and ran off in a different direction. Her black sundress billowed in the wind and multiple guys turned to check her out. I couldn't blame them.

I saw the booth she'd gone to and groaned. Only Greta would do this. It read 'Non-Creepy People Watchers'. "G, no way."

"What?" she asked with wide eyes. "I love watching people. It's not creepy. It says so in the title. Duh." She grinned with an agenda in her crazy eyes. I should've persisted more, but she just went back to signing her name up. I gripped her hip with one hand, pulling her away from the disturbing group. I appreciated how her entire body reacted to me. It wasn't part of the plan. But shit, she looked fine as hell in the dress.

"Pookie." Her tongue went to the side of her mouth. "Are you getting hands-y again?"

"Uh-huh." I sat on the faded park bench, pulling her onto my lap. "It's the damn dress."

"Oh, you like it?" Her blush pleased the hell out of me. "I'm glad."

"It gives me quick access." I slid a hand up her thigh, her smooth skin a little piece of heaven. "Ah, does she wear panties or no?"

I stopped my hand, waiting to see what she would allow. I expected her to swat me away but instead, she shrugged. "Find out yourself, Ronnie."

I didn't wait a second longer. I cupped her bare ass and groaned into her neck. She wore the tiniest string of fabric. That was it. I traced her ass, my dick throbbing to be inside her again. *It hasn't even been a day.* "Fuck."

"You wanted to play the game, well, guess who's the loser?" She lifted her mouth to mine, biting my bottom lip. "You have to walk around with a massive wood. I don't."

Then the little tease got up. She winked at me, leaving me stranded on the bench alone with exactly what she said—a massive wood. I mouthed "*You're dead*" to her but she stuck out her tongue.

Score one for Greta.

It wasn't until a painful twenty minutes later that I found Greta again. She stood under an old oak tree, laughing with a group of girls. I hadn't seen them before and walked toward them when Greta waved me over. Four pairs of eyes stared at me with each step. I plastered on my smile. "Ladies."

"Hi, Aaron." A shy, petite girl held out her hand. I shook it, giving her a long grin. She blushed, Greta smacking me on my side.

"Don't lay on the charm, Ronnie." She put her arm around my waist and dug her nails into my skin. *Message received.* "These gals are in my cohort for teaching. Be nice to them."

"I'm nice to everyone, Gabs." I winked at her friends and Greta rolled her eyes. "Nice to meet you guys. Mind if I steal my girlfriend for a second?"

"Oh, no. Go ahead. We'll chat later, Greta," the short one squealed and Greta smacked my ass.

"God, you are such a flirt." She tried to move her arm from me, but I kept it there. "You about killed poor Kim over there. She's going to talk about that for weeks."

"Nah, she'll be okay."

"You're wrong. People are sort of obsessed with you. It's disgusting."

"Thanks for that," I said without emotion. "You're not charming when you're jealous."

"Not jealous." She looked up at me with fire in her eyes. "It's anger. To me, you're just Hilly. To them, you represent what they can't have. You're sex on a stick, a hell of an athlete, and popular. I haven't told you how many people I haven't spoken to since freshman year texted me asking about you. I've dodged invitations to hang out from girls I can't stand."

And any one of them could be the mysterious author of the post defaming me. I wanted to thank her, hug her, do something, but before I could, she grabbed my face in her hands. I had no choice but to taste her minty lips. She swirled her tongue with mine, her chuckle making my heart squeeze. "Greta," I said between kissing her. "You're getting me hard again."

"Sorry," she said, her face telling me she felt no remorse. "I saw someone on my shit-list."

"You have a shit-list?" I fought a laugh.

"Uh, yeah. Doesn't everyone?"

"No. I don't think so. Do you carry it around with you or what?"

"Ronnie." She sighed and picked up a Frisbee that had landed in front of us. She threw it back with a huge smile. The sun hit her hair the perfect way and I felt sucker-punched in the gut. "I carry it around in my head. I know who's on it and who isn't."

"Who the hell is on your list?" I refused to believe she had one. She liked everyone and everything. I'd witnessed her become friends with an asshole who'd taken her parking spot. She could not possibly have a shit-list.

"Hm, well, Jenn and Travis Fish."

"Who the fuck are they?"

"My neighbors growing up. They always threw parties and my brother was old enough to go. I wasn't. They looked fun."

I rolled my eyes. "You're on my shit-list."

"Nah, you've already told me I'm your favorite person." She smirked, a little too much confidence on her face.

"Goddamn it, I shouldn't have told you that." I laughed. "Don't get cocky on me."

"Don't say the work cock, *Aaron*." She mocked me and feigned a sigh. "I should go. You should, too."

"Wait, why?"

"I work tonight. Plus, you should check your email."

I froze. "Why, Greta?"

"I may or may not have signed you up for every club I walked by." She grinned like a lunatic. "Have fun at the Non-Creepy People Watchers Club."

Then she took off running toward her place. I shook my head, watching her. I couldn't believe she'd done that. What an asshole.

My little lunatic.

Chapter Fifteen

Greta

My first day of classes flew by—the opposite of everyone else I knew. Callie stressed about her internship, the guys stressed about fitting workouts into their already stacked schedule and I hung around with a smile. The guys were encouraged to take more classes in the fall as their season made them miss a lot of class in the spring. It made sense but taking twenty credit hours would not be easy. I offered to help, but they insulted my fifth-grade math class. Sure, it was simple math, but not everyone could do long division like I could.

I smiled, listening to Zade and Callie zing each other back and forth on who had harder classes. For a pitcher, Zade was crazy smart. Callie, on the other hand, worked harder than anyone I would ever meet in my entire life. So, when they fought, I had no doubt my girl Cal would win. To prove my point, she picked up a pillow and threw it at his face.

"Callie, don't be a dick." He laughed and pulled her into his arms. I sighed, happy for them. Only a tiny, miniscule part of my heart felt envious. A speck. A dot. "When are you going to cook for us? We're withering away."

Another reason I loved Zade — he was just as obsessed with her cooking as I was. I shared a look with him, and he winked. "Is Aaron coming over?"

"No idea. Haven't talked to him at all today." I shrugged. I had to play it cool. The last thing I wanted was to get emotionally attached to Aaron and look like a damn fool in front of all our friends. It was a disaster with a capital *D*. I'd had sex with guys before...ones I'd never gotten feelings for. It could be done. "If Callie cooks like she promised, he'll show up. He's like a damn dog."

"That's true. I don't know how he knows. I swear, I started cooking chicken Parmesan a couple weeks ago and he showed up. Zade didn't even know." She grinned with a glint in her eyes. "He's a wack-a-doodle."

I rolled my eyes. "He's something all right."

"How's the fake dating going?" Zade directed all his attention to me. I fought a groan. Zade had a face that belonged on calendars. Hell, Aaron did too, but Zade's face was more masculine. Aaron bordered on pretty. Now that I thought about it, I could make some money selling calendars bearing them half-dressed. I'd have to ask Callie about it later. "I haven't heard anything more about Aaron's little scandal."

I nodded. "It's going well. We hang out all the time anyway. We just added some making out and shit."

"Yeah." He shared a smirk with Callie. "We saw."

"What does *that* mean?" I fired back. I despised being on the end of a joke.

"The night of your show." Zade ran his hand over his mouth, not hiding his smile at all. "It looked a little heated."

I fought a blush. My body tensed. *They can't know, right?* "Guys. It's kissing. Aaron's hot. A kiss is just that—a kiss. You could do it with anyone without feeling. I could kiss Callie right now and not feel a damn thing."

"Really?" Zade's brows disappeared into his hair. "Callie?"

Callie laughed, pinching him. "Calm down. We aren't going to fulfill a secret fantasy."

Zade directed his gaze on me and said right as Aaron walked in, "Prove it, Greta. Make out with Callie."

Aaron froze at the entrance to the living room, his gaze going straight to me. He looked ready to pounce and that couldn't happen. I burst out laughing. "Have a good day, Ronnie?"

He chose to sit on the armrest of the chair I sat in, his back as stiff as a board, and I wanted nothing more than to mess with him. I put my foot into his side. "Cat got your tongue, playboy?"

"What did I walk into?"

"Greta was just explaining to me how she could kiss anyone without feeling. Like at your show," Callie explained, giving Zade a pointed glare.

"I told her to prove it. Like any guy would. She can talk the talk, but can she walk the walk?" Zade attempted again, raising an eyebrow at Callie. I chuckled. "Hmm? Ladies?"

"This isn't *Friends*. We aren't going to make out to win an apartment." I threw one of the remotes at Zade. He caught it and looked back at me a couple more times. I flipped him off and left them in the room. I needed a damn beer.

"Watcha grabbing?" Aaron's smooth voice followed me into the kitchen and I ignored how good he looked. It had been two days and my legs turned to jelly. He moved his hand to my hip and I glared at him. "Woah, why the face?"

"Our friends are here," I whispered at him, swatting his hand. God, it felt good, but they couldn't know. "Behave."

"They're so into each other, they'll have no idea." He lowered his voice and tingles broke out on my neck. He cornered me into the nook between the refrigerator and the counter. "I'm not happy with you. I got ten fucking emails about clubs. Ten." His eyes heated over, flicking to my mouth for a long, drawn-out minute.

I laughed and he shook his head, slow and methodical. I gulped. "Boom."

"I'm going to get you back." He ran a finger over my bottom lip. "Somehow, someway."

Tanner walked into the place, followed by Jeff. I shoved Aaron away. They greeted us and each carried a food item or beer. They were learning – when they ate us out of house and home, it was only polite to replenish our stock. "G!"

"Hey, guys." I pushed past Aaron and hugged them. I was a hugger. An aggressive one, depending on who it was. "How were your classes?"

"A bitch." Tanner scratched his neck and nodded to Aaron. "Hilly."

"Johnson." Aaron's tone worried me. It was too tense. I looked back at him and noted his flared nostrils, tight jaw. *Uh-oh.*

"What did you bring?" I asked, desperate to rid the tension that overtook the kitchen. "Potato salad?"

"No, Greta." Tanner laughed and put his hand on my shoulder. "I brought extra chicken, rolls and pasta. If Callie's cooking Italian, I want to overeat. Carb-load for a workout tomorrow."

"Boys." I rolled my eyes and grabbed the food from him. "Callie, get your cute ass in here. I'll help you cook." I didn't want to go into the room with Tanner and Aaron. Nope. Not when Tanner clearly knew something and didn't like it.

"No way, G." Zade appeared in the kitchen and put on a dorky apron. "I'm her sous-chef. She likes bossing me around. It's part of the kink."

"Shut the hell up, Zade." Callie hit him with a spoon and joined the five of us all squished into the small room. I backed into Aaron's chest to let her pass and he put his arms around me. Tanner saw. I began sweating. "Everyone out of here or you don't eat. Out! Now!"

Jeff laughed and held up his hands. "Listen to the woman."

Aaron kept his hands on me until we entered the living room and I shook him off. This was getting weird. Unease filled every part of my body to the point where I couldn't relax with him near me, so I chose the single person chair. Aaron couldn't try to sit on it.

"G, when do you work next?" Tanner sat on the ground at the foot of my chair. Good. It was better that he sat there, not Aaron. His strong back leaned against the footrest and I tucked my feet so they went underneath me and not against him.

"Hmm. Thursday through Sunday. Four nights in a row. Ugh." *Money is hella good, though. Don't complain.*

"You play on Saturdays, right?"

"Yup. For the next three weeks."

"Cool — I'm planning on going every time you play. I still can't get over how good you are. You know, you could forgo this teaching thing and explore music." His eyes filled with pride and my heart melted.

"Thanks, TJ. That's sweet." I glanced at Aaron and wished I hadn't. His fists rested on the couch as he glared at us. *God, this is hard.* "Education is a sturdy career. Solid. A demand for it will never go away. I need the consistency."

He sighed. "Yeah, I get it."

"On the other hand, I could get replaced with computers and robots soon. So maybe I should say to hell with it and form a band. Travel the world. You guys could be my groupies! Yes! I would be more famous than you. Maybe you could form a fan club." I cheered, all of them chuckling.

"Greta's G-Thangs?" Jeff attempted, getting booed. "G-Moneys?"

"Nah, those suck. What about…" Tanner stuck out his tongue, thinking. "Greta's Gang?"

"Oh, I like that one." I pushed myself up closer to him. "Greta's Gang. Rolls off the tongue, yeah? What you think, Ronnie?"

"G-Spotters." He deadpanned. "Greta's G-Spotters."

Then we all burst out laughing. Even Aaron's stoic face curved into a grin. I wiped tears from my eyes and shook my head at him. "I think we have a winner."

"I'll make the shirts." Aaron stretched his long arms over his head, a sliver of his tight abdomen sticking out. My throat became heavy. "I think we need an episode of *The Sopranos.* Nothing gets me more excited for Italian than mobsters."

"Oh, not again." I got up and switched the cable to hook up to our premium channels. "You and your mobsters."

"I vote we have Italian Mondays," he yelled, Callie and Zade joining in. They agreed and now, I succumbed to the fate of watching mob shows and eating pasta on Mondays. *Not a rough life.*

An hour later, we sat around the table stuffing our faces. Dinner tasted like a small piece of heaven. The six of us laughed and passed the food around like a damn sitcom. I smiled at my group of friends, my heart constricting with how much I loved them. *Damn it.* Aaron kicked me under the table and I gave him a pointed look.

"You had a weird look on your face, Gabs."

"Yeah well, I had a brief lapse of emotions."

"PMSing? Great." He crossed his eyes, a small smile on his lips.

"Asshole." I kicked him back, harder than he had. But he caught my foot in one large hand. He rubbed it with the hand not shoving food into his mouth and he winked. I tried to remove it, but he held on. It was our little secret.

I forced myself not to react to how he softly traced my bare foot. He rubbed the base, and my eyes closed in pleasure. It felt amazing. I never knew my foot could turn me on. *Interesting…* We needed to explore that later. He kept his hand there for ten minutes, teasing me beyond reason, and I wanted nothing more than to throw the dishes on the ground and have him fuck me senseless. All from him touching my foot.

I needed to get a grip.

His knowing eyes didn't help either. They kept widening and heating at me. I swore everyone at the table had to know. They had to. Aaron was emitting sex waves as we spoke. Tanner broke me out of the trance. I turned to look at him and hoped my face wasn't flushed. "Come again?"

"You said you have a weekend off in three weeks, yeah? I say we all go camping or take a road trip. You guys down?"

I nodded, looking at Callie. "I'm down."

"Hell yeah, what about you ass-hats?"

Zade and Jeff agreed but Aaron's stare stopped me. He looked down at his plate, shoulders sagging and body deflating. My heart wanted to reach over the table and squeeze him. "Aaron?"

"I'm going home that weekend."

His words silenced us all. Home meant hell for him. We knew that. *Fuck the rules.* I reached over and squeezed his hand. "I'll go with you. It's part of the plan, yeah?"

His sad eyes warmed for a second before he nodded. My eyes stung. He clenched his jaw before replying, "Okay. I'd like that."

"Shit." Tanner sucked in his lip making a wet, awful noise. "Now I feel like an asshole."

"Don't. You didn't know. Go camping." Aaron waved him off, but he was hurting. "It's fine."

"We can talk about it later," Tanner added, sounding desperate for someone to lighten the mood. It got real heavy, real fast. Nothing happened and he stood. "I'll clean up. You all hang out, I got this."

"Thanks, TJ," Callie said, her eyes still narrowing at Aaron. We shared a look. She wanted to help but didn't know how. I shook my head at her and brought my plate to the sink. Aaron still looked like a deflated balloon and I knew what would cheer my best friend up. I ran my hand down his.

"Want to go watch *Goodfellas*? I have it on my laptop."

His ears perked up and surprise filled his eyes. "You have *that* movie? Why?"

"I went through a phase." I shrugged. He'd assumed I hated mob movies. I never said I did so I'd let him think it. "Let's go."

He pushed out of the chair, sizing me up to see if I was lying. I waited, not giving a shit if the rest of the group watched us or not. I tuned them out. Aaron's sadness took priority. "Come on, Ronnie."

I didn't wait—I went to my room and opened my laptop. Sure enough, I had it in my video library along with an eclectic list of movies I liked. Not two seconds later, Aaron walked in with such sad eyes my heart turned over. "Come on, lie down."

His flat lips didn't move, but he obeyed. He stretched his long body next to me and I began the movie. We didn't talk. We didn't move either, the entire two and a half hours. My head rested on my hands while his arm remained around me. I hated to break the moment. I knew he needed the escape. I patted his hand. "Great-ass movie."

I sighed when he didn't respond. Instead, I shut the computer and finally took a glance at him. His gray eyes assessed me with a slow heat behind them. I bit my lip, the temperature rising a hundred degrees. I whispered, "Are they still here?"

"I don't care." He set my laptop on the side table and nipped at my mouth, his body covering mine. "I want to fuck you right now."

"Mm, yeah?" I closed my eyes, arching my back. "I've been wet since dinner."

"Fuck, Greta." He closed the distance between our mouths and kissed me hard. Aggressive. Rough.

I fucking loved it.

I matched his tongue with each stroke and loved how he tore at my clothes. I moaned and he stilled. "You need to keep quiet, baby, can you do that?"

"Uh-huh," I whispered. This time he licked his bottom lip with such a heated look that I had never felt so wanted in my life. He got up and carefully locked the door. When he turned around, I shivered. God.

He stripped out of his clothes and walked over to me with his beautiful, perfect cock ready to go. He threw my shirt and bra across the room, his fingers knowing what to do. I arched, grabbing a pillow to cover my mouth. The pillow served as a blindfold and holy shit, I was turned on.

He bit down on my nipples, his fingers already going to my soaking-wet panties. He slid them aside, chuckling. "You're drenched for me. God, I fucking love it."

Soon, I was moments away from my first orgasm. His fingers knew me like my pussy was a controller. He thrust and flicked and I cried into the pillow, the pleasure blinding me from everything else. "I hate that I can't hear you say my name."

I moved the pillow and his mouth hung open. I don't think I had ever seen Aaron look so goddamn good as I did that second. I sat up and crushed my mouth to his. I pushed him down, grabbed for a condom in my drawer and slid it on him. He groaned, fisting my hips with his hands as I moved.

"Fuck." His eyes closed, jaw tensing. "You feel tight as hell."

"Yeah?" I felt bold, pulling myself off him before spinning around so my ass faced him. And I rode him. I built up the speed, the pressure hitting me right where I needed it, and I used my fingers to give me the extra help I needed. I exploded on him, his body shaking underneath me. He didn't let me stop—he moved my hips with his hands, pushing deeper inside me with the motion. "Aaron, yes."

"This is so fucking sexy," he said with a hoarse voice. Sweat pooled between our bodies and we fucked to a slow, rhythmic pattern. He moved one hand and placed it onto my lower back, pushing down to change the angle just enough for him to moan. It worked, because not a minute later he thrust harder into me, tensing as he shook beneath me. My name left his lips as he held onto me. "Greta, my God."

"Goddamn." He chuckled with heavy breath. "Hot, G. That was really hot."

"Yeah?" I slid off him and expected him to get up, but no. He disposed of the condom then joined me on the bed. His eyes sparkled. "Wh-what are you doing?"

"You need more. I have a good memory." He grinned at me, a full-fledged Aaron grin, and found my center again with his talented fingers. "What do you say…we put in another movie and I just play with you until you pass out?"

My body hummed in response. *Movie and orgasms I don't induce myself? Sign me up.* "I'll press Play."

"Good girl. I want to break your record. I like winning things."

Chapter Sixteen

Aaron

School had never been my thing. I understood its purpose, sure. But the concept of learning and taking notes did not excite me. Zade, well, he loved it. Jeff and Tanner didn't mind their classes. I got no joy from acing a test. My one requirement to keep the scholarship pertained to my GPA. I had to keep a 3.5, which was the only goddamn reason I carried my laptop to the library to meet with a cohort for a study session. We had a marketing concepts test the second week of classes. Our professor was an asshole.

"Hey, guys." I gave a curt nod to the group and frowned when I recognized one of them — Cindi's friend Jill. Jill was hot, and she knew it too, but that wasn't why I disliked her. It was the way she looked at me. She studied me, with her phone pointed right at me. *Great. More gossip about me. She's not even trying to hide it.*

"Hilly, have a seat, man." Cory pointed to the chair next to him and gave me a smile. He was a nice guy. So was his girlfriend, Lisa. They were why I'd agreed to this session. "We split up the assigned Chapters to create cheat sheets. I can't believe he's testing us over six chapters. What, does he think we don't have lives?"

"Obviously." Lisa rolled her eyes and handed me a list. "You'll do the first two since they're short. We'll take three through five and Doug here will do the last one. Does that sound okay?"

I eyed the key terms and concepts I had to create a cheat sheet for. My heart sank. This would take hours and I wanted to be on the field or at the bar with my friends. The craving to drink had gone away. It was the atmosphere and Greta, if I was honest with myself. I took too long to respond and Lisa cleared her throat. "Sure. Sounds great."

"Good. Upload into Google Drive when you're done and we can end by going over our Chapters. Happy note taking, y'all!"

I dove into the Chapter and ignored Jill. I finished the first chapter, feeling proud of myself for buckling down. Maybe I needed to do study groups more to hold myself accountable. I stretched my neck and saw Jill licking her lips at me. I cringed. Her small sighs and paper shuffling had annoyed me the entire two hours and I wanted a break. "I'm going to grab a coffee. Anyone want anything?"

"If you have a cigar, I'm not above trying it in the library." Doug chuckled and shook his head. "I'll take a black coffee."

"Yeah, me too. Thanks, Hilly," Cory replied and went back to his notes. I prayed I would walk there alone but I should've known Jill would follow.

"Aaron," she purred. "I'll join you."

I didn't respond. I quickened my pace to the coffee shop on the main floor and ignored her. There was a fine line between being polite and telling her to get the fuck out of my face. I was so close to breaking that point. Her steps tapped on the floor and I knew she stood right beside me. "Aaron, why are you being so rude?"

I wiped my face with my hand, turning to look at her. "What do you want, Jill?"

She had the gall to look hurt, which annoyed me more. "I-I don't want anything."

"Doubtful." I went back to the line and she followed. Ignoring her little sniffs, I ordered the drinks and paid the barista. I hated being a celebrity on campus because I had no choice but to offer her one. I turned, jaw tight, and hated asking, "You want anything?"

"Oh, you're so sweet!" she squealed and put her arms around me. I froze, the wall probably more comfortable than me. She pulled herself off me and I pinched the bridge of my nose. The last thing I needed was any more goddamn pictures. The barista narrowed her eyes at Jill and I swore I saw a little pity there, but she masked it and handed me the drinks.

"Thank you." I took the small carrier and left Jill standing there. I didn't doubt she was tweeting or Snapchatting me. I saw the angle she held her phone and *Shit*. I'd never cared before and now I wanted to smash her phone. *Could she be the one posting the photos of me, ruining my life? Maybe Cindi?*

Fuck, if I ever found out…

"Thanks, Aaron." Cory clapped my back and took the drinks from me. He lowered his head, his voice dropping, and forced us to turn the other direction. "Just wanted to give you a heads-up about Jill. She's…she's uh, she's trying to get with you. Lisa is friends with her and she mentioned it to me. I didn't know before today, man. Sorry to put you in a bad spot."

I just nodded. Cory wasn't a bad guy—he was solid, so I trusted him. "No worries. I'm probably gunna take off. I'll send you the second Chapter tomorrow."

"Sounds good. Sorry again."

"See you." I picked my stuff and got out of there as fast as I could. I felt used—the irony wasn't lost on me. I'd used girls for sex and nothing else my first year. This was karma. It had to be. And it sucked.

I had a couple of hours before Greta's show and I preferred to see her than do homework. Hell, I preferred her over about anyone else. My brain went straight to what we'd done two nights ago—her hair spilling over my pillow, her nails digging into my back. Greta was a spitfire.

Great. Now I had a boner in a library.

My thoughts eventually pushed Greta and her body to the side and focused on the project. I buckled down and dove into the material, knocking it down in two hours. I sighed in relief. I could finally go to the bar.

Cheap beer it was. I walked in, the crowd larger than it had been the past two times. It was a packed house. My chest filled with pride. I hoped Clyde was giving her at least three hundred dollars, because it sucked waiting in line for a drink. I briefly thought about how chill it used to be here on Saturday nights where I could enjoy a drink in peace. Good for Greta, though—her talent brought everyone here.

"Hilly!" Zade yelled to me, his arm around Callie. "Come join us. I bought some pitchers."

"Thanks, man." I took a sip and Tanner gave me a nod. I wasn't certain, but I would bet money Tanner had either heard Greta and me the other night or guessed it. He hadn't been cool with me since but, hey — it wasn't his goddamn business. "How was her opener? I got caught up with some work."

"I'll say." Callie smirked and rolled her eyes at me.

"What does that mean?" My chest pinched. The anxiety I hated filled my lungs each second as I waited for her answer. *What now?*

"I saw some pictures of you online. Getting chummy with Jill, eh?" She raised her brows and the sinking feeling in my gut came back.

"Whatever she posted, it's false. I went to a study group and she followed me, getting all in my space." I wanted to leave, to get away from my friends and their accusatory glances. Callie's eyes softened, her body relaxing. I knew she believed me. But I still hated to talk about it.

"I'm sorry, Hilly." She leaned into Zade and he gave me a tight smile. I avoided Tanner altogether, choosing to watch Greta. She wore a full shirt this time, thank god. I was far too pissed to deal with her lack of clothing. The jeans, though — they left little to the imagination and thoughts of eating her all night pleased me. Callie interrupted my daydream by holding the phone at me. "You should take a look at them."

I sighed and glanced down. Sure enough, the moment Jill had thrown her arms around me and when I walked away, she'd stolen pictures of me. If I had learned anything, it was that pictures told only part of the story and could be manipulated to fit someone's agenda. Like these. Right now, the pictures clearly looked like I was cheating on Greta with our faces pressed together. Fake or not, it was not good news for my social media presence. "Shit."

"Don't respond to her. It's not worth it. She's grasping, Aaron. If you respond, it'll get more attention than it deserves. Do you remember last year when girls would show me pictures of them with Zade?"

"Yes. I do have a fond memory of Catty Callie trending on Twitter." I grinned, but stopped when Zade narrowed his eyes at me. "But you're right. I hate it, though."

"Focus on you. You're doing a great job." She'd attempted to make me feel better, and it had had mollified me a little. I shrugged it off, though. I wanted to watch my girl perform.

She killed it. Her throaty voice and the fedora she wore made her even more attractive to every guy in the bar. Hell, I already thought she was amazing and I wasn't a fan of watching a bunch of guys drool over her. I needed to send another message to these asshats that she was taken. Real or fake, she was mine until January. I had no plans to share.

When she announced her short break, I went right up to her and dipped her real low before planting a wet kiss on her. She grinned, her teeth hitting my lips. "Ronnie. Hello there."

"Gabs, you amaze me each time." I smiled at her. The tension in my chest relaxed and I felt loads better. "A couple of guys were getting too aggressive with their staring. I had to show them who's boss."

"Damn it. I was hoping for a dick-measuring contest. I'm sure Clyde has a ruler and you could whip it out right on the table," she teased and kept her arm around. "I'm for real. Whip it out."

"Don't be a Pita." I pulled her close and found an empty corner. I knew what had been bothering me the last twenty minutes I'd watched her. "Look, there's something I need to tell you."

"Is it about those pictures?" She rolled her eyes, putting a hand on my chest. "Please."

"Wait, you saw them?"

"Yeah, of course I did. I'm addicted to social media. It's a sickness." She put her other hand on my hip so we faced each other. Her brown eyes filled with concern, narrowing as she took in my appearance. "Were you worried?"

"Yeah." I wanted to kiss her again but held myself back. I deserved an award. "I thought you would've been upset. The pictures were taken out of context. She cornered me. I couldn't push her away. It sucked."

"Hey, I believe you." She ran her fingers over my forehead and bit her lip. "Don't frown so much. You're going to get wrinkles there. You already have them."

"Wait—you're worried about my wrinkles and not the pictures that look like I'm publicly cheating on you?" I asked, flabbergasted.

"Ronnie, I trust you more than anyone. Except Callie, but she doesn't count. Why would you break that when we're doing this for you?" She shook her head with a laugh. "You might be ridiculous, but you aren't stupid."

"Well fuck." I blinked a couple of times. "I never thought about it that way."

She flicked my forehead. "Now, relax. Have a couple drinks. I'm going to mingle."

I released her when she walked away and her words hit me. *I trust you more than anyone.* After my past, all the shit I had done, she still trusted me. That put an unknown emotion in my chest. It felt like confidence and something like contentment. It was a new feeling, and I barely had time to register it before my phone went off.

Why would my sister call at this hour?

"Kenzie? Are you okay?"

"Come home." Her voice cracked. "Dad's in the hospital."

"What happened?" My throat turned to ice, the calm I'd felt seconds before nowhere to be found. A pain I was familiar with. Regret, hopelessness and despair replaced it. "Kenzie, tell me what the hell happened."

She sniffed. "Due to the chemo, he's easily susceptible to the flu. He got a bad flu a week ago and it kept getting worse. His fever is a hundred and three right now."

"Shit. I'll leave now."

"Please." Her strong façade broke and I heard her soft cries. "Please come home."

Chapter Seventeen

Greta

I laughed at Callie — she did the perfect impression of Zade. He didn't laugh but that was okay. "You have to come on stage with me for a song. Come on, Callie."

"Ah, maybe." She scrunched her nose, looking at Zade. "Not tonight. Let's practice some more beforehand."

"I'm holding you to it." I held out my pinky finger, making her pinky promise. It was a sacred vow. I don't care whatever anyone says. "Good."

"You're a dork, G," Tanner said and put his arm around me. He gave me a hug and it felt nice. Nothing like Aaron's arms...no, those were a beast. "Woah, what happened to Aaron?"

I frowned, following the direction of his gaze, and sucked in a breath. Aaron looked crestfallen. Devastated. Forgetting my friends, I ran up to him. "Aaron, what happened?"

"I need to go." He didn't focus his gaze on me. He glanced from person to person, scattered and distracted. "I need to go now."

"Where?" I put my hand on him and he jumped back. *What the fuck?* "Aaron, you're scaring me."

"My dad." He closed his eyes, his hand shaking. "He's in the hospital. My sister called. I need to go."

"I'll go with you." I nodded, more to myself than him. He couldn't drive. I wouldn't let him. Not with his shaking hands and scattered brain. "Let me tell Clyde."

"No," he demanded, still not meeting my eyes. "I can go."

"Aaron Hill." I waited until he met my eyes. It took a minute, but he did. "I am not letting you go alone. Let me tell Clyde and we'll go together. I'm driving."

"Greta—"

"Don't argue. You know what, come with me." I dragged him toward Clyde. His eyes widened, perhaps sensing the clear panic coming off me. "Clyde, something came up and I need to leave right now. You know this is serious, I've never done this. Beg, bribe, do what you can to get Callie up there. She can play for an hour."

"Wait, what?"

"I need to go with Aaron. Family emergency."

And Clyde nodded. He knew. Everyone knew. I took that as permission and I half ran, half pulled Aaron toward Callie. "Cal, I'm driving Aaron to see his dad. He's in the hospital. Please play for an hour, take care of my guitar."

"Of course." She hugged me and I kicked into action. I led Aaron outside to his car and yelled for the keys.

"I can drive."

Oh, so he can talk now. Good. "No. You're shaking. Let me do this for you."

He sighed, resigned, and passed me his keys. We hopped in and I adjusted the seat. I didn't even think to stop at our places for clothes. I didn't think about a charger or toothpaste. I just thought of Aaron and his family. My heart hurt. "You want to stop for food? Have you eaten anything?"

"I'm okay."

"Can you tell me what happened?" I pulled onto the highway, hoping I could remember the two-hour drive. Luckily, it wasn't farther. "What can I do?"

"He's been going through chemo. You know, trying to lessen the size of the tumors in his lung. It increases the risk of sickness. He got the flu, my sister said, and it got worse. He has a fever of a hundred and three right now."

"Okay. Okay, well. He's at the hospital. They'll put an IV in and get the temperature down. That's their job." I spoke more for my benefit. "He'll be okay."

"Yeah." He grunted.

"Do you want music? Silence? Questions? I feel helpless, Aaron. I want to help you." I glanced at him and felt his pain in my core.

"Just talk. I like your voice."

Sucker-punch to the gut. Then to my heart. "Okay."

I hummed for a bit, then went into stories. I told him about my childhood. My deepest secrets, which weren't scandalous at all. I talked about my brother and his divorce and how that made me nervous for love. I talked about my favorite toys I played with and how I used to create these elaborate stories with my brother's action figures, totally forgoing dolls and dressing up the masculine robots into girly clothes. He didn't laugh, but he released a quick breath and I took that as a good sign. "Do you want to stop and get any food?"

"No." He still stared straight through the windshield, as though the interstate had all the answers in the world. "Do you?"

"I'm fine, thank you." His question warmed me. "I think we're almost there. Can you direct me to the hospital from here?"

"Yeah, turn left at the next two lights. You'll see it." He gripped the *oh shit* bar hard enough to turn his knuckles white.

Ten minutes later, without a single word spoken between us, we parked at the hospital and walked hand-in-hand to the entrance. I couldn't remember who reached for who, but I squeezed his hand. I would support him any way possible. I couldn't imagine this hell. "You can do it, Ronnie."

He squeezed it back and asked the nurse what direction his dad's room was. She pointed down the hall with a smile. I took that as a good sign. Aaron pushed the door open with his fingertips and I wasn't sure if I should follow or not. He answered for me, pulling me in with him.

His mom and sister ran up to him, hugging him hard. My eyes stung at their raw emotion and I was shocked when his mom hugged me too. "Thank you, Greta, for coming with him."

"Of course." I met his gaze over his mom's shoulder. "How's he doing?"

"Stabilized the fever. He's still weak." She squeezed me one more time and put her arms around her son. "He's been pretty out of it for a while, at least the last hour or so."

Aaron removed his arm from his sister and went to stare down at his dad. My heart did something funny but I pushed the emotion down. This was so not the time for any thoughts like *that*. His sister hugged me and kept her arm around me. "Want to go find a drink with me?"

"Sure." I waited to see if Aaron looked up or acknowledged that he'd heard me, but I got nothing. "Ronnie, you want a drink?"

He slowly glanced at me and shrugged. "I'm okay."

"I'll get you a water anyway. Mrs. Hill?"

"A water would be great, thank you." She smiled warmly at me and joined Aaron at the edge of the bed. Kenzie motioned toward the hall and I followed. "How are you holding up, Kenz?"

"Kenz?" She laughed and flicked her long hair over her shoulder. "You must hang out with Aaron. He's the only one to call me that."

"Well, yeah." I shrugged, pursing my lips. "I know you as Kenz. Sorry. Kenzie? Mack? Mackenzie?"

"Hell, no. I like Kenz. That's just fine." She collapsed into a plastic chair near the vending machines and let out a loud heart-stopping sigh. "I needed out of that stifling room. Aaron has it lucky not having to live this every single day. I hate it. Does that make me the worst human alive?"

I got the water from the machine and sat next to her. It wasn't my place to comfort—hell, I had my own issues—but the plea in her eye called to me. The sadness in the room, the tenacity of this family as it changed a year ago… If my words could help ease her pain even a little bit, it would be worth it. "You are not the worst person at all, Kenz. No. I can't relate to your situation, but seeing your dad struggle every day, and your mom, has to be hard as hell."

Moisture filled her eyes and she wiped them quickly before looking back at me. "It's the worst. I can't enjoy my senior year. All I want to do is get away, go to college to try to be happy. But I can't do that to them. I won't. Look, I'm sorry I'm venting to you. This is humiliating."

"Stop, it's okay. I'm a good listener." I squeezed her shoulder, my eyes stinging. "I can't speak for Aaron. However, we hang out all the time and you aren't the only one struggling. He handles it in different ways. Talk to him."

"Thanks." She sniffed again and stood. "Ready to go back?"

"Yup." I smiled at her, seeing her put her bravado onto her face piece by piece. My heart hurt again. I couldn't imagine being the kid at home during this time. One parent struggling, the other in pain... I shook my head. I would think about all that later.

We entered the room and I passed out the water. Without thinking, I went up to Aaron and slipped my arm around his waist. He smiled down at me, putting his arm around me and gripping my hand. No one spoke as we watched Aaron's dad breathe, the machine monitoring his vitals next to him. It wasn't until a bit later, maybe an hour or so, that Aaron's mom cleared her throat.

"Why don't you kids go back to the house and come back with food in the morning? I'll stay here with him. They'll come and kick you all out once they realize you're here."

"Sure, Mom," Kenzie replied and took the keys from her. "We'll call in the morning for requests, but if anything else happens, call us immediately."

"Of course. I love you both, so much." She went to Kenzie first, enveloping her in a tight embrace. She did the same to Aaron and I gasped when she hugged me too. "Thank you again, Greta, for coming. See you all tomorrow."

We left the room. "Did you drive here or do you need a ride, Kenz?"

"I need a ride." Her gaze flicked to our joined hands, but she didn't say anything. We went to the car in silence, the worry and sadness present with every breath. He volunteered to drive and we sat in silence. When Aaron pulled into the driveway at their house fifteen minutes later, I felt I could breathe again. Kenzie strode off into her room. "I'll see you guys in the morning. Bye."

That left me and Aaron. He appeared more relaxed, his shoulders not as tight as before and his face not a blank stare. He faced me and smiled — not the full one I loved, but a half one. "Come here."

I obeyed and walked into his open arms. He squeezed me, putting his head into my hair. I closed my eyes and tried to give him all my strength in that hug. It lasted for two minutes, the comforting scent of him filling my nose. "Let's go to bed, Ronnie. You gotta be tired."

"Okay." He put both hands on my shoulders and guided me toward the basement door. "My room is down here. I've always been a bit crazy. They put me down here to block out the noise."

My stomach tightened. Did he mean — no. This was not the time for *that*. I went down the stairs and spied the baseball shrine that was clearly Aaron's room. I chuckled at the baseball beanbag chairs, the posters from the nineties and early two-thousands teams. Pictures of teams, trophies, ribbons and jerseys all hung up on the walls. I went to look at them, but he grabbed my elbow, dragging me. "What?"

"I need you right now." His eyes were haunted, dark. His sadness and worry poured out of him and I tensed.

"Okay. What can I do?" I would do anything for him to help get that look off his face. *Anything*. No one should deal with this pain. His chiseled face was meant to smile and laugh.

He didn't reply, instead cupping my face. He closed the distance between us and kissed me hard. It wasn't painful, but it wasn't soft. He danced his tongue against mine, searching for something that I wanted to give him. He moaned into my mouth and the sound startled me. It wasn't pleasure...it was sadness.

"Aaron, come on." I pulled back, dragging him to his bedroom. I shut the lights off, and stripped off my shirt. It was easier without the lights. I could lose myself in the pleasure of the moment instead of the rapid pace of my heart, which was trying to tell me something. I ignored it and focused on Aaron. My best friend. I pushed him onto the bed and straddled him. I kissed his neck, pulling his shirt off and tossing it to the floor. His muscles felt tight and hard. I dragged my tongue down his impeccable abdomen, stopping when I reached his belt. He moved to undo it, but I stopped him. "Let me."

I undid it with shaking hands. The darkness surrounded us, cutting off any distractions besides our bodies. I slid off his clothes and took him in my mouth. No more thoughts of his family. No more thoughts of our fake arrangement. None of that. It was about him. And me.

"God, Greta. Yes. So good." He fisted my hair on the top of my head, pulling ever so slightly, but the pain enticed me. I sucked a little harder, using my hands to bring him as much joy as I could. His legs stiffened and I knew he was close, just a little longer. "Stop."

I froze at his command. I glanced up at him even though I couldn't see much. The sheets rustled, the tension between us drowning me. My limbs shook with need and *something* but Aaron cupped my face before I could think. "Baby, I want you to ride me. Can you do that?"

"Yes," I whispered between kisses. I gently shoved him back down, fumbled with a condom and put it on him. Then I straddled the beast of a man. I slid down, farther and farther until he entered me. "Jesus." He cupped my breast, applying the right pressure where he knew I would tremble. "Aaron, please."

"Mm," he hummed, his strong hands gripping my hips and forcing me to move up and down at the perfect pace. I matched it, figuring out the exact momentum we needed and I rocked. I arched my back, shoving my hips forward as he pushed up and the result was... It made me scream. "Shh, baby."

He sat up and moved my legs around his waist. Flesh to flesh, chest to chest, I had no time to think before he kissed me. This felt different. He tasted like leftover gum and desperation. My eyes stung at the tender way he held me, but I forgot about all that when the first wave of an orgasm hit me. I bucked against him, his mouth swallowing my cries. He didn't stop, though. No, he knew me. He knew I was just getting started and he continued our gentle escape from reality. He tilted me back and hit me at an angle that sent me over the edge, and this time, tears leaked out.

It wasn't until later, way later in fact, that my eyes closed for the night. Aaron's body surrounded me, his legs intertwined with mine as our breathing matched. We hadn't spoken. We didn't need to. But I was royally fucked.

I'd fallen in love with my best friend, with my fake boyfriend, with a guy with an unhealthy aversion to relationships. *Great.*

Chapter Eighteen

Aaron

Three days later, Coach called me into his office with a half-smile on his face. My chest felt about the size of a peanut with all the anxiety I had. My voice came out gruff, raspy, as if I'd smoked a pack that morning. "You wanted to talk?"

"Hilly, I heard about your dad this weekend. How's he doing?" His large, lean frame plopped into the chair with a soft thud. I gulped, wiping my palm on the hem of my shorts.

"He was released yesterday. He's doing good. Just a bad flu. It escalated quickly because...well, you know why." I cleared my throat and met his eyes. "How did you know?"

He chuckled softly and typed something into his computer. "I didn't read it anywhere, don't worry. Zade told me, that's all. I wanted to check. I know you aren't open for discussions all the time. I have good news for you, son."

"Yeah?" Hope blossomed from the pit of my stomach.

"The athletic director and I had to meet to go over stuff you'll never have to worry about. Quite boring, if I'm honest with you. Anyway, he asked about your situation and said no one has inquired about the photographs and no one at his end is worried about it. I've had a handful of scouts contact me about observing some workouts. Not a damn word about what happened."

"Jesus." I released a long breath of air. It was like pounds of stress left me. "That's awesome news."

"Yeah, I thought that might make you happy." He shoved his computer around to me and pointed to the picture on the screen. "There's going to be a charity function for the chancellor in a month. I'm not saying you need to go, but I don't think it would hurt. Bring Greta. Behave. It'll do a lot. Network. What do you think?"

"I'll talk to Greta about it. If she's in, I'll be there."

"Good. I'm asking Zade and one of the younger kids, too. You could all go together if you want. You figure it out. Let me know tomorrow, okay? If not, I'll find another schmuk."

"Yes, Coach. Thank you." I stood to leave and he motioned for me to wait.

"You've been playing well. Keep it up."

I nodded and left his office. I leaned against the wall outside, rubbing the spot right between my eyes. The headache that seemed to live inside me softened. I knew better than to get my hopes up, but damn, I needed that news.

I took my time walking back. I was in no rush—I had no homework and no one would be back at the house. Sitting in a silence sounded like an awful idea. The shops and little downtown area always had people and laughter. I preferred sound to silence. A couple of guys nodded at me, the girls smiling with hidden meaning. I ignored them and found myself standing in front of a jewelry shop. Kenzie had rambled on when Greta and I had taken her out to brunch before we left. She'd rolled her eyes about how silly girls were nowadays, how they wore a necklace with the name of the guy they were 'with'. She'd scoffed but I think Greta and I both knew she wanted one. She would never admit it, but Kenzie had a major crush going on.

I would be the second to last person she would talk to about it, the first being our dad. I chuckled at the thought of making fun of her as soon as I found out who. The gold chain caught my eye, and although it was stupid, I smiled. Aaron wasn't an entirely odd name and I found it without much trouble. I bought it, wrapped it in a white tissue-paper thing and put it in my pocket. I smiled.

Greta: Did I just spy you leaving a hipster store? Who are you?

I glanced around, wondering how Greta had seen me, but that blonde hair was nowhere to be found. Blue Street stood in the center of the east campus and contained a multitude of stores and restaurants, but not many class buildings. I checked my watch. Greta had class right now.

Aaron: Are you skipping class?

Greta: Never. I'm glad to see you worried about my education.

Aaron: Where are you?

Greta: Muahah. I like this.

Aaron: I don't. Damn it, Gabs. Well, are you almost done? Want to grab a drink?

Greta: God yes. I'll meet you at the Cams in twenty?

Aaron: I'll be there.

My mood improved and I headed toward the bar. It wasn't quite happy hour and I managed to enter the campus favorite without being noticed much. Sure, the bouncers all shook my hand, but they remained cool about it. It wasn't until I found a back booth that a group of girls, all looking like they planned to hit a high-class club, spied me. They sauntered over, bringing with them an assaulting array of perfume.

"Hilly, can we buy you a drink?" a tall, leggy brunette purred at me. She didn't ask before sliding into the chair across from me. "Please?"

"Ah, I'm meeting someone here. I'm good. Thank you, though." I smiled, tight and fake, and my heart beat faster. Her friends held out phones by the bar and sweat beaded on my forehead. They held up the phones in our direction and I gripped the table. *Jesus. I'll never trust a girl again.*

"Oh, come on." She pursed her shiny red lips and a waft of her sweet perfume hit me. She leaned over the table with her face a foot from mine and I leaned back as far as I could, my back hurting from how hard I pushed. "One drink, Mr. Hill."

"I said no." Anger seethed from my voice, her face flinching for a second. "My girlfriend is on her way. She wouldn't appreciate this."

"Ah, yes. Greta, is it?" She leaned back and crossed her arms, her ample cleavage at least four inches long. Her too-full lip curled on one side as her voice lowered. "Rumor has it the entire relationship is staged. I write for the *Who's Hot, Who's Not?* blog on campus and I came over here for an interview."

I didn't react. I couldn't react. Instead, I smiled a tad menacingly and leaned toward her this time. *That's why she's here.* "Regardless of what I do or don't say, you're going to write whatever the hell you want to get views and traffic on your site."

She licked her bottom lip, flashing her eyes at me, before shaking her head. "No, actually. I don't write bullshit."

"Sorry, honey, have you lived under a rock? I don't trust anyone." I ended the conversation with a finality to my tone. She got the message and nodded at me before rejoining her friends. My stomach tightened until they left the bar and I prayed I hadn't made things worse. Something good was happening and it would only be a matter of time before something fucked it up. That was the pattern of my life.

"Ronnie!" Greta's voice broke my self-deprecating thoughts as she waltzed into the bar with the joy very few people had. "Where's my boyfriend?"

I smiled and pulled her into my lap. I smacked a kiss on her, then another ten. She made the softest, most perfect moan and I deepened the kiss so our tongues molded together. I refused to stop and we continued until she pulled back, red splotches all down her neck. I grinned. "Hey."

She flicked my forehead before moving to the seat the blogger had just left. "What a welcome. Did you order drinks?"

"No, not yet." I felt stupid. I should've done that.

"Okay. I'll go grab some. Liquor or beer? I know what you like." She stood and held out a hand to prevent me from standing. "Chill, let me buy you a drink."

"Uh, beer. If you insist."

"I do insist." Her gaze went from my eyes to my mouth for a split second before she went to the bar. I studied her. For the first time in my goddamn life, I was thankful to have a girlfriend. Yes, it was fake. Yes, the sex was the best I've ever had.

She liked the same things I did.

She had the same humor.

She cussed.

She ate anything.

She could kiss like a damn porn star. She craved sex just as much as I did. And she didn't give a flying fuck about me playing baseball. My palms sweated as she walked back, an uncomfortable and unfamiliar feeling overwhelming my chest. "I got you a craft beer, Ronnie. It's very hipster. I figured since you stopped in the hipster store. Are you going to wear fake glasses now?"

"I'll think about it." I grinned and held my beer up to hers for a cheer. "Thanks, baby."

Her eyes widened for a second, so fast I almost missed it, but I knew every one of her facial tics. "You're welcome."

We each took a long swig, not breaking our eye contact. The gift in my pocket now weighed ten pounds. My voice resembled a primitive caveman's rather than my normal tone. "I bought you a present."

"What?" Her mouth curved up, her perfect white teeth on display. "I love gifts!"

"Yeah. I know. I saw it and thought of you. You might not like it. Well, maybe you will. I don't know." She bit down on her lips, fighting a smile as I stumbled over my words. I chose to stop talking then and there. I handed her the small package and watched as she opened it with a wild expression in her eyes. *Buy her presents all the time if she smiles like that.*

"Is it a necklace?" she whispered, twisting the gold chain in her fingers. "What does it say?"

Suddenly, I broke out in a sweat. It was a terrible idea. The worst. I tried to take it out of her hands, but she was too quick. "Is it your name?"

I nodded. "You heard Kenzie at brunch about what girls wear now. Girls should wear their guy's name around their neck. It's a message, you know? I figured it would be perfect for our ruse."

Her eyes dimmed, slightly, before she nodded. "Yes. The ruse."

"I can return it. Here, it's stupid." I tried taking it from her again, but she shook her head.

"No." She pursed her lips and stood. She sat on the edge of my side of the booth and put her back to me. She lifted her hair and exposed the nape of her creamy neck. I gulped. "Help me put it on."

She handed me the necklace and I let it fall against her skin. The clasps were so damn small it took me three tries before they latched. "There."

She turned around and puffed her chest out. "How does it look?"

I fisted my hand. It looked incredible. *Good lord.* My name fell right above her delicious-looking tits and something fluttered in my stomach. "Good."

She lifted the edge of her thin black shirt and tugged down, the result showing more of her porcelain skin above her chest. I clenched my fist. "Are you wearing anything *under* that?"

Her eyes flashed at me. "No."

I stared at the front of her tight shirt and, soon enough, the peaks of her taut rosy nipples showed and I slammed my eyes shut. My anger at her made no sense. She could wear whatever she wanted. She wore shit like that all the time. Now? I wanted to cover her up in a goddamn parka.

"Aaron, what's the problem?" Her voice had the perfect amount of trepidation, as if she knew the littlest thing would send me over the edge. I opened my eyes and pointed to her chest.

"I can see the outline of your nipples. If I can, then that means anyone can, *Greta*." I sneered her name, hating myself.

She glanced down, saw what I was referring to and shrugged. "Who the fuck cares? Free the nip is a very real thing."

"I don't like the fact others can gawk at you." I closed my hand tighter around the bottle.

She assessed me with her clever eyes. Lips pursed, not unlike the blogger, but hers were the right color, the perfect size. "Are you jealous?"

"Fuck yeah." I laughed like it was the simplest thing in the world. "Fake or not, I don't like sharing what's mine."

"Am I *yours*, Aaron?" Her eyes clouded, briefly, before staring back at me.

"For three more months, every part of you, yes."

"Fair enough." She gulped and her throat moved with the motion, "I didn't realize you knew how to be jealous, Ronnie."

"I'm assuming that's what this is. I'm not sure." I ran my finger over the crack in the table. "Do you want people to see your tits?"

"Aaron!" she gasped, a red tint to her cheeks not coming from a blush. "What kind of question is that?"

"An honest one." I leaned forward, studying her. "Am I not satisfying you sexually? I thought your five orgasms this weekend were sufficient."

She laughed. The echo of it rang across the bar and a handful of people looked over at us. She mirrored my pose and positioned herself inches away from me. "I like looking good. It's not for anyone but *me*. Ruse or not, no one is changing that. So, get that through your obnoxiously large head." She paused, licking her lips, tantalizing me. "Now that I know this drives you crazy." She ran her fingers over the outline, my dick straining to be inside her. "I feel like I'm going to be going braless for a while now."

I grunted. "You didn't answer my question."

"I know." She ran her fingers up and down the bottle, the motion not unlike stroking a cock. "I guess you'll have to figure it out for yourself."

"Let's go. Right now." I stood, chugging the rest of my beer. "You're killing me."

"I'm not done with the beer *I* bought." She smirked, looking smug as fuck. "Sit down, horn dog. I'm yanking your chain."

"I know what you could be yanking." I sat back down, adjusting the waistband of my shorts, which were way too tight. She brought the bottle to her mouth, taking her sweet-ass time, and sipped. She did it again, silently.

Then, she stretched, the fabric pulling tight against her and the necklace peeking out at me.

"Jesus, Greta. I'm dying."

"Too bad. I'm hungry. I think I want ice cream. You can come if you want." She got up and walked out of the bar. I ran after her like the pathetic chump I was. And we got ice cream before we went to my room. *Finally.*

Chapter Nineteen

Greta

The vacuum drowned out everything and I found peace in the repetition. Cleaning did that to me. It was therapeutic, in a sense. My parents used to tell me I was a slob, a tornado who always left damage in my path, but I'd figured it out. I liked to create the mess so I could clean it later. It was a sick, wonderful cycle I had had my entire life.

Why would my relationships be any different?

I couldn't talk to anyone about it. Aaron was my best friend besides Callie, and we'd agreed not to tell our tight-knit crew. That left me alone, to deal with the range of emotions I wasn't used to. I hated it. Despised it. Loathed who I was becoming.

Thus, the insane cleaning I had done all week. The necklace with Aaron's name on it reflected the light from the window I'd dusted earlier, mocking me. *You're mine for the next three months.*

Okay. Three months. Then what? That was the million-dollar question I refused to ask because I already knew the answer. *No, don't go there. Be chill. Be cool.*

I stopped the vacuum and wrapped the cord around to pin it on the back. I had dusted, mopped and wiped every crevice in the place and still felt restless. I ran my hand over my chest and rubbed it, like that would ease the anxiety. It didn't help. I completed all my homework, worked ahead in two of my classes and scheduled two more slots to tutor. I still had too much free time, and free time meant trouble.

And trouble meant making crazy decisions to calm the storm inside my head.

Greta: I'm going crazy. Want to get a tattoo with me?

I texted Aaron. If anyone understood anxiety, it would be him. I damn well wouldn't tell him *he* was the main source, but I could use his company. Despite the battle going on inside, he made me happiest.

Aaron: Are you getting a typical, 'basic' girl tattoo? I don't support that.

Greta: No idea. I'm in a weird mood, like I need to do something crazy.

The last time I'd felt like this, I'd gone out with Todd. It reminded me of a girl who'd pulled the fire alarm during high school. When I'd asked her why, she'd simply said she was bored and needed a distraction. I'd never understood how they connected, but I had this underlying desire for *something* and it was either a tattoo or dying my hair green.

Or confessing things that shouldn't be said to Aaron. And I would rather shave my eyebrows off than ruin it.

Aaron: I like crazy. I'm finishing up at the gym now. I can pick you up.

Greta: Okay. Maybe I'll get a tramp stamp. Or a lightning bolt on my forehead.

Aaron: If that's the path you want, you might as well get an entire book cover on your back.

Greta: It's settled.

I laughed at his suggestion. My rebellious side rarely took precedence, but I figured this called for it. I was stuck in a battle of my mind and heart and I didn't have time to figure it out.

"G, I'm here." Aaron's voice carried through the door sometime later. I smiled—he always came to the door and I loved it. Too many guys honked when they came to get me. Or called. Or yelled. But Aaron, he *always* came to the door.

I glanced down at my black cut-off shorts and purple crop top. I'd chosen them hours ago, not intentionally forgetting to put a bra on. Our conversation at the bar came to mind again, the thought warming me at his jealousy. With my purse in my hand, I headed out of the door and he smiled as he took in my outfit. "Hot damn, Gabs."

"How's it going, Ronnie?" I grinned as he tightened his hold on my hips, the predatory glint entering his eyes. He wasted no time before darting his tongue into my mouth. He tasted like mint. "Mm."

"Your mouth gets me hard."

I drifted my hand down to his tented pants. I giggled into his neck. "You told the truth."

"I don't lie." He pushed back, hissing as he moved his fingers up my stomach, touching the bare exposed part. "Fuck, what is this?"

"A crop top. They're in style, Ronnie." I used a finger to tilt him away. "You like it?"

I spun around, the four inches of my abdomen breaking out in goosebumps. A deep growl started in his chest and a part of me enjoyed it. I felt smug. "Greta."

"What?" I stopped, putting my hands on my hips. My position had me sticking my chest out, the slope of my tits on full display. He didn't reply. His eyes went from heated to glacial and I walked right past him. "You think you'll get a tattoo?"

"No." His hand went to my lower back, his fingers pressing into me harder than normal. "What are you getting?"

"No idea. I've always wanted a tattoo or something ridiculous to regret in my nineties. I never had the time or money and with the bartending job...I deserve a reward."

"I thought you were going crazy?" He opened the door for me while his jaw continued to resemble concrete.

"I am. You've talked about it before. The itching in your chest...the urge to do something." My heart beat fast, the anxiety building. "I've had it the past couple days and I need to release it."

"We could just have a lot of sex."

Boys are dumb. I scoffed. "Yes. Let's solve all our issues with sex."

"I could fuck you hard enough you wouldn't remember your thoughts."

I gulped as he shut my door and headed toward his side. *Dear lord.* His words hit me in the groin and the thought of doing *that* sounded better than anything. "Well shit, Aaron."

"Just saying. You could've asked me to do just that and I would've had no problem." He shrugged, putting the seatbelt on. "What shop are we going to?"

Where were we going? Oh yeah. Tattoo. "On Blue and Lincoln Street." My voice shook. Thoughts of him thrusting into me repeatedly made me lose focus. "I've always liked the idea of a yin yang. You know, the good and the bad in life balance each other?"

He shrugged again. *I see he's talkative today.* "Get what you want. As you said, it's *your* body."

"Ronnie, I sense an attitude. What's up your ass?"

"Nothing."

"Ah, yes. The infamous *I'm fine* line guys steal from girls. Fine. Be a bitch." I hid my smile when he gave me a side glance. I knew to wait it out. Eventually, I'd learn the truth.

Five minutes later, he sighed. "Tanner posted a picture of the two of you yesterday out to eat. I don't think that's part of the plan. People could gossip and that's the last fucking thing I need."

"Did he?" I pulled up my social media apps and scrolled through. Sure enough, Tanner had a picture of the two of us, huge smiles and tacos. I'd run into him after a class and the idea had made sense. I didn't think twice about it when he suggested it. Not long ago, Tanner, Aaron and I did almost everything together. *And I crushed on TJ. Different time.* "It's an inconspicuous picture. What's the problem?"

"You're supposed to be *my* fake girlfriend. We still have eight weeks left. Just, keep the flirting down."

My temper flared. *Flirting? No way.* "Where the hell is this coming from? I don't... Aaron. Come on. I'm doing this for you."

"Shit. You're right. I'm sorry." He reached out, squeezing my knee. "I'm being a dick."

"Holy shit. You just apologized."

"Okay, no need to make a huge deal out of it." He dug his fingers a little harder into me. "I meant it. I'm sorry."

"Twice now." I pretended to faint. "I can't handle all this."

He chuckled, the air in the car becoming clearer and less tense. I could relax. "I'll be interested to see what you get."

"Me too, because I don't have a goddamn clue."

Ten minutes later, I felt like a fool.

I hated needles. The woman in the chair closed her eyes, wincing as the needle buzzed for everyone to hear. Her daughter held her hand, becoming paler by the second, and suddenly, I did not want a tattoo. *Nope.* I couldn't have the buzzing needle death machine come near my skin. My stomach clenched. *Nope.*

"You decide what you want yet?" the hip, young, and attractive tattoo artist asked, appearing next to me.

A picture caught my eye. A close-up, graphic picture of a nipple piercing. *Rhianna has them, Bianca from high school has them. They would be my little secret.* Now I knew what I wanted. "I changed my mind."

"Yeah, what you wanna do, doll?" Tony, the handsome, tatted-up guy, grinned when he followed my vision. "You wanna get both or just one?"

I bit down on my lip. "I'm sure the pain sucks. What's better? What do you think?"

Jaqueline Snowe

"Might as well get both."

"All right. I'm doing it."

"Follow me." He motioned me back and Aaron perked his head up from the binder of designs he was rifling through.

"What did you decide?" He set the binder down and followed us. "Are you getting a butterfly?"

I laughed, my nerves dancing in my stomach. Suddenly, telling him made me sweat. I stuttered. "I-I'm getting my nipples pierced."

"Shut the fuck up." He laughed. The asshole laughed loud. Tony turned around with a look to make me cringe, but Aaron ignored him. "No, you're not."

"Yes. Yes, I am." I stomped harder toward the back room. Tony pointed to a chair and I sat.

"All right, doll, let me get the supplies. Do you want rings or barbells?"

"I liked the picture out front. The rings." My entire body shook with adrenaline and excitement.

"Nice choice. I'll be right back." Tony eyed Aaron, but left the room. In his absence, I swore fumes were coming out of Aaron's ears.

"What the fuck are you doing?" he snarled at me, teeth bared. "Your nipples? Really?"

"Yeah. It's what I want to do." I jutted my chin out at him. "You can leave if you want."

"The hell I'm leaving." He crossed his arms, his gaze not moving from my chest.

"Then stop glowering at me. It's making me nervous."

Tony walked in, ignoring Aaron yet again. "What's got you nervous, doll? This guy?"

"No. Needles do. Do you use a needle?"

"I use this." He showed me a clamp of sorts, kind of like a pair of scissors with holes at each end. "I clamp down on your nipple, pinching it quite hard, then I slip this inside it real quick. The harsh pain is quick, I insert the ring and it's done." He smiled. "You'll handle it great."

"Okay. Do it." I leaned back in the chair, closing my eyes. Tony laughed.

"First, I need you to lift your shirt to your chin and keep it there. Are you okay with him being in here?"

I opened one eye to see Aaron staring daggers at me. Part of me wanted to say no just to see what would happen, but I chose the other route. He would cause a scene of epic proportions, and I wasn't feeling that cruel. "Yeah. He's good."

"Okay, I'm shutting the door." The light thump of the wood had my chest heaving. "Shirt up, doll."

I lifted the small crop top to my neck, both my breasts exposed to the two men. Aaron looked murderous so I chose to focus on Tony's face. He put gloves on, the sanitized materials on the small tray next to us. He grabbed an alcohol swab, cleaning each nipple. The coldness of it had them both perking up, higher than I had ever seen them.

"Nice. This is good, actually, more to clamp onto." Tony swiveled in the chair, grabbing the scissors. "This will feel a bit cold and like a pinch, okay?"

I nodded as he used his hand to grasp my breast, the clamp going around my tip and pulling. I flinched. It was cold and painful but when he brought out the needle, I closed my eyes. "I'm inserting it now."

He did, the white-hot pain instant as the metal circle clung to my body. He released me, making me open my eyes. "One done. Nice job."

I looked down at my swollen, bleeding nipple, but the ring looked badass. "Hell, yeah."

"One more." He went through the same process with the other nipple, the pain having me clench my jaw. But soon enough, it was over. He placed Band-Aids over each nipple, going over cleaning care and directions for the next couple of months. I listened, not wanting the infections that scared the shit out of me. I paid, Aaron not saying a word the entire time. I tipped Tony, smiling at him. "Thank you. They look awesome."

"They really do. See you again sometime."

"You think?"

"Once you get one, you'll want more." With a wink, he went back down the hall. Aaron led me outside with aggressive stomps. *Great.* He slammed the door when we got into the car and didn't say a word for the short drive. My bravery faltered the longer we sat there in an awkward, tense silence. "Aaron. What's going on?"

"I just had to watch some fuck handling your tits, Greta. I'm fucking livid and I want to fuck the shit out of you," he growled as he pulled into his driveway. "Don't push me right now. Go upstairs and get naked."

My thighs shook with need at his words. Normally, I'd smack him for talking to me like that but the desire... The sick game I'd played choosing the nipple piercing had all led up to this. And I wanted it. I wanted it bad.

I sprinted into the house, stripping off my clothes as soon as I entered his room. My heart hammered with anticipation. *Will I like it rough?*

I laughed. Of course I would. My nipples throbbed with each beat of my heart. All the blood went to the sensitive buds, causing a bit of pain to the recent piercings. But I loved how they looked. Aaron entered the room seconds later, dangerously calm and quiet. I turned to glance at him.

"Get on the bed," he ordered. I obeyed. "Spread your legs for me, as wide as they go."

I did. *Holy shit I'm turned on.* He stripped out of his clothes and crawled on top of me with an intense focus. "Don't move your hands from where I put them."

He lifted them over my head, his strength pushing them into the bed. Then he dragged his other hand down my chest between my pulsating nipples and slipped his fingers inside me. "Did the tattoo artist get you wet, Greta?"

"Wh-what?" I tried to sit up, but he forced me right down. "No. No way."

"Do you know how *hard* it was to watch him touch these?" He fisted both of my tits, being careful not to touch the piercings. "His fingers pinched and twisted these beautiful, perfect tits of yours."

"I'm wet for *you*, Aaron," I whimpered. His eyes heated darker than I had ever seen.

He added another finger and pushed harder. "They look so fucking hot I can't wait to suck them when they're healed."

"Yeah?" I managed to say between moans. I was already so close. I groaned, arching my back, but he pulled out his fingers.

"No. You're coming with me inside you today. Don't you come yet." His growl sent shivers down my body. He sheathed himself in a condom and didn't wait another second before plunging into me with an underlying fury I couldn't grasp. "God, you're fucking tight."

He kissed me. Hard. Claiming me and ruining me for anyone else I would come across for the rest of my life. "Tell me you're mine, Greta." He gritted his teeth, pulling out of me. I gasped at the loss. "Say it."

"I'm yours," I cried out. I needed the release. "I'm yours, Aaron."

Ravenous, predatory and soft. All those emotions crossed his face before he plowed back into me. I screamed in the best way. My hands were held captive over my head, each move more aggressive than before. Every kiss, bite, thrust, orgasm was rough and exhilarating.

When I exploded around him some time later, he held me tight in his arms as he released himself. We had never done it like *that*. Ever. Our bodies pooled with sweat, the evidence of what we had done all over the bed. "Can you shower those babies?"

He carefully traced the outline of my new metal rings, placing the softest of kisses on them. I shivered. It was so gentle. "G?"

"Yeah. I can shower," I whispered.

He didn't respond. Instead, he lifted me up and walked me toward his bathroom. He turned on the water and we both went inside.

Something changed in the scope of that ten-minute shower. Aaron washed me, kissing almost every part of me. Feelings I never wanted or knew existed hit me in the chest as we lay in bed together. Aaron, the goofy baseball boy with an aversion to relationships, had snuck his way into my goddamn heart and made me fall completely in love with him.

Goddamn it.

Chapter Twenty

Aaron

"Let's go!" I yelled, pounding on Jeff's door. "We're gunna be late."

"Dude, I'm in the bone zone. Go without me," Jeff yelled and I burst out laughing. *Bone zone? What did that fucking mean?*

"His latest and greatest is in there." Zade joined me at the end of the hallway. "I bought you a stack of *Playboys*."

"Dude." I laughed at the bag he handed me. "You get sick of using them or did Callie make you throw these out?"

"Asshole." He grinned. "It's been some time since you and Greta started the deal. I figured you needed them."

"Thanks. Let me lock these in my room before we leave for the stadium."

"Sure."

I joined Zade within a minute and we headed toward a leadership presentation for the captains. As we walked out, the door slammed and a tall girl ran off in the other direction.

"Damn, did you see her necklace?" Zade asked, laughing.

"Yeah? What about it?" She had a black, collared thing around her neck. Greta wore one every once in a while, and they were in style.

"I call those blow job black belts."

I thought about it, then doubled over in laughter. "Shit. You're right."

"You're welcome." He patted my back when I kept laughing. "Callie even agreed with me. Now, every time we see one we burst out giggling like teenage boys."

"Callie has the humor of a teenage boy," I quipped back. He knew Callie had a soft spot in my heart. "Speaking of your sexy woman, why hasn't she cooked for us in a while?"

"Her classes picked up. Trust me, I'm suffering, too."

"Yeah. Suffering," I mocked him. The guy walked around with sunshine coming out of his ass.

"You ask Greta about the charity thing coming up soon? I know Callie knows about it but I'm not sure if I demand she goes or if I gotta ask her. What you think?"

"Shit." I ran my hand through my hair. "I'm not sure. I haven't asked Greta. I should today."

"What are you gunna do for her after all this is done? I mean, it's your call, but I would buy that girl a car or something." Zade said it so casually, I had no reason to react to his words. There was no reason for my blood to turn to ice and sheer panic to replace the calm.

I *knew* it would come to an end. But we still had weeks left. Plenty of time to deal with all that later. I pushed the unwarranted, annoying feeling down. It made no sense to have a feeling of dread. I was almost in the clear. I should be living it up, celebrating. I shook my head. "I hadn't thought about it."

"Think about it. You owe her. Your life has been a hell of a lot better the past four, five months, don't ya think?"

"For sure, man." I wanted to change the topic. Anything. "How's your sister?"

"Zaria?" He laughed. "Student teaching. Can you believe she's gunna be teaching high school math?"

"Hell yeah. She's smart as a whip." I'd always had a little crush on Zaria. But she rarely hung out with us and was the female version of Zade. It would've been weird regardless of how good-looking she was. "She still trying to get to know your half-siblings?"

His face blanched and I regretted the question. I wanted the attention away from me but not enough to upset him. "Never mind, not my business."

"No. Don't worry about it. She's...yes. She's seen them about three times. She's getting resistance, though. Apparently, their mom had another son from a previous marriage. He's causing some problems. Preventing her from getting to know them. She didn't explain it the last time I talked to her, but I'm picking up that he thinks she's after his money."

"Dude. You both donated the money he left you. Why the fuck would he think that?"

"No idea. I'm going to the next meeting they have, though. I don't like this guy at all."

"Let me know if you need help, man." I hit his back.

"Will do. Now, let's get this leadership course over with. I get the need for it, but I don't enjoy doing it on a weekend."

"What, you don't want to work on your leading abilities? For starters, don't be an ass. Encourage. Inspire. Have integrity. Blah."

"You're already there." He chuckled. I hadn't been invited the year before and the thought that Coach wanted *me* to go meant a lot. It meant I wasn't a total failure. "Why haven't you embodied those qualities?"

"Fuck off."

* * * *

Hours later, Zade and I were joking around with the rest of our teammates who'd gone. I remembered, my freshman year, how some of the older guys went out of their way to welcome the newbies. Sure, they might have hazed us a little bit, but I'd felt right at home. I wanted to do that to the new ones. Zade had the humor and unique ability to make anyone feel comfortable. That wasn't my style. I was messy. I came with baggage.

I wanted to be the guy that our team could turn to when shit hit the fan. I was great at helping others pick up the pieces, just not myself. Coach pulled me to the side after it concluded. Zade said he would wait and I walked toward Coach's signature stern look. "Hilly, glad you made it."

"Thanks for the invite, Coach."

"Be a sponge. Soak this up. Shortstops are the hardest position to find a lot of success. You need the mental stamina and you've been through the wringer. You might not know it yet, but others follow you."

I nodded. I'd always assumed people followed Jeff and Zade with their pitching and catching combo. "Thank you."

"I didn't just call you over here to butter your ass. I have some scouts coming to watch practice next week. You're one of the names."

"Excellent." My throat constricted with emotion. This was it. This was what I wanted more than my next breath.

"Have you Googled yourself recently?"

"No. I prefer not to. I've only posted stuff with Greta the past four months."

"Well, most of the stuff that pops up is your stats and about your dad. You need to think about doing an interview or something to generate talk."

"No. I don't want to do an interview," I scoffed. "Too personal."

"Think about it, Hilly. These scouts are going to Google the hell outta you. If I can stumble across the post with those pictures, so can they. I'm not telling you what to do, but think about it."

"Fine. I will." My lifted mood plummeted. "Thanks for looking out."

"I'm not lecturing you, kid. I'm rooting for you."

I ran my hand down my face. "I know. I just… Putting my life out there scares the shit out of me."

"It's better to control what press you can. That's all I'm saying. Now, go out and have fun tonight." He clapped my shoulder and joined the other coaches from the staff. I spotted Zade laughing with a punk named Elijah.

"Eli, Zade. How does a beer sound after sitting for four hours?"

"You know I'm not twenty-one yet, Hilly." Eighteen-year-old Eli frowned. I chuckled.

"There are some perks of being on the baseball team and with us. I can get you in. But no drinks."

"Really? Fuck yeah!" He clapped. "Let's go now."

Zade and I shared a look—this kid had too much energy. "What did Coach want?"

"He thinks I should do an interview." Eli didn't know about the fake relationship, but everyone on the team knew about my dad and the shit-storm photos. Eli was smart enough to let Zade speak first—he was older and one of my best friends.

"Damn. I see his side. But I know you."

"What's the harm in a little interview? I don't get your holdup," the punk-ass replied, his gaze darting between the both of us as he realized he was the opposite opinion. "Shit. I mean. If you do a small interview and have premade questions done in advance, you could control the conversation, you know?"

I hadn't thought about that. It still didn't sit well with me. But I'd table the idea and think about it. Coach had never steered me wrong before. "Thanks, Eli. That's not a half-bad idea."

He smiled, relieved. "Now, how about this bar?"

We laughed, talking shit about him the entire walk to where Greta was playing. I knew she was on stage when we walked in. Her throaty voice never got old. My heart raced and my mood became better without explanation.

"Damn, Hilly. Damn," Eli said, his gaze directed at Greta on stage. She wore tight black jeans, a grunge tank top and a goddamn fedora.

Her looks stopped me in my tracks.

Fuck.

"What, you aren't going to smack me for checking out your girl?" Eli's voice brought me back. On cue, I hit the back of his head.

"Thanks for the reminder."

Zade snorted and disappeared to find Callie. I joined them, not able to take my eyes off Greta. Her fingers strummed her guitar, the vibration of her voice hitting me in the solar plexus. She used to play with her eyes closed, but now she searched the room with those soft-brown orbs and landed on me.

Something squeezed around my heart, the sensation so unfamiliar I frowned. Greta saw my reaction, a briefly noticeable look of concern crossing her face before she looked elsewhere. "You got it bad, my friend."

I recognized Callie's voice, Zade nowhere in sight. I smiled at her. "What you mean?"

"You have feelings for Greta." Her kind eyes didn't mock me, no. But they assessed me a little too much.

"Greta's my best friend, Cal. You know this." I rolled my eyes, avoiding her gaze. "Come on."

"I know that look on your face, Hilly." She patted my arm. "It's okay. I won't tell anyone."

"I don't know what you would tell," I lied, lied, lied. "We have almost two more months left. That's it. Then things go back to normal. Greta can date and I can go back to my whorish ways."

My stomach soured. Callie smacked her lips together, snorting. "You're going to be okay seeing Greta make out with another guy? *Really*?"

I clenched my fists. Thinking about her with someone else turned my blood hot. Rage, not dissimilar to how I felt about the pictures, consumed me. But Callie's knowing gaze and tone pissed me off. "Callie. Yes. It's part of the deal."

"Okay, sorry." She pulled back, and I imagined her frowning hard at me. I didn't have time to think about it when Greta announced a short break. The crowd cheered, Eli's voice a little too loud. *Idiot.* I didn't want him to get into trouble for being at the bar.

I wanted to run up to her but I waited. I watched as she hugged friends, guys I'd never had seen before, and had to take a calming breath when Tanner appeared next to her with a huge hug that lifted her off the ground. *What the fuck is he playing at?*

"Johnson, I swear to god." Her voice carried over, filled with happiness and amusement. My chest tightened.

"You're so tiny and cute, I can't help it." He set her down and I saw red. I took four strides and stood directly in front of him.

"Stop flirting with my girlfriend," I barked. A group of people around us turned in our direction, but I didn't care. Tanner's eyes widened, a slight tremor of fear replacing the shock. Greta put her hand on my forearm, pinching me enough to get my attention.

"Ronnie, did you forget to eat today? You're hangry as fuck."

I laughed, the tension disappearing as soon as it had appeared. "Shit. Maybe."

"Come on, crazy." She tugged me and flipped Tanner off. "I know your weakness, TJ. I'll get you back."

He said something, but I ignored it. I wanted to touch Greta. I knew the breakroom was small, just a table and two chairs. She opened the door and shoved me inside. "Hey, asshole."

"Asshole?" I attacked her neck, running my tongue down it and tasting the salty mixture of sweat and perfume. "I don't like the fact he touches you a lot."

"Aaron. I don't have feelings for Tanner." She looked up at me, the dark brown eyes blinking and pleading with me.

I wanted to ask if she did for me.

I desperately wanted to know…but I didn't ask. If she said no, I wouldn't survive it. Instead, I lifted the edge of her grungy shirt and saw she was braless again. "How are my favorite nips doing today? Sore?"

An unreadable expression crossed her face before she grinned. "They're fine. They hurt when they rub against something."

I gently ran my finger over both of them, careful not to touch the metal rings. "God, I can't wait for these to heal so I can suck them."

She gulped. "Are you trying to get me wet right now? I have to be up there in five minutes and trust me, this table has never been cleaned. I'm not having a quickie on it."

"You're no fun." I put her shirt down, telling her about the scouts and the conversation I'd had with my coach. I quickly chowed down on a protein bar as I told her and her reaction made it all worth it.

"My Ronnie is making his dream come true. Shit. I'm proud of you." She wrapped her tiny arms around me, her head positioned right over my heart. "I can't fucking wait to hear about it. They're going to love you. I mean, besides those shitty pictures, you're the perfect recruit."

I squeezed her shoulders, letting myself enjoy her words and warmth for another minute, then pulled back. "My coach suggested this charity event. It would do well for me to have good publicity. He thinks I should take you. Want to go?"

Her face fell, just enough for me to notice. I had no idea why, but I blew out a sigh of relief when she nodded. "Sure, when is it?"

"Two weeks." I pushed a piece of her hair behind her ear. It escaped from her crazy hairdo, where half of her hair was up in a stylish bun and the other half hung loose. "You look good today."

She rolled her eyes. "Thanks. I'll see if Clyde will let me off. It's close to the holidays and we always get a larger crowd."

"I'll make it worth it." I weaved my arm around her waist, pulling her into my chest. "I promise."

"How so?" Her voice rose. Good. I liked when my body affected her. I ran a finger over the outline of her piercing, her body tightening in response.

"Trust me. You'll enjoy every minute of it."

"Do I have to wear a fancy dress?" She pulled back, putting a distance between us. Her tongue wet her lip and an urge so strong, so sudden hit me. I had to kiss her. And I did.

"Sorry. Your mouth... I needed to kiss you. But yes. You wear a fancy dress. I wear a black suit. We get pictures. Food. Expensive wine."

"You had me at expensive wine." She patted my cheek, her neck blotchy from a blush. It wasn't a hickey, but I felt damn proud to knew I'd put it there.

Chapter Twenty-One

Greta

"I lit the entire three-wick candle with one match. I'm going places in life today." I blew out the match while Callie chuckled. "Really, I never can do it all in one match. This is a record."

"Your life is sad."

"Fuck off, mate." I took a long whiff off the lavender scent and checked the time. "Are you heading to the guys today?"

"Nah, I need to work with Nicole on more meal plans." She crossed her eyes. "I love it, but I'm ready for a break."

"We're almost at finals baby. So. Damn. Close."

"I have clinicals with football. I don't have actual tests except for some econ class I had to take. I have so much to do, I won't be able to study for it until the day before. I'm fucked."

"You'll do great. You always worked hard." I meant my words, too. "Well, let me know if you need anything. I'm heading over to see Aaron."

Callie paused, narrowing her eyes at me. "Greta. Can I ask you about him?"

"What about it?"

"Is it real for you?" She glanced at the ground a couple of times while her teeth dug into her lip. That was her signature sign when she was uncomfortable. "I know it's not my business and I don't care either way. It just seems like more, you know?"

I blew out a raspberry. It was now or never. "I think it is… I'll have to tell you everything. But not now, you're busy and I'm running late. Soon, though. I promise." I held out my pinky finger, waiting for her to do the same. She did, interlocking our fingers, and we kissed the bases of our fists. "Okay, now go study your ass off."

"Thanks, G, have fun." I waved at her, but she spoke again. "I think it's real for Aaron, too."

I just smiled.

I wondered if he had developed feelings for me too, as the moments became more intense and intimate. But as soon as I thought maybe, just maybe he reciprocated my feelings, he would say something dumb.

Like how his coach wanted him to ask me. Not him. Or weeks ago, when he'd said I was his for the time remaining. Or how I shouldn't flirt because of his *image*. Our relationship had always been friendship, the purest form. With the added intimacy, I was gone. The walk to the house didn't last long—the excitement of seeing Aaron overtook all my emotions.

It would be the last time before he went home for Thanksgiving. He would only be gone for four days but it still saddened me. I smoothed down the edge of my dress, a tight leather one I'd found a couple of weeks ago. It fit my body perfectly, and Aaron would die. He hadn't told me what our plans were, just that he wanted to teach me things. I shivered with need. I wanted to learn anything I could, especially if we were both naked.

I texted him, waiting outside the door. I knocked, twice, but still no answer. I tried the handle and the door creaked open, but no one was in sight. One of the guys was always in the kitchen or watching TV. It was never this silent.

Aaron knew I was coming. He either greeted me outside, which I assumed was for show for the neighbors, or waited for me to come to his room. I ventured toward the long hallway. They must be in the basement. I turned off the TV they'd left on upstairs, then headed toward their man cave. They used to throw pretty badass parties there, but now it served as a game room where they could be dumb boys. Voices carried up the hall when I began my descent and I froze, my name echoing off the brick walls.

"You're *fucking* Greta? Are you shitting me?" I recognized Tanner's agonized voice. "How the fuck could you do that?"

"Chill out," Aaron replied, anger seeping into his voice. "It's not a big deal. We both like sex. It doesn't mean shit. Also, not your goddamn business, TJ."

"You... It's Greta. What happens when this bullshit is over, huh? Have you thought about that?"

I hadn't moved a muscle, his answer becoming *everything*. We had one more month for the 'plan'. Four more weeks. My throat constricted, my pulse skyrocketing in anticipation.

"Yeah—nothing. We go back to being friends. It was part of the plan. Why are you being such a dick about it?"

Aaron fired back, my stomach souring in the worst way. "It's just fucking. You get around enough to know. We fuck. We pretend."

"Jesus, I can see your bullshit," Tanner yelled, the easy friendship between the two of them nowhere to be found. "Who the fuck cares if you have feelings? I'm just saying—"

"I'm not in love with her, Tanner."

"Greta has always been off-limits. Her friendship is important." Someone hit the wall, the loud boom echoing off the stairwell. "That's why I *never* let anything happen with her. You're a fucking idiot. So, you're telling me when this shit is done, I can ask her out?"

I stopped breathing. My entire body turned into a rope of angst, fear and heartbreak, his one-word answer deciding everything for me.

"Yeah. Jesus, it's her decision." A cold, unnatural tone came from Aaron. An unrecognizable one.

"God." Tanner hit a wall again. "You're fucking her over. You're going to hurt her."

I wanted to move, I really did. But I couldn't. My legs stood stiff, glued to the old carpet on the stairs. If he was going to hurt me even more, I wanted it to be pouring salt into a wound. And he did.

"She agreed to this, Tanner. She knows I don't do relationships. This was to help me and my career. She chose to accept the terms. Stop making it a big goddamn deal. She's handling it better than you."

"Well, when you fuck this up, Aaron, because you will—you fuck everything up—I won't help you."

I sensed footsteps coming toward the doorway and moved into action. I couldn't be caught. Without making a sound, I exited their house and took off running toward my apartment. Tears fell, betraying my tough attitude. *We fuck. We pretend.*

I'd prepared myself to feel this way. Like a stake had been shoved into my chest and pulled out only to repeat the process. I recalled that first day we'd talked about the notion, way back in July. *I don't want you to hate me at the end.*

God, I shouldn't've agreed to this. Tears fell harder, my vision becoming blurry as I dropped the keys twice. Callie must've heard me, because she swung the door open, took one look at me and wrapped me in her arms. "Oh, Greta. What happened?"

I sobbed into her shoulder. I told her everything, all the way back from the beginning. She didn't interrupt or ask questions. She just listened and patted my back. Right as I was about to tell her what I'd heard, my phone began ringing and didn't stop. Callie winced at the phone. "It's Aaron."

"Ignore it." I sniffed, wiping my nose on the back of my hand. "When I got there today, I —"

It rang again. I silenced it and hammered out a text.

Greta: Something came up, sorry. I'm not feeling well.

Aaron: Wait, really? What's wrong?

I closed my eyes, another bubble of emotion hitting me. "He said it was just fucking. He's not in love with me. And that if Tanner asked me out…"

Aaron: Greta. I'm worried. Pick up, please.

I ignored it again. "Aaron said he would be fine if Tanner asked me out."

"Aw, hun." She rubbed my back again. "I fucking *knew* something else was going on. When I asked Aaron about it...fuck."

"What?"

"What if I did this? Like, put the notion in his mind and he's acting out because of me?" She gasped, her face blanching.

I chuckled with a stuffy nose. "Cal, not your fault at all. Knock that shit off. It's his words, his actions. Not you."

My phone blasted again, my annoyance at him reaching a high. I snapped at him as I answered. "What, Aaron?"

"What's wrong? Are you hurt?"

"No. I'm just not feeling well, okay? I'm staying home." My voice shook a little bit, and I hoped I didn't give anything away. "Look, we'll talk later."

"Greta, did you talk to Tanner?"

"No. I didn't. I'm sick. I'll text you tomorrow. Bye."

I hung up, another wave of emotion flowing through me. "Cal, what did I do? I didn't mean to fall in love with someone unable to love someone else."

"Fuck." She ran her hand through her long hair, her teeth going to town on her lip. "I think you need to sleep it off. Maybe a small break from him will be good, yeah? Four, five days without him around every second. That'll help."

"Yeah." I wiped the mascara from my eyes. "I think I'm going to lie in bed and mope. Maybe put on an old movie."

"Are you sure? I can lie with you."

God, I loved Callie. I shook her off. "No, go do your stuff."

"I want to punch his perfect teeth."

"He didn't do anything wrong. That's what sucks. He told me all this beforehand, made me promise this wouldn't happen. This isn't his problem. This is all mine. So, I have to learn how to deal with it."

"You're being so rational about it."

"I don't have a choice right now."

I went to my room and sulked for a good half an hour. I should've known better. I really should've. But it had to be a good dose of karma for my rash decisions. Because why else would I give my heart to an *allergic to feelings* guy?

I was in a pretty deep pity party when a loud, obnoxious banging on the door made me jump about four feet in the air. It repeated, and Callie's soft footsteps padded to the door. I listened through my door, already knowing who it was.

"Aaron, hey. Uh, she's not feeling well."

"Yeah, I brought her stuff." Aaron's strangled voice carried to my heart, squeezing it. "Let me in, Callie."

I knew Callie stood no chance when he used *that* tone. Seconds later, my door opened and Aaron's gaze shot straight to my face. Unnamed emotions flitted across it before he sat on the edge of my bed. "Hey. I brought you some stuff."

"I heard. I told you" — I avoided his assessing gaze — "I would text you tomorrow."

"G, in the almost three years I've known you, you've never been sick. I figured this was big. So" — he grinned, the smile so pure it hurt to look at — "I brought you soup, crackers, soda and the entire first season of *The Sopranos.*"

I smiled, despite my inner turmoil. "This is a lot."

"I wasn't sure what you had. I figured soup and crackers make anyone feel better. The soda helps with nausea and, well, *The Sopranos* was for me."

He reached out and squeezed my foot over the comforter. His warmth traveled all the way up my body, the need to have him touch me overtaking everything else. "Here, what would you like first?"

I swallowed, hard. It hurt the back of my throat. The emotion trying to escape, the battle between head and heart, and the combination of his earnest, sincere face had my head spinning. "Soda."

"Coming right up." He left, returning seconds later with a glass of ice, and I observed him as he poured it. He set it on my nightstand and lifted the covers I had over me. "Scoot. I'm joining you."

"Aaron." My throat still sounded raspy from crying. "I don't want you to get anything. You can go home."

"Not a chance, Greta." He used his sheer strength to push me over, but not roughly enough to hurt. He lifted me up without much effort and set me between his legs so my back hit his chest.

"Wh-what are you doing?" My heart hammered. He *had* to hear it.

"Relax." His arms enveloped me, his hands coming up to my neck. He began massaging it, right below my ears, and I turned to putty. Straight putty in his arms. "There we go. I can feel you loosening up. I'm here because I want to be with you. I won't get sick. I take too many vitamins."

"Whatever, weirdo." I tried to fight it. The emotions and desire to keep him there. But his hands and soft words made all the reasons why I should say no go away. "Mm. That feels amazing."

"Good." He chuckled in my ear, his hands moving down my neck toward my shoulders and upper back. "I can't believe you tried to get out of seeing me today. I leave tomorrow for home."

His words caused my stomach to tighten again, the conversation I'd overheard replaying a third or fourth time in my brain. *He promised me this would happen.* His lips touched the side of my face, right near my temple, and I closed my eyes. It was too easy to pretend it was real. The words, the actions, the way our bodies knew every part of each other. "I'm going to miss you."

Goddamn it. Goddamn him and his words.

"Now, you rest and sleep. I'm putting in the show. Want any soup before we start?" He slid out of the bed, looking more handsome than ever. His dark eyes warmed at me and another wave of emotion took over. "Ah, baby, what hurts?"

"Nothing. Just, I'll get it out." I cried into the pillow, hugging it around my body like a damn lifejacket. Aaron just rubbed my back, whispering things he didn't know or mean. How could he possibly know I was crying because I'd fallen in love with him...and he would never feel the same way?

Chapter Twenty-Two

Aaron

Kenzie stared me down. Her beady eyes showed no mercy as she set down a draw four, ensuring she won the round of *Uno*. I threw my hand on the ground, flipping her off. My mom and dad chuckled from the couch and for that brief second, it was like everything in the world was normal.

My family had had their turkey meal. We'd watched the parade and football. We'd played games and watched movies for two days and there'd been no shadow of *cancer* in the air. The experimental medicine my dad was trying had begun working. The tumor had stopped growing, stopped spreading throughout his body. It was too soon to celebrate, but we could all take a deep breath for the first time. The combination had everyone in an odd mood, excited for progress but too afraid to express it.

"Want to go again, bitch?" Kenzie said under her breath. She *still* got scolded for language. I didn't.

"What was that, Mackenzie? Did you use a curse word?"

"*Fuck you,*" she mouthed at me. I laughed.

"Aaron, how was Greta's Thanksgiving with her family?" my mom asked. I'd found myself talking about her the whole damn weekend. Her classes, her music, what we did together, yet my mom's question made me tense up. It wasn't her fault. She had no idea that Greta hadn't responded to me. Or that things had been weird since she got sick.

I knew Greta. She said she was sick, but it didn't sit well with me. Something else was going on. And avoiding me or lying were not options.

"It went well," I lied. I checked my phone for the hundredth time to see if she'd responded. My unread messages sat there.

Aaron: Hey, how's your holiday going? I have awesome news for you.

Aaron: Yo, give me a call when you have a chance. I haven't heard you gab in two days. I miss your stupid jokes.

Aaron: Okay. I take it back. Your jokes aren't stupid all the time. Just most of the time.

Aaron: G? You okay?

It wasn't like her to play games, so something had to be wrong. My mom nodded at my bullshit answer. My dad's health had her ridiculously happy and she went back to focusing on him. That was fine by me. I excused myself from the room to try calling her. It rang and rang, but the second I was about to hang up, she answered.

"Hello?" She was out of breath, like she'd run a mile to get to the phone.

"Hey, G." The coil of nerves growing in my chest left the moment I heard her voice. "I've been worried about you."

"Oh, I'm sorry. I've been busy." Someone shouted in the background—loud music playing and every impression she gave me about her family was not *this*. "What's up?"

"I wanted to talk to you. Do you have some time?" Fuck the rules about being needy. She was my best friend.

"Sure."

A pit formed low in my stomach. Something was wrong. I knew her too well. "Gabs, are you still feeling *sick*? You don't sound like yourself at all."

"No." She released a deep sigh, her breath making a loud sound through the phone. "I'm feeling better. Thank you."

"Then what is it? I know you." We didn't keep things from each other and my patience snapped. "Something's wrong."

"Okay, you're right, Aaron." Her voice sounded resigned, like she'd rather do anything than talk to me. "Look, I promise I'll talk to you when we get back. I'm going through a weird time. It's not you, okay?"

"What is it?" My anger turned to worry. *I fucking knew it.* "How can I help?"

She snorted, sounding more like herself than she had in three days. "You can't. It's my deal. I'm trying to work through it. I'll fill you in."

"Okay, I don't like waiting, but I felt like you were avoiding me for a bit. I hated it," I admitted, sounding like a damn idiot. A pathetic idiot who wanted his fake girlfriend's attention every second.

"I'll try not to do that again. I saw your text, though. What's the news?"

"My dad!" I shouted. "The experimental drugs he tried helped. It hasn't spread and there are tiny measurements of it shrinking."

"Fuck. I'm so damn happy for you guys." Real emotion poured out of her voice. "How's he feeling?"

"Pretty good. They keep asking about you." *And wanting to know when I'll bring you home.*

"Ah, tell them I'm so happy for them!"

"I will. Hey, when are you heading back? I want to see you."

"I play Saturday and Sunday night for Clyde, since I'm taking off next weekend for the charity event."

The charity event! Yes! "Are you excited?"

"Yeah, I think so. I need to get a dress for it. You wearing a tux or a suit?"

"Just a black suit. You look good in anything. Wear the red one you have." An image of it popped into my mind and my dick jumped to life. It had been too long without being with her. "Speaking of how good you look, can I stop by tomorrow night after your show?"

"For a booty call?" She laughed. "I'm on my period. That's a firm no."

"I don't care about that shit."

"Still a firm no. Listen, I gotta head out."

"I'll see you soon, okay?"

"Bye, Aaron."

She called me Aaron twice. Not Ronnie or Hilly. My gut churned, but I chose to trust her. I preferred to talk to her in person about something bothering me, so I understood. We would talk about it next week. I would make sure we did. I joined my family back in the living room just as my parents excused themselves to bed. "Want a beer?"

"Wait, really?" Kenzie's eyes widened. "They'll kill you."

"Nah, you'll be fine. Here. I'm sure this is your *first* one."

"Asshole." She laughed but took the brown bottle. "You know, you've impressed me this year."

"Yeah?" I grabbed a baseball off the shelf and tossed it in the air. It was an old homerun ball with the date from high school. I couldn't believe my parents still had it.

"Look, I feel I should tell you. I saw those pictures, Aaron."

From her tone, I knew what pictures she meant. A wave of paranoia, guilt, anxiety had me stopping in my tracks. If she knew about them…

"Do Mom and Dad know?" I tossed the ball up into the air, catching it right before it hit my face. I repeated it over and over, the motion calming my anxiety.

"No. I made sure they didn't find out."

"I owe you." My voice came out clipped.

"No, you don't." She got up and put her hand on my shoulder. "It's about time we stick as a team. You would do the same for me. And I'll do it again in the future."

"Wow, Kenzie." I blinked back emotion at her fierce tone. "Of course we're a team."

"Good. I'm going to college next year, at the same university, and I want us to remain friends. I've seen siblings torn apart because of them being 'too cool' or some shit."

"Uh, stop watching shitty movies. We aren't going to turn on each other," I scoffed at her. "Where is this coming from?"

"I loved you before, Aaron — before the diagnosis — but the guy you were *before*, well, I'm afraid you'll go back to that."

I missed the ball. It hit my face but I didn't care. I sat up, staring at my younger sister. She avoided my gaze and the meaning and fear behind her words upset me. "Kenzie."

I waited until she made eye contact. "This entire experience changed me. We all grow up at different times. You had to earlier than I did."

"Is Greta real?"

"What? Of course." I shook her off, the question almost making me laugh.

"No. You two." Kenzie bit on a hangnail so forcefully it made my fingers hurt. "The relationship began right after those pictures came out. What sane girl would willingly date a guy with *that* reputation? Greta isn't crazy."

"Ah, well. She is, but in other ways."

"Um, ew. Gross."

"No! I didn't mean... Ah shit." I covered my face. "No!"

"I'm just messing with you." She laughed, but her face turned serious again. "But, please be honest with me."

I sighed, figuring this was the best time to tell someone. "Yeah. It was staged."

"At first, right? It's real now, though."

"Wait — why do you ask that?"

"Because, Aaron, I've seen you two together. And I know you. It's okay, you know. To actually develop feelings for someone else." She crossed her eyes at me with a small smile. "You can trust me, ass face."

"I trust you. I do." I cracked my neck, the conversation my friends had recently had with me coming back to me. "I haven't seen her in almost three days. It sucks. I miss her. It's weird for me."

"Are you sleeping together?"

"Kenzie! Jesus." I choked and wanted to be anywhere but the room we were in. She held up her hands, surrendering.

"What? I'm not a kid. I'm going to take that as a yes. Okay, new route. If she were to sleep with someone else, what would you do?"

"Kill them."

"It's settled. You're in a real relationship." She patted my knee. "Congrats."

She left me there, where I waiting for the feelings of panic and anxiety to hit me. *Real relationship? Please. Can it be true, though?*

Yeah. Greta's mine.

"Shit." I ran my hands through my hair. We only had a couple more weeks left of the ruse. I did my damnedest to make it clear it was fake every chance I had. But the charity event was coming up. Everything built up to the event. Black tie. Dinner. Dancing. Falling into bed together.

I would show her it was real.

* * * *

Saying goodbye to my parents wasn't as daunting as it had been before. The progress had changed *everything*. I didn't feel that leaving made me the devil, like choosing to go back to school meant I chose school over my dad. That would never happen. As they waved at me, while Kenzie flipped me off with a huge smile behind them, my chest expanded. I would be back for Christmas break in a couple of weeks, and there wasn't a countdown of time left with my dad.

I knew his chances were still slim, but the timeline was put on hold and it made a world of difference. The energy I had burning up inside me consumed me. I needed to find Greta and do whatever the hell she felt liked doing. I just wanted to be with her. She balanced out the bad with all her good.

I shot her a text, letting her know I was on my way to the bar. Her final show for the weekend wouldn't be busy with most kids gone for break. She never responded, but she never did on stage. Fuck her rule about a booty call. My game had changed and she needed to adapt to the play.

Hours later, I walked into The Lion and heard the deep tone of her voice, the perfect rendition of Amy Winehouse taking over the bar. A few stragglers hung around the stool where she sat, the spotlight showcasing her blonde hair. It was braided tonight. Her plaid shirt and dark jeans gave her a punk rock look and my heart sped up. I didn't order a beer or talk to anyone. I watched her.

Is this real? A real relationship? My first one?
Fuck yeah.

I grinned at the same time as her brown eyes found mine. They widened a fraction before she winked at me and continued playing. Once she'd announced her break, I wasted no time in walking up to her. "G, come here."

I opened my arms, and instead of her falling into them, she hesitated. *What the fuck?* I wrapped myself around her, grabbing her chin with my hands and kissing her. "I missed your mouth."

"Mm," she hummed, a slight blush creeping up her cheeks. Her eyes warmed at me, the knot in my chest lessening. "I didn't realize you were coming."

"I told you. I missed you." My hand remained on her chin, the desire to do anything she asked crossing my mind. "You sound amazing, baby."

She bit her lip, glancing away for a second. "Thank you. The Winehouse song was a new one. First time playing it live."

"Yeah?" I twirled the end of her hair. "You killed it."

"Really?" She scrunched her nose, the gesture damn near killing me. "Thanks."

"You're an amazing performer." I kissed her forehead. "Can I come back with you?"

She frowned for a second, so quick and so hard it made lines appear on her face. "I don't know. I'm on my period and I want to watch shitty movies. Maybe cry. Maybe eat all the ice cream in the county."

"I like shitty movies. And crying. And ice cream."

Her teeth met her lip again, but I knew I'd won her over. She smiled, her shoulders relaxing. "Okay. If you insist."

"I do. And I'm a barbarian. Don't mess with me."

"I'll be sure to remember that. Aaron the Barbarian." She fought a laugh and lost. "Wow. I'm pissed I haven't figured that out before now. Aaron the Barbarian has a nice ring to it, don't ya think?"

"I prefer Ronnie from you. Or *oh god, yes*."

"Aaron!" She hit my chest, my hand catching hers. I spun her around, forgoing all masculine cards society deemed I should have. "What—what are you doing?"

"I wanted to check you out. My girlfriend is hot." I whistled, the red on her neck giving her away. "I'm a big fan of these jeans."

"Look, can we talk about something?" A line appeared between her brows, her dark chocolate orbs dulling somehow.

"Yeah, what is it?"

"I've been thinking about the break-up, you know?" she said in one, quick breath. "It's in four weeks. Will it be a big super-public one? Where we stage a fight? Or passive and quiet? What do you think? Because it's coming up soon and I think we should plan it. Or talk about it to know what to do."

It felt like ice water poured down my veins. "Woah, slow down."

"What?" She pushed away, the distance between us growing more than a couple of inches. "I'm trying to prepare myself for it. The downfall. The looks. The *I told you sos*. What do you think? Just an amicable one?"

"Greta, we don't have to talk about it now." I became pissed. "Hell, we still have weeks left." *Tell her, idiot. Tell her.*

"Fine. I want to be prepared, that's all." Her normally warm eyes froze over. "I have to go back up on stage."

"Okay, I'll wait until you're done." I leaned in, hoping to kiss her, but she moved her face at the last second, giving me her cheek. "Greta?"

"Sorry! Gotta go play!"

And for the first time, an uncomfortable, unfamiliar pang hit my chest that had me questioning everything.

Chapter Twenty-Three

Greta

"You look amazing, G. Perfect." Callie eyed me, my long hair tumbling down my back. She'd been helping me do it all afternoon. I wanted to look *the* best. I wanted Aaron to forget how to talk. Why? I had been asking myself that all day, and no answer made sense besides to have one final, amazing night I would never forget.

The last hoorah. After tonight, things had to end. One final night of him pretending and me holding my heart together. My plan to save my heart had backfired — when I distanced myself from him, I ended up craving him more. Guys want what they can't have, and his behavior had gotten more erratic. Showing up unannounced more often, buying me coffee every day, more social media posts and hand-holding.

I ate up the attention, even found myself pretending it was real. One side of my brain would bitch-slap the other and I forced myself to focus on the reality. It was fake. *Fake. Fake. Fake.*

Tomorrow. I would think about the end tomorrow. Tonight was for me. I would enjoy him one more time. Because Aaron loved like a flame, and the slightest wind would put it out. So, tonight was about burning, in all the good ways.

"You sure you can do it?" Her voice dropped low, her words chosen with care. "This charity event is big, but he can do it alone."

"Yes." I smoothed the red chiffon material down my thighs. It fit like a glove and was my favorite dress I owned. Aaron had also suggested a red dress, but this one had cut-outs on the sides. I wasn't egotistical, but I rocked the hell out of it. And my confidence needed all the help it could get. Especially tomorrow. "Yes. I can do it." I released a long pent-up breath. "When is Zade coming to get you?"

"In an hour." She waltzed to the mirror and finished her own makeup. "I love fancy dinner dates. Who would've thought?"

"It's like high school prom again. Only this time we don't have those petty teachers watching us," I quipped. *Sure, use humor to avoid feelings. Totally normal.*

"Yes!" She cackled, our eyes meeting in the mirror. "Do you remember how Katie got thrown out of prom, but showed up at the after-prom party anyway?"

"Epic. That year was epic." The laughter relaxed me. The ball of anxiety inside my chest had taken root over the past week and the balloon of tension released some air at the fond memory. I needed to chill the hell out. "Whatever happened to her?"

"You know, I'm not sure. Last I heard, she moved to Chicago and is dating a hockey player."

"Good for her. She knew how to break it down." The minute of silence was enough to build the tension again, the smile on Callie's face a mix between pity and concern. I knew she wanted to say something, but I held up a hand. "Cal, don't. I'm fine."

"I hate knowing you're hurt. I hate it so fucking much." Her clenched fists told me everything. That girl never got mad unless she was defending someone she loved. I happened to be on that list and I would be forever grateful.

"I agreed to it. I'll be fine." I blanked my face, found my battle mask and put it on. No more feelings. No more worries. No more thoughts about how all of this would be a mere memory the next day. The tall bottle of whiskey caught my eye. Without asking her, I poured two quick shots and gave her one. We clinked glasses, threw them back and winced. The burn felt good. "I'm going to dance my ass off, ride the shit out of Aaron and come back here for pancakes in the morning."

"Fair enough." She fought a small smile, not able to remain stoic much longer. "If you need anything tonight, let me know. Please."

"Will do, C." I hugged her, squeezing her tight against me, so hard she made an *umph*. "Love you."

"Yeah, yeah. I think he's here." She pushed me away. I chuckled to hide the nerves. The faint thump of a car door traveled through from outside and Aaron's heavy footsteps soon followed.

"Here goes." My voice didn't shake. Nope. Not at all. My palms didn't feel like wet towels. And my legs weren't trembling. I was calm, cool as a cucumber. *Yeah, fucking right.*

He knocked on the door three times. I lifted my arms, airing them out from the nervous sweat. *Jesus. Why am I so goddamn nervous?* My clammy hand clenched on the doorknob, turning it, and as I pulled it open, the familiar, enticing scent of Aaron hit me. *God, he smells good.*

"Hey," I spoke first, leaning against the door. He'd dressed to the nines in a sleek dark charcoal suit with a bright red bowtie. Aaron's old style, the flamboyant playboy, was back. And damn it, he looked good enough to eat. "You look amazing."

He cleared his throat, his gaze roaming every inch of the front of my dress. It mollified me to see him struggle. The sick, twisted part of me wanted him to suffer. I knew I looked good, but speechless? *Color me pink.*

"Greta…just… Wow. Spin around."

His caveman voice had me weak at the knees. I obeyed, showing him the back of the low-dipping dress. Because of the back, I was braless and he sucked in a breath. I guessed he'd figured it out when his gaze zoned in on my chest seconds later. "You're perfect."

It's fake. Fake. Fake.

"Ronnie." I fought a heavy blush. "Thank you. Don't be ridiculous."

"No. You're perfect." His large hand held my waist. The grip almost hurt. *Almost.* His other hand found my neck and tilted my face up to meet his. "Your red lips tease. I can't walk away from them."

"Yeah?" I puckered them, closing the distance and enjoying every taste of him. The dance our tongues did teased for what would come later, a slow-burning fire that I would cherish for the rest of my days. He bit down on my lip, pulling me toward him so we were chest to chest. He moaned into my mouth, the sound hitting me in the groin.

"God, you taste so fucking good. I should stop or we won't make it. Coach told me to be there, so I need to go."

"Of course." I wiped my fingers over my wet lips, his arm slipping into mine as he guided me down the stairs. I shivered once the wind hit my back. The price of beauty was going sans coat.

"Greta, do you not have a coat?" An accusatory tone entered.

"Couldn't ruin the outfit." I shivered again, his jacket going around me. "What's this? Your jacket?"

"Yes. Keep it on until we get there."

"How gentlemanly of you." I smirked. He smacked my ass in reply. "Watch it, bud."

"Or what?"

"I'll bend *you* over and have my way." I joked with him, but his eyes widened. "Don't get any kinky ideas yet. We have hours until then."

"Yeah? I can't wait." He opened the passenger door, helping me inside for the sake of touching me. I relished it. He wasn't assuming I wasn't capable. I was. He knew it. He wanted to touch me, help me, and damn it, I loved it.

"Where's it at tonight? I realized I never asked."

"The swanky hotel off-campus. Not too far. I've heard about the place but never been. A lot of the alumni stay there when they come back to campus. Makes them feel cool, or whatever."

"Ah, yes. I can't wait to be cool and come back, strutting my stuff about how adulty I am and shit."

"Adulty. Don't think that's a word, Gabs."

"That's okay. I'll make it official when I have a big job and you're playing baseball making the big bucks. You can endorse me."

He laughed, his fingers coming back to rest on my knee. "Yeah? What else is going to happen when we're adults and shit?"

"Hmm." My heart clenched. The visions I'd always had about the future contained Aaron, but the thought of him being with someone else felt like a knife in the gut. *Damn it.* I pushed it down, way down, and focused on diffusing my inner turmoil. "Well, any time you're in town, obviously, we'll rent out an entire buffet so you can eat your body weight. I'll probably have a dog. I'll name him Hilly. Make him wear your jersey."

"I like that." His low throaty laugh had me clenching my legs together. "Will you, too, be wearing my jersey?"

"Aaron. That is about the stupidest question you've ever asked me. And you've asked me some pretty dumb questions."

"Like what?"

I rolled my eyes, the playful banter making everything better. "One time, you asked me if I've ever used my bra as a slingshot. Or if I tried to eat dog poop. Or that one time you literally thought girls' periods were preventable. Need I go on?"

"I see no need. You made your point." He trailed my smooth skin right above my knee, the sensation feeling damn good. "How are my favorite piercings doing?"

"Take a look yourself."

I pulled the light fabric to the side, made easy by the low neckline. We weren't around any cars, it was almost night, and goddamn it, I loved getting him fired up. My piercings had been coming along nicely, the exposed tips of them hardening in the cool air. "Think they look healed?"

He glanced over at me, then did an immediate double-take. "*Jesus Christ.* Greta. We're in a fucking car."

"No one is around, Ron. Calm your balls. They're all twisted up." I laughed at myself, but his grip tightened again and his breathing came out harder. "You're no fun."

"No. I'm a jealous person. I don't want anyone else seeing those. Now, are you going to behave tonight? You seem amped up."

I sighed. "I'll behave in front of your coach. But with you? Probably not."

"I expect nothing less."

* * * *

"Dance with me." It was an hour or so later and Aaron spoke so low, his lips touched my ear an. "Come on, Gabs."

I rolled my eyes, fighting the urge to run far, far away. Dinner had been amazing. The food was top-notch, and Aaron's coach had introduced us to the bigwigs in the athletic world. I had no idea who the people were, but seeing Aaron's face light up had been worth it. He smiled more that night than he had in a long, long time. He traced his finger right below my ear, making me shiver. "Greta? Give me your hand."

"For a slow dance?" I bit my lip nervously. There were so many people. And I wasn't the best at slow dancing. I preferred more of a free-style dance, where I could flail my long arms around in circles. I could *rock* that move.

"Yes. It's easy. Put your arms around my neck like this." He entwined my hands and set them around his neck. "Good. Now, sway side to side with me."

"I know how to dance, Ronnie."

"Then why are you nervous?" The littlest frown line appeared between his eyebrows, the urge to touch it surprising me. It was so damn cute.

Good question. "I'm not used to attention like you are."

"Please." He held the back of my head so it rested on his chest, his body leading the rhythm. "When you're on stage, no one can take their eyes off you. Even now. You're stunning, Greta."

Don't cry. My eyes stung, but I swallowed it down. "I guess, but the music is a shield."

"Well, luckily, you're with me and my dazzling dance moves will distract everyone." He let go, spun around with a leg kick and the smile on his face looked funny. It was too big, too expressive. "See?"

I laughed. All eyes were on him, as they should be. His newfound joy, surely to do with his dad making a breakthrough, almost put an aura around him. He radiated happiness, and people began gravitating toward him. Callie and Zade danced to the right of us, their eyes locked on each other as lovers do. My eyes stung for a second, knowing I would never have *that* with Aaron.

"Want another drink, babe?" He guided us off the dance floor, his hands never leaving me. "Let's stop at the bar back there, where there isn't a line."

"Sure." A drink sounded great. "I'm going to use the restroom."

He winked and strode off in the other direction. I couldn't complain. I was having a hell of a night, but it was so much *Aaron*. The escape to the ladies' room was well needed. After using it, I wiped my face down with a damp cloth and stepped back into the main hallway. I almost ran into Tanner, who turned around and smiled widely when he noticed it was me.

"Greta! Hey, look at you." He hugged me, his body just a little taller than Aaron. I returned the gesture, but didn't get an ounce of warm tingles like I used to. *Nada.* "You look beautiful."

"Thank you, TJ. You look handsome, as always. You come here with a date?" I glanced to his side, not seeing anyone. No one had been in the bathroom either.

He blushed, the slightest shade of red on the top portion of his cheeks. "No." He ran a hand over his face. "I came to network. I assume you're here with Aaron."

"Yeah." I looked at the ground, the conversation between the two of them coming to the forefront of my mind. *Shit.*

"Look, I'm not sure how to say it." He cleared his throat and checked the surrounding area. He lowered his face to mine, a deep frown replacing his earlier smile. "I just, I care about you, G. You know that. I don't want you getting hurt. I don't know when this *fake* relationship turned real for you, but Aaron still thinks it's fake. I'm fucking pissed at him."

My eyes stung again. But, I swallowed down the lump in my voice. "Thanks, TJ. I'm under no illusions that it's real."

"You're not hurt?" He reached out, squeezing my shoulder. His eyes bore into mine, searching for the truth. But I didn't let him find it.

"I know what I'm doing, TJ. Thank you for looking out for me. I appreciate it." I went to hug him as a thanks, but right as his arms closed around me, just inches from my ass, Aaron rounded the corner with a furious expression on his face

He remained silent as I waved bye to Tanner, who headed in the other direction and avoided the angry glare of Aaron. I walked over to my hot-headed, perfectly handsome, *fake* boyfriend and patted his chest. "Stop. Whatever you're thinking, stop."

"Why were you hugging him?" His eyes never left the direction Tanner walked in. His chest was as stiff as a board.

"He was being a good friend. I told you, there's nothing there. He won't ruin anything, Ronnie." I comforted him, connecting our hands and leaning against him. How fucked-up was that? I was in over my head and he would hurt me, yet seeing him jealous or worried made me comfort him? I was fucked.

"Hmm," he grunted, putting his arm around me again. "What did you talk about?"

"Nothing of importance, trust me." I stood on my tiptoes, kissing his neck and biting his ear. "Are you wanting to stay or head out?"

That got his attention. He turned so our chests had no room between them. "Well, I've been a desperate man to rip this dress off."

"Do you need to stay any longer?" My heart picked up with his intense look. It might be the last time I gave in to him, but it would be the best. I lowered my hand, tracing down the front of his shirt and ending right when I got to the belt buckle.

"Fucking hell. Yeah. There's a scout I need to talk to around ten." He checked his watch with a tight jaw, his grip telling me all I needed to know. "Shit."

"I have an idea. Do you trust me?"

"Of course." His charcoal eyes lit up.

"Come with me." I checked the hallway for signs of life. There wasn't a soul in sight and I pushed the door to the ladies' room open. "Come on."

"Greta, what—"

"Shh!" I giggled and went to the baby changing room. It had a private door, one that locked. No one would ever see us. I dragged him, pushing him up against the

Jaqueline Snowe

wooden door. I lifted the bottom portion of my dress, wiggling my eyebrows at him. "Think you can perform under pressure?"

"Jesus Christ. Yeah, no issues." His heated gaze darkened to black when he noticed my bare opening. "You-you... Nothing underneath?"

"I like being risqué."

"You'll kill me. Kill me." He ran his hands down my waist and lifted me up onto the sink without effort. "God. Your lips. Your pussy. You're so wet already."

"Fuck me, Aaron. Hard." I held on to the porcelain sink and braced myself. "You've looked at me like prey all night. Own up to it."

He growled. His fingers went to his pants and he lowered them enough for his huge cock to bounce out. "Fuck."

"What?" I moaned. *If he leaves me wanting with need, I'll murder him.*

"I don't have a fucking condom." He ran his hand over his face while the other gripped my side. "Goddamn it."

"I trust you."

His face transformed. He flashed his eyes open and bore into me. I knew what my words meant to him. I could see it all over his face and the quick bathroom fuck turned into more. My eyes stung with the tender look he gave me as he slid his bare cock into me. I moaned as my head hit the wall. "Keep your eyes open, Greta."

And I did. I watched as our bodies connected physically and so much more... Each thrust was words we couldn't say. Each groan was feelings we couldn't name. He devoured my mouth just as I savored his.

"You're fucking perfect," he whispered into my ear as he thrust faster. He brought his fingers down to my clit

250

and knew the magic combination to have me gasping for air. The look in his eyes did it—the passion. I fought a cry when I convulsed around him and seconds later, he joined me.

"Greta... Oh. Oh god." He gripped me so tightly it bordered on painful. Then, it was over. "Beautiful."

"Here." He kissed my mouth.

"Here." He kissed my chest.

"And here." He kissed my clit. It started as a sweet, tender press of his lips but then I bucked. "I know my girl. You need more."

Boy, he knew me. He flicked his tongue against the already swollen nub and dragged me into his mouth. It was hot. It was messy. And the way he watched me with his dark eyes would forever be burned in my brain.

It wasn't until thirty minutes later I came down from my high. Aaron brought a warm paper towel to me. "You need help cleaning up?"

I shook my head. Words were too hard right now. I was seconds away from fucking ruining everything. I grabbed the towel from him and, without any embarrassment, cleaned up the evidence of our sex. He chuckled and washed his face in the mirror. It was such a *couple* thing for us to hide the fact that we'd fucked in a nursing room. It wasn't until we left the room that he slung his arm around me and dropped a bomb on me.

"I've never done it bare before. I will never forget this for the rest of my life."

"Yeah?" The thought alone made my stomach drop. *Good.*

"Yeah. Just you. And damn, I can't go back. Felt way too good." He kissed my temple. "Who would've thought?"

I nodded but the nagging feeling about who would be next turned my happiness to dread. *No. Not now. Enjoy it.* "It was amazing."

"Yeah—hey, there's the scout. Come with me. I can't wait to introduce my girlfriend to him."

Shot to the heart. I wouldn't survive.

Chapter Twenty-Four

Aaron

A soft rustle woke me. It was the sound made by clothes sliding across the floor. I rubbed my eyes, taking a second to remember everything. *Greta. The charity event. Greta... God, last night was amazing.* Every kiss. Every touch. I didn't know *feelings* could go that deep. I didn't get it until I did. And I wanted her. For real.

I had to tell her the truth — it had become real for me. *But what if she doesn't feel the same way?*

She had to. Right?

The looks, the touches, the way her face softened at me. I couldn't be imagining it. It had to be two-way. Or I'd force her. *Make* her understand. I couldn't walk away.

The bed was too cold next to me and I opened my eyes. I spied her by the door, half-crouched over. *Why is she on the floor?*

She must've forgotten something in the damn car. Or had an errant thought she had to write down. She could be odd at times, and I loved that.

"Get your gorgeous ass back in this bed." I pushed up onto my elbows and admired the view. Her plump ass was facing me. And my brain had already thought of a bunch of things to do with it...but she didn't turn to face me No. She remained frozen in place, not making a sound. She didn't remain quiet unless something was wrong. And a tiny, very present bubble of anxiety appeared in my chest.

I sat straight up. "Greta, what're you doing?"

She spoke slowly, in an almost inaudible whisper. In those next few seconds, my blood turned to ice. Like someone had doused me in cold water. "I need— I should go."

"Why?" *She must have something early. Tutoring. Work. Homework. Anything.* "I'd prefer you stay in bed with me. But if you need to leave, I can drive you if you give me a second." I stretched, the meaning of her words not hitting me quite yet. "What time is it?"

"Don't drive me, Aaron."

Now she had my attention. All of it. I swung my legs out of bed. "Wait—why?"

She sighed, her back still as stiff as a headboard. She turned to face me with an expression I had never seen before. She had a look of revulsion. As if speaking to me was the last thing she wanted to do.

My stomach churned, the beers from the night before on the verge of coming up. *This can't be happening.* "Last night was pretty amazing. But let's call this for what it is—a sham. It was part of the plan for you."

"But—"

"No." The aggression in that word stopped me. Her coffee-colored eyes stared into me, but they were blank. Empty. Just like my heart felt. "Aaron, I can't continue the next couple weeks. We would've staged a break-up, big or small, I don't know. But the charity event was the final thing for your image. We both know it."

"Wait...what?" My sleepy brain didn't compute her words. Or their meaning. It wasn't possible. I had plans. Plans to tell her. Keep her. Be with her.

"This is done, Aaron. I can't do a fake relationship anymore." Her usual warm gaze was long gone. There was no heat behind her eyes. Sadness, sure, but...a determination I knew well. I had just never borne the brunt of it. She clutched her neck with her free hand. "Last night was my final act."

Spiraling, my heart stumbled over itself trying to find words, but none came. I just stared at her. Her mouth moved, but I didn't hear it. "Did you hear me? I met someone else."

She bit her goddamn lip and avoided my gaze.

Act.

Someone else.

This is done.

A sham.

Done.

"Are you fucking *kidding* me?" Anger, so ripe and so raw, ripped through me. It hurt, unlike anything I had ever felt. Like someone had poisoned my blood.

"No." Her luscious bottom lip trembled. The same one I had sucked and licked hours earlier. "I'm s-sorry."

"I— Who the fuck...? You're seeing someone else? You're *sorry*?" Each syllable took effort, like cotton balls had forced themselves down my throat, making speech almost impossible. "Who?"

"The tattoo artist." She avoided my eyes, backing toward the door.

"*Tony*? Fucking Tony?" I stood, bare-ass naked but not giving a shit. I was beyond mad. "You slept with me, did all last night with me and you're…you're seeing another guy? What the *fuck*, Greta? No."

"I didn't cheat on this *fake* relationship. I would never hurt your future, if that's what you're worried about. Your image is fine. But I'm interested in him. I want to explore it. And I can't with you."

I had no words. They'd left. All of them.

"Now, I need to go." Her voice broke at the end, just a little bit, before she ran out of the room. It took me two seconds to snap into gear. *Fuck this.* We were talking about it. It was Greta. My best friend. We talked about everything and I'd rather die than lose our friendship.

I threw on old jeans and a sweatshirt, forgoing shoes to find her before she was out of view. It didn't take long. The dumbass didn't have a jacket and was running in forty-degree weather.

"Greta, goddamn it." I jogged up to her, the two-second lead she had not enough to escape me. "Stop. I'll drive you. It's fucking freezing."

"N-no. I-I… I'm fine." She shivered, her teeth chattering. She still refused to meet my eyes. I gripped her arm. Not painfully. "Let me go, Aaron."

"I'm pissed as fuck at you. But I give a shit so I'm driving you back." I didn't wait for some snide remark. I was beyond pissed. Annoyed. Shocked. All of it. And it wasn't a good combo.

I picked her up, her hands hitting my back as I carried her back toward the house. It wasn't more than a block and no one was up or out at the time. I ignored her screams. The ridiculous notion of her… No. It couldn't be true. She was being dramatic.

"Aaron. I swear to god. Put me down, now."

"You're being a dumbass. No." I gripped her tighter. Her resolve lessened and her legs became limp. "I'm driving you home. We're talking."

She remained silent until we reached the car. As soon as I set her down, she jumped into the front seat and crossed her arms. *She broke my goddamn heart and she's pissed at me? Fuck that.*

"Greta, are you *really* interested in Tony?" I started the car and waited, hoped and prayed she said no. I needed her to.

"Yes." A long exhalation filled the silence. "This has been fun, but that's all it was, right? Fun. Fake. Staged. We both agreed to it."

Knife to the heart. My own pain masked how she said the words like a question. I selfishly thought how she'd hurt me, and ignored the look of pain that flashed across her face. She continued talking as I headed down the street toward her place. It was amazing how, within twelve hours, I'd gone from the highest to the lowest moment possible. "It started the day I went to get the piercings. I ran into him at one of my shows you didn't go to. We chatted and, well, I figured I'd like to give it a shot. It's only ending the sham two weeks early. This means you can go w-wild at New Year's."

I glanced at her. The face I loved, wanted, craved was turned away from me. Her brown eyes didn't meet mine, and when they did, they wouldn't be filled with *love*. Not anymore. "Greta." My voice broke once we got to her parking lot. "Look, I think—"

Her eyes filled with hope. They widened, an expectant look on her face. God, how could I prevent her from being happy, even if it wasn't with me? She was always honest with me and if she wanted a chance with this guy... I couldn't stop her. I had no right after everything she'd done for me. I was a selfish guy, but not *that* selfish. With a throat full of cotton and a stomach filled with rocks, I asked, "Will we still be friends?"

Her face fell. I would've preferred a punch to the gut. "Sure, Aaron. I gotta go. Thanks...for everything."

She got out of the car, not looking back once when she got into the apartment. She'd gone above and beyond for me, playing the game and being my best friend. I shouldn't feel so miserable. *Right?*

* * * *

Aaron: Hey, want to grab a coffee?

Greta: Nah, I can't today. Sorry.

Aaron: When's your next show? Tonight?

Greta: Nope, next Saturday.

Aaron: Want to grab a drink before or after?

Greta: Can't. Plans already, sorry.

Aaron: Are we okay?

Greta: We're fine. Just super busy.

Aaron: I want to see my best friend. Tell me when.

Great: Soon.

I fisted my phone, the urge to smash it against the tile in the kitchen seeming like a damn good idea. Every attempt I had made to talk to her, see her, *fuck*, even text her had been unsuccessful. How could she, after everything we'd been through, just cut me off?

One week. One week without seeing her or talking to her and I was about to lose my goddamn mind. My world felt off-balance, the yin and the yang not aligning, and I don't think I smiled the whole time.

Is this what heartbreak is? It sucks. Big-ass balls.

"Dude, you look ready to kill someone."

"I might." I nodded at Zade. "You just get back from throwing?"

"Yeah. 'Bout to head over to Callie's for some grub before the Bears play. You wanna come?"

I froze. I could go and see Greta. "Would they care? I wasn't asked to come."

"Hilly, it's G and C. When have you ever asked?" he scoffed, motioning toward the door. "Let's go."

Zade rambled on about the season and the speed he'd increased with his pitches. I wasn't selfish. I was beyond happy for him, but my mind wasn't in the right place. I mentally cringed at myself. My dad was getting better, my sister and I were closer, the scouts, my stats, everything was on the up *except* for Greta. "Hilly, what's going on?"

"Ah, nothing. Sorry. It's great to hear about your increased speed, though."

"I asked how you were doing since the fake relationship ended." He glanced at me, worry in his eyes. "You haven't announced it yet, right?"

"Nope. Next week." The smallest, tiniest flicker of hope filled my chest. *What if I can convince her to keep it going?*

"It's not my place, man, but you guys seemed good together." He parked the car, not letting me respond. He got out and headed up the stairs two at a time. *That used to be me.* Now— I regretted coming. I was dying to see her. Talk to her. But if she looked at me with cold eyes, I would break.

And I couldn't do that.

"Hilly, you coming?" Zade's voice sounded so hopeful. I shrugged. *Fuck it. Pain can't get worse.*

I trudged up the stairs to their apartment and the familiar smell hit me. Callie had to be cooking something delicious. I spied her in the kitchen and she gave me a quick hug. Her smile didn't reach her eyes like it normally did. *What the hell?*

"Cal, you made enough for all of us, right?" Zade asked the most important question. If I had to suffer through a football game, then I deserved a good meal. I relaxed when Callie nodded.

"Greta's in her room."

I knew she'd spoken to me. But I ignored it for three seconds until Zade gave me an odd look. *He has no idea. Tanner never opened his big-ass mouth.* "Okay. Thanks."

And so I went into the living room and fought the urge to run. *This sucks. Fuck this. God. Why did she have to meet someone else?*

But, I knocked on the doorframe. "Hey."

She sat on her bed, her face lighting up for the briefest of seconds. It was worse than a sucker-punch to the gut. She was so fucking beautiful. But the joy left her face just as quickly. Her hooded eyes were downcast. Every little thing about her made me crazy. Made me want to do things I never imagined. "Aaron."

No Ronnie. Hilly. A-A-ron. Kick me in the heart, Greta. Do it.

"It's been a while." *Seven days. Seven days since I touched her.* "How've you been?"

"Busy."

"So you've said."

"Yeah. So I've said."

I gripped the back of my neck. Fuck. This was awkward. And miserable. "This sucks ass."

She chuckled and pulled on the end of her hair. "Yeah. A bit."

"Are we not friends anymore?" I snapped. "Because this shit wasn't supposed to end like this. You avoid me. You look like you'd rather be anywhere but here because I'm here. So what gives, Greta? Are we not friends anymore because…" My voice broke a little. "I don't think I can handle that. I need you in my life."

Her bottom lip trembled, enough for me to see, but she turned away. "Yeah. We're friends."

"Then why ignore me? Why look at me like *that*?" I pointed at her. My anger, hurt and misery built up inside me. "You decided to walk away. Not me. You."

Her brown eyes widened. A flicker of *something* crossed over her face. But she just sucked that bottom lip into her mouth and gnawed it. "It would've ended in a week anyway. I got it over with."

"Because of fucking Tony." Rage…rage I could barely contain. "That's why you walked away? After everything we did together."

"You made it clear, Aaron, we had a *fake* relationship to help your future." Her words were hard. Like punches to my gut. She wasn't wrong.

"Yeah, but—"

"But what? The sex was a fun part of it. Additional bonus. You've slept around. You know you can just fuck." Her fiery eyes burned. And it wasn't with passion.

If I were a smarter guy, I would've got her reference. But I wasn't a smart guy sometimes and right now, all I saw was hurt and anger. My chest hurt in the worst way. "That's all it was to you?"

She flinched. "What was it to you, Aaron? How do *you* feel?"

"I miss you and I can't stand the thought of you with that guy." *There. I said it.* My heart raced. Maybe…maybe things would go back to normal.

She ran her tongue over her teeth with a sneer. "Well, I don't know what to tell you. I'm sorry you're having a little bit of jealousy but how do you think it'll look t-to Tony if I'm constantly hanging around my so-called ex?"

Oh god. "So. That's it."

"For now, yeah." She pushed her long hair out of her eyes and, with a shaky hand, held up the phone. "Excuse me, I need to take this."

She walked out of her room. She left me there with all the memories and laughter, pictures of the two of us all over the room. *When did it become real for me? Why did I think…why did I think it was real for her, too?*

I'm a fool.

I deserve this.

"Hilly—you ready to eat, bro?"

Zade's cheerful voice snapped me from the guilty pit of misery my brain went to. I took a deep breath. I'd lived without being in a relationship my entire life, I could continue doing just that.

I would just do it without the joy that Greta brought. *Yeah right—I'll be miserable.*

Chapter Twenty-Five

Greta

My life turned into a sad shadow of happiness. I sat for three continuous hours watching world championship cornhole games on TV. Callie joined me an hour ago and became invested. So now we cheered for Charles from a hick town in Missouri to win the grand prize to help raise his Labradors at home. *I define the word pathetic.*

"I'm really living it up my junior year. I'm going to be alone on the night before Christmas Eve watching Charles celebrate a comeback win." I studied the drink in my hand and finished off my third one of the night. "When are you heading out?"

"I don't know." Callie's face was an open book. I knew she felt guilty about leaving me alone with my private heartbreak. But it was a big night with her eating with Zade's family. I saw her nerves and attempted to bottle up my anger. But I failed. Her wide eyes and hesitant smile gave her away. "I can stay here with you."

"Cal — go have fun with your man candy. It'll piss me off if you're here for pity." Popcorn fell off my shirt, landing between us on the carpet. It was symbolic. "I have no qualms about watching Charles and drinking myself into a slumber."

"I hate this shit so much. I envisioned something quite different for the holidays. All of us with eggnog, at a bomb New Year's party." Her twisted lips came together.

"Yeah, well, I did too." I tucked my knees to my chest. "Please go. I'll feel even worse if you stay here. I'll be okay. I have lists. Plus, I'm leaving tomorrow morning to head home."

She flicked her gaze toward the coffee table. I had a bottle of champagne, a stack of Harry Potter books, and papers everywhere. Did I mention a box of tissues? Because I was a crier now. I cried at commercials. At couples when they danced to my music at the bar. I missed Aaron. He was like the air. Without him, breathing was hard. Enjoying moments was hard. *Everything* was hard.

If this was what love did to people, I wanted to exclude myself from it. From every part of it. It had been a week since I'd seen him last. Since he visited me in my room, we hadn't spoken. He'd stopped texting. Stopped calling. Stopped visiting. But that didn't stop me from checking my phone every second with the small, outrageous belief that this hadn't happened.

And yesterday was the official, final date of our proposed relationship. My eyes stung again. He'd announced it on social media — per the plan. But it was like a knife to the gut. *Don't cry. Knock it the fuck off.*

"Greta?"

"Yeah, Cal?" I sniffed and hoped my eyes weren't red. "Why are you looking at me like that?"

"He's suffering, too."

"He misses his friend. And I can't go back to that. I can't." My voice broke. I took a breath. "I need time. I hope I can find it in me to be friends again. But not yet."

Callie frowned harder and put her arm around me. "Why don't you see what he's doing tonight?"

"Ha! No fucking way." *Probably already with someone else.* The thought made me want to throw up.

"Why? What do you possibly think he's doing?" Her eyebrows rose and I didn't like her speculative look one bit.

"Cal. I appreciate you. I do. But we said what we needed to say." I stood and crumbs from the cookies I'd snarfed earlier fell. I didn't have enough feelings to be embarrassed. I'd showered that morning and considered that a big fucking deal. "I'll have to figure out a way to move on. It won't be tonight, or tomorrow, but it'll happen."

She twisted her fingers in her lap. Her outfit and appearance were so beautiful — all but the pitying expression. "I hate leaving you."

"Girl, if you don't leave, I'll cut you. Not everyone finds a guy like Zade. Go cherish that hunk of a man and bring me leftovers. That's all I ask." I jutted my chin out, daring her to argue. She sighed. *Score.* "Now, leave."

"I'll come back after the dinner."

"No. No you won't. Stay the night. Get freaky." Her pain took precedence and I found my normal voice. "You're my ride or die. Sister from another mister. My thunder buddy. But, right now, go be Zade's girlfriend."

"Okay. Call me if you need anything. Anything at all."

"Yes, *mother.*"

"Fuck you," she joked and I knew everything was fine. "You're the best, G."

"Yeah, yeah." I brushed her off and busied myself with a true-crime novel. Nothing got me more in the mood to feel sorry for myself than a book about crime.

She left soon after and the unwelcome silence seemed loud. I heard every creak of our upstairs neighbors. Every echo of laughter from someone. I laughed without humor. *Good for them for being fucking happy.*

The large vacuum mocked me. Yeah, he knew I liked to clean to distract myself, so what better way to spend a Saturday night than cleaning?

Clyde had wanted to give me a night off since I'd been playing so much. I think he felt bad for me. The Robot had shown emotion and let me sulk. I appreciated the gesture but loathed the fact that I was stuck with my thoughts. I would've preferred to be at the bar, faking it. Sometimes escaping my own thoughts in a crowd of superficial people felt better.

And I knew Aaron was out tonight. Social media never let anyone go unnoticed. He was out with the baseball team—the wild ones—and I couldn't imagine what he was going to do. Because he could now.

Fuck, it hurts.

I blasted some Dashboard Confessional and allowed myself to cry and clean. It was a hot mess of an experience. It wasn't until an hour later that someone knocked on the door. *Is it Aaron?*

I ran to the shitty mirror in the hallway and rubbed under my eyes. I had remnants of mascara on but, other than that, I didn't totally look like trash. I took a calming breath and wiped my palms on my yoga pants.

I opened the door with my heart in my throat. But it was a UPS guy.

"Hi there. This is Unit 232B, right?"

"Yes," I replied with a loud grunt. *Not Aaron. Just Frank.*

"Here you go," he said with way too much cheer.

"Wh-what's this?" I eyed the cardboard box.

"A package for you, ma'am. You are Greta Aske, right?" His mustache twitched and I thought of a million jokes about it I wanted to tell Aaron—but then I remembered. *Oh. Yeah. We don't talk.* "Ma'am?"

"Yeah, sorry. I'm Greta." I took the pen and scribbled my name. The cold air slammed against my face and I wanted to close the door. But, Mr. Mustache-Man sighed. "Thanks."

"Have a good night. Happy holidays."

"Yeah, you too," I mindlessly replied. I shut the door and eyed the brown box. I hadn't ordered anything and no one in my extended family cared to know my address. I found scissors and tore it open. *Maybe I ordered shoes?*

Shoes could solve world problems. Paper rustled and I ripped it open. A typed letter stuck out and my gaze slid to it. It was as if a fist had plunged into my chest and squeezed my heart. *Aaron.*

Dear Gabs,

Forgive me for being cheesy—I had a couple beers before thinking this was a great idea. It might suck. But fuck it. Your smile is worth it. God, when you smile, it's insane. I get this feeling in my chest I can't explain.

The bracelet is a phoenix. Like, new beginnings. And the cycle of life. I liked the symbolism of it. I felt like with you, it was like starting over.

God, I'm awful at this.

Thanks for doing this for me. I'm hoping to convince you to keep it going. So, what do you say? Care to make this the real thing?

Ronnie

I reread it. Twice. But the words blurred together with tears. I frantically searched for a date. "When did you order this, Aaron? Shit. When?"

It made such a difference. *Oh my god.* My heart raced. If this was ordered before *that* night...then god... I didn't know. I cut my finger on the paper and I brought it to my mouth. "Come on, come on!"

But, after two minutes of searching for a date, I remained in the dark. The bracelet shone at me. The silver flashed. The intricate design of the phoenix was beautiful. So unlike anything I had and I loved it. I put it on my wrist and the guilt of not being honest with Aaron hit me like a truck.

What if...what if he'd developed feelings, real feelings, and I'd ended it out of fear? *No. That can't be.*

I paced. I walked back and forth across the living room, eyeing the note. Did I call him? Go over there? Ignore it?

"Gah!" I kicked the edge of the couch and regretted it instantly. *Fuck it. Fuck it all to hell.* I dove for my phone. My fingers hurt, I typed so fast.

Greta: I got the bracelet.

The three dots appeared as he typed. But then they disappeared. It happened two more times and I grew about ten gray hairs in frustration. Patience was not a virtue I had.

Greta: When did you send that?

Aaron: Does it matter?

Greta: More than you know.

Aaron: How's Tony?

Greta: When did you send it, Aaron?

Aaron: I'm giving you space. Enjoy it.

Greta: You're frustrating as fuck. Why can't you answer the question?

Aaron: I'm busy right now.

I clenched my eyes together, imaging him with woman after woman. *Why is the pain not getting better?*

"Fuck." I stared at the bracelet, spinning it around my wrist. It weighed about an ounce but felt like ten pounds. *Aaron has feelings for me. Real feelings.*

I punched the pillow on the couch and had such a restless, terrifying feeling in my chest. It started small, then grew, pushing on my heart. My breathing came out fast, too fast. And I hated the pact. I hated the deal I'd made with him and how I had to protect my feelings. I hated it all.

"Fuck this." I needed another drink. A distraction. *Anything.* The anxiety in my chest scratched to get out and I had no sane path to help it. I just didn't want to be alone—so to the bar it was. Two pitchers to myself. A hangover from hell. All of it sounded better than knowing I'd thrown it all away. Fuck my resolve to be in control.

* * * *

"Greta—are you sure you're okay?" Clyde frowned, hard. I'd already downed three glasses of shitty beer. My life didn't seem *that* bad after drinks. Nope. The tingling in my neck felt great because it blocked out the pain in my chest. *Yup. Beer is good.* "Greta?"

"Yes. I'm *fiiiiine.*" I pouted like a damn child and didn't give a fuck. He was raining on my pity parade. Some nice-looking guys strolled in, giving me *the stare* I knew well, but nothing happened.

No butterflies. No interest. Not even a flicker. I didn't return their gaze and stared at the amber liquid. *They aren't Aaron.*

"Is your posse all home for the holidays already?" Clyde attempted to converse again. The man literally had no social skills, because he was not picking up on my mood. "Where are the barbarians?"

"Busy." God, I hated how snotty I sounded. I cleared my throat and made an attempt. He did not deserve my attitude. "They aren't home yet—most of us leave tomorrow."

"Ah, well. I feel bad I'm not having you play tonight. It's a decent crowd." He scanned the bar and I agreed. There were more people than usual for a holiday weekend. "Oh, there one is. I figured as much."

"There who is?" I turned, and felt like a train had hit me.

Aaron stood there, looking straight at me. With another girl. My chest squeezed so tight, I thought I would burst. Then, a numbness took over.

"Aaron, my man, it's been a while." Clyde's voice held joy—the two of them had become some version of *amigos* during our dating scheme. But now, I hated Clyde. I glanced back at the beer and gripped the edge of the bar. *Leave me alone. Leave me alone, Aaron.*

"Hey, Clyde. Happy holidays." His deep voice held the perfect undertone of playful.

"You too. What can I get you?"

"I'll have a pitcher, and you, Ambar?"

Ambar? Fucking Ambar?

"Whiskey is fine."

God. She's cool too, drinking whiskey. I slammed my eyes shut and thought about leaving the rest of my drinks. But nope. Aaron chose a stool three away from me. I felt his stare and gave in. I met his dark eyes. "Hey."

"Hey, how's it going?"

"Great. You?" *Fuck fuck fuck.* I glanced at Ambar and she stared right back at me with wide eyes. *Good. I hope I scare her.*

"Good." He ran his hand through his hair. His gaze flicked to my wrist, the phoenix bracelet sticking out against my pale skin. But he didn't react to it. He bit on the inside of his cheek for a second before saying in a neutral, emotionless tone, "Have a good Christmas."

"You too." I fought the urge to cry and threw a ten on the counter. I couldn't pretend. I couldn't. Not when he had another date. "I need to go, Clyde."

"Wait, Greta—"

"I'm sorry." My voice cracked and if I didn't leave that second, everyone would see me melt down. "I need to go."

And I ran out of the bar.

Chapter Twenty-Six

Aaron

"That's not the look of someone who's happy, Aaron." Ambar's observation was not alone. My thoughts traveled too fast for me to clasp onto one idea. Greta's dark brown eyes were dull and her face looked off without a hint of a smile. An uncomfortable pit formed in my stomach before I remembered her words. *She wants space. She wants fucking Tony.*

"We came here for a reason. Let's get to it." I didn't dislike Ambar, but I didn't like her either. It was an odd combo, but she had a purpose. "I want to get this over with."

"She thought we were together." Her voice dropped and I mentally rolled my eyes. "She looked like she was crying."

"She wasn't. Greta... Let's just forget about that." I grabbed our drinks and sat in an abandoned booth.

"Thank you for meeting me the Saturday before the holiday."

"Yeah. No worries. I live in town." She pulled out a spiral notebook and placed it on the grungy table. "Before we start, what made you want to do this? I thought you were out with the bros tonight."

"It was suggested to me and if I have to do it, I'd rather control it the best I can. And I had a drink with them — I just didn't want to partake in their actions tonight." My body was as stiff as a board. Every part of me hated the idea of doing an interview, but my brain overrode them. Coach said it was *a learning experience* about media.

'Either control what you can or deal with it. If you give one full-access interview, then people will back off. But it's your choice, kid.'

"Fair enough. How did you hear about me?"

"I asked around for an unbiased, not psycho journalist. Your name came up." *And she hasn't slept with anyone on the team or looked at me with crazy eyes.*

"I appreciate that — but we both know you had other reasons. It's all the same. Where do you want to start? We have a couple angles here — your baseball career, your dad, or your relationship with Greta that gained a lot of popularity on campus."

"They're all connected." I gripped my large glass of beer. "It began with my dad's diagnosis. No, before then. Shit." I sighed. "This is harder than I thought. Do you have questions for me?"

"I can ask some, but this interview is about you. A feature on our campus' troubled playboy. What direction we go is your call. Now, what's your goal from this?"

"To tell the truth. Plain and simple, no bullshit."

"Then let's cut to the chase. The pictures."

"Christ, I guess that's where it all kind of started." I cracked my knuckles and a deep, inexplicable calm took over me. *The truth will set you free.* And that was what I wanted. "After those pictures came out, I needed to clean up my reputation."

"And that's where Greta came in?"

"Yeah." I smiled. "She was my closest friend, best friend, since I came to school here. She didn't give a shit I played baseball or treat me any different after I told her about my dad's diagnosis."

"Sounds awesome. You started dating shortly after the pictures? That created a lot of buzz."

"Yeah. Simple, really. We hung out all the time, so we threw a label on it to keep attention on *us* rather than my wild excursions. We have followers online — it was easy enough. We agreed nothing would change." The pang in my heart hadn't left since the night after the charity event. I was almost used to a piece of me missing constantly, but talking about it hurt. "We promised to always stay friends."

"What was in this for Greta? I'm curious. Our female readers will want to know." She clicked the pen three times and I focused on the question. *What was in it for her?*

She'd told me it would prevent her from making bad decisions about guys. But that wasn't solid enough. She'd just had a rough patch. So, why did she?

"I think… Greta has one of the biggest hearts I've ever seen. She didn't view it as getting something out of it — "

"You honestly don't think she used you for fame? Cleat chasers are pretty well known. Some would say she was the ultimate chaser." Her pen stopped and she arched one eyebrow almost to her hairline.

Anger flashed through me. "Greta is *nothing* like a cleat chaser. She helped me out because she's loyal as hell, one of the best people I know, and can make a selfish, fucked-up guy like me feel like a million bucks."

That shut her up real good. Her fingers shook a little at my aggression, but she received the message. "Any more questions about Greta?"

"No. I have enough to write about." She took a long sip of her drink and I felt a little bad. I backtracked.

"Look—I had no intentions of ever falling in love. If that's what happened. I never made time for anyone besides her and my life isn't the same without her. I got so used to seeing her every day with all her energy and compassion. At some point, it turned real, but I never told her. I behaved like a typical asshole and made sure to remind her constantly it was fake—but I think it was how I coped with it." I rubbed both palms in my eyes, trying to erase the picture of Greta's crestfallen face as she'd flown out of there. *Give her space.*

"Wow." Ambar smiled. "You got it bad, man. This will be an awesome piece to write. Emotional and statistical."

"Statistical?"

"Yeah. We need to talk baseball now. Your past, present and future goals. You're rumored to be drafted, along with the rest of your testosterone-filled house. Is that okay?"

"Sure. I live for the sport. Tell me when to stop talking." And I began from the very beginning, when I knew baseball was for me. It wasn't until an hour later that we left the bar. She promised she would let me read the draft before she published it and I trusted her. It was something about her. I hoped I didn't regret it.

I headed back to the house, my mood worsening each minute. The relief from the interview was short-lived. I couldn't get Greta out of my mind. My chest tightened and I thought about her texts.

Why couldn't I tell her I'd sent the gift the day before she ended it? Why couldn't I have fought harder, told her how I felt? *Because I'm a dumbass. I'm not a good bet.*

Beer. I needed a beer and a diversion from my mental scolding. And it was the first thing I grabbed when I walked into the house.

"Dude, why you here tonight?" Jeff plopped onto the kitchen chair with a stupid grin. "I figured you'd be out going wild with your new freedom."

"Nah." I thought about how to answer. Tanner must not have told everyone. *Damn.* "Just wanted to hang here."

"Good for you. You don't look happy, though. I told you going to talk to Ambar Henderson was a bad idea. What's up, man?" Jeff and his damn inquisition. He could always read a mood, but never had jack shit to help it. His use of her name would normally have piqued my interest. But not tonight.

"Greta and I... We didn't end on the best terms." There. That was sort of the truth. "You know how close we are."

"That sucks ass, man. I'm sure it'll get back to normal. It has to be hard faking a relationship for that long. Give her some time." He smiled, like his suggestion was the best fucking advice in the world. *My friends are idiots.*

"Sure." I took a long swig of beer, emptying half the bottle. "Wanna play some Madden?"

"Hells, yeah, it's been a while."

"Why are you here?" I asked him as we sat on the couch. "You're trying the relationship thing, right?"

"Dude, I can't do it. There's too many options. It's rough. Like, if you're at a buffet, you wouldn't settle for one food, right? Women are like that. I can't just choose the orange chicken if there's beef and broccoli, sweet and sour chicken and kung pow chicken. You know?"

"Holy shit." I howled with laughter. "You're such a dumbass."

"Makes sense, though. Laugh if you want. But I've known you to eat an entire buffet in a week's time. You better not judge me, Hilly." He powered on the game and tossed me a controller. "You're going down, fuck face."

"Whatever." But the idea of competition had my blood pumping. I welcomed it. And an hour later, I had one game on Jeff, but the pain in my chest hadn't really lessened. "Suck it, I won."

"God. I hate this shit." He paused and flipped me off. "Fuck you."

I laughed. "Sucks to suck."

"Why are we even here? Let's go get laid." He tossed the controller, but I didn't join him when he stood. "Are you coming or what?"

"Fuck, I don't know. I'm not up for it."

"Don't be lame. You're single. Lonely… We're playing videogames on a Saturday night. You've been celibate for, what, months?"

Someone cleared their throat and Callie appeared in the room. *Shit. Shit. Shit.* "That's right. You've been *celibate.*"

"That was part of the deal, right?" Jeff asked, confusion dripping in his tone. "Did you sleep around on Greta?"

"No — I didn't," I said between clenched teeth. I glared at Callie, but she didn't back down. Nope. Not her.

She persisted. She moved to stand directly in front of me. "Why aren't you up for getting some ass? You *always* get the best-looking gals. Why the hold-up, Hilly?"

"Let it go, Callie," I warned.

But she stood her ground and jutted her chin out. Jeff had no fucking idea what was happening, but I didn't give a shit. This didn't involve him. "You make a better window than a wall, Callie."

"Good one, but we aren't nine years old. Man up, Aaron." She crossed her arms. Her pursed red lips matched her dress and my thoughts went straight to the charity event. God. *Greta.*

"I'm man enough. When you're tired of Zade, come find me," I snapped.

"Asshole," Zade replied behind me. "That's a neck." And he slapped the back of my head. "I'll punch your pretty face if you say that to my girl again. I'll forgive you because I know you're a miserable sack of shit right now."

"I'm not miserable." *Liar. Idiot.*

"Wait—why are you miserable?" Jeff decided to join in. *The more the fucking merrier.*

"Hilly, I need to tell you something and you're going to listen."

Her tone alarmed me. "Okay. Is Greta okay?"

A brief smile appeared before she shook her head. "Yeah, physically she's fine. But I've sat by idly long enough. It's not my business but neither of you are happy. She lied about Tony."

"Wait—what?"

"Greta came over here a couple weeks ago and happened to overhear a conversation between you and Tanner." Her brow furrowed as she waited for me to comprehend her words. I couldn't think past the fact Greta had lied. If there was no Tony...

"Why did she lie?"

"Dude, piece it together. What did you and Tanner talk about that day?" Zade cut in and joined Callie in front of the damn TV. They reminded me of parents looking after their kid. And I was the kid. "Hilly!"

"Shit, sorry. We uh... Fuck." It hit me. "No. No way. She...she heard it wrong."

"What's going on?" Jeff asked and I didn't have patience to explain shit. I waved him off.

"She heard exactly what you said, both of you. Imagine if you'd heard that."

"Heard what? Guys. Fill me in."

I froze. *It's just fucking'... Oh my god.* "She lied. Because of me."

"Yes. Why else would she lie about Tony? She was protecting herself, Aaron." Her frown deepened and she grabbed my wrist. "Go talk to her."

"Someone explain to me what the fuck is going on!" Jeff yelled.

"It became real with Greta, okay? I need to go!" I shouted.

It took all of two seconds to jump into gear. Heart racing, palms sweating, chest heaving. I forgot to grab a jacket. Before I stormed out of there, I picked Callie up and squeezed her. "Thank you — so fucking much."

"Go get our girl!"

Raw hope flowed through me. Not unlike the feeling I got when my dad's tumor was shrinking. It was like someone had lifted a weight off my chest and breathing became easier. I couldn't drive fast enough. The goddamn stop signs had me sweating. *We still have a chance!*

The ten minutes seemed like an hour, and I slammed it into Park before flying up the stairs. I knocked — I pounded the door so loud it hurt my wrist. "Greta! Open up, please!"

But only silence remained. I called her five times, each one going to voicemail.

Where the hell is she?

Chapter Twenty-Seven

Greta

No fucking sweets at the apartment — and if this didn't call for chocolate, I wasn't sure what did. So, with a bag full of candy ranging from dark to white to caramel-filled chocolate, I headed back to my place.

I would've called an Uber but I'd left my goddamn phone at the apartment and the short walk home was uneventful. I should've worried about walking alone, but I didn't — the train of my thoughts swirled around one person and one person alone. *Aaron.*

If he'd sent the bracelet before the charity event, then I'd thrown everything away for nothing. The thought of being stood up, or turned down... I couldn't forgive myself for not taking the chance. *But it's Aaron. He doesn't do feelings.*

But that bracelet said different. And talking to him wasn't an option because of that girl... *God, I want to hate her.* I squeezed my eyes shut and clenched my fingers around the white plastic bag. *Think of the chocolate, all of it.*

I was pretty deep in a self-deprecating thought when a familiar car raced down the road toward me. The bright lights lit up the entire block, like a spotlight from a helicopter was shining down on us. I gasped. It was Aaron's SUV.

Is he driving drunk? Shit. I waved my arms in the air and ran up to the vehicle. "Stop. Slow down, psycho."

"Greta!" he shouted and jumped out of the car, a crazed look of desperation on his face. "My god... Greta."

And he crushed me with his weight. He closed his massive arms around me, the familiar scent of him overtaking all my senses. And it felt *right*. As though he was the final puzzle piece to complete everything. He kissed my forehead and, with shaky hands, cupped my face. He forced me to meet his eyes and the intensity in his gaze hit me deep in my chest. "It was real for me. Fuck, it was real. All of it."

"Me too," I whispered into his warm chest. His body relaxed in my arms, and my heart raced to meet his. The combination of our heartbeats sounded like a loud stereo, and I wanted to pick him up, I was so damn happy. "Me too, Aaron."

He pulled back and just stared at me, emotions swirling in his eyes. My heart continued to race. He traced my bottom lip with his thumb so sweetly that my eyes stung, and he pressed his mouth to mine. Each stroke of his tongue answered a question I had, just as each moan of mine told him how I felt. Seconds, minutes — time didn't matter at that moment. Nothing mattered. Just him. His mouth, heart, happiness.

"Ronnie, should we—" He interrupted by kissing me. "Ronnie—"

"Shh. I fucking missed you."

"Let's go back." I put my hand on his chest and swore he trembled. "Come on."

He took me and helped me into the car. "That girl wasn't a date tonight, just so you know."

"Tony wasn't real, just so you know."

He grabbed my hand and held it tight where it was almost painful. "I just found out. God, I'm sorry I didn't tell you. I can't believe you heard—"

"Heard what?"

He paused and faced me rather than start the car. Turmoil was etched onto his face and I tensed. I prepared myself for the worst.

"I can't believe you heard what I said to Tanner. I—"

"Callie told you." It wasn't a question. He nodded and all my thoughts jumbled and mixed, and the previous drinks I'd had didn't help. My stomach churned and I held up a hand. He backed away and began the drive to my apartment.

How do I feel about Callie intervening? Angry? Betrayed? Would Aaron even be talking to me if she hadn't told him? Why can't I enjoy the moment?

"G, you look like you might be sick. Do you want me to pull over?" he asked in a calm, sweet tone. I shook my head and kept my arms crossed. We rode in silence the short distance and he helped me out of the car. "You about scared me to death. I sprinted over here as soon as I found out and you didn't answer."

"Chocolate. I needed chocolate." I held up the plastic bag and he chuckled. I welcomed his arm around me, but we still had a lot to talk about. He kissed my temple, neck and shoulder when I stopped to open the door and I shook him off. "Aaron. We need to talk first."

"Okay. Anything." His reluctance to argue should've been a good sign. But I wasn't ready to jump up and down yet. Lots of hurt had happened. "Can I get a bite of that chocolate?"

I hesitated. "I got this because of you and that…girl at the bar."

"Ah, baby." He frowned and cupped my face again. "I haven't touched anyone since you—hell, I don't have room for anyone else when you're all I think about. No room in my shallow thoughts."

Goddamn it. This is good. I blinked back tears. "Here. Have a piece of chocolate."

"Thanks," he replied with a huge grin. "God, you and your sweet tooth."

"It's part of who I am." I took a huge piece of the dark and moaned. "Good shit."

"I love you, Greta."

He didn't waste time. I gulped and left the half-eaten bar on the table.

"I'm not done." He closed the distance between us so my back pressed against the counter. He lifted me up, positioning himself between my legs. The look in his eyes…

"I didn't know what love was like before you. It's hard to figure out for a guy like me. But all I know is you're my future. Every single thing I want in life is with you. I can promise you, I'll do whatever I can to make it work. I know when you need tea, wine or whiskey and how you need the fan on at night or you can't sleep.

"I also know you pretend to like football but we all know you don't. But I know I love you." He grinned so wide.

"God, Aaron." I wiped my eyes. "I love you, too. But it sounds silly now."

"No. No it doesn't because those words coming from your mouth…they're the best thing I've ever heard. Say them again."

"I love you." *Fuck the what-ifs. Live in the present, bitch.* I plastered my mouth onto his and took my time tasting him. I swirled my tongue with his and enjoyed the way he moaned into me. I pulled back and wiped my mouth on the back of my hand.

"I love your fear of roller coasters. Your secret killer dance moves. Your ridiculously nice wardrobe. And your unwavering loyalty to those you care about. I feel so blessed I'm one of them."

"Baby, don't cry." He blinked a handful of times before bringing our mouths together again. "I'm sorry. I'm so fucking sorry you heard that and thought it was true. I—"

He stuttered and looked so unlike Aaron that my heart broke for him.

"I didn't know how to handle what was happening. A guy like me? I'm not a good bet and falling in love with you wasn't the plan."

"Trust me. I know." I nodded and wiped my eyes.

He chuckled and picked me up. "I know we need to talk, but I need your body with me now. All of you."

"Yes. Okay." I moaned and broke out in goosebumps. Each kiss, touch and sound would forever be etched in my memory. The way he set me on the bed, the way he slowly undressed me like I would break and the way his eyes were on fire. All for me. It was mind-blowing.

"I missed you." He pressed a kiss on my forehead and removed my jeans down my legs. "Your beautiful, perfect body. You're amazing, Greta."

I trembled something fierce. It was like nothing else in the world mattered at that moment. Just Aaron. And his hands.

Those strong hands peeled off my panties and didn't ask permission before touching me right where I craved. I moaned and throbbed with need. "Oh god."

"I need to taste you—it's been too long."

He kissed me on my clit and took it between his teeth. It wasn't painful but, holy shit, it was hot as hell. He swirled his tongue around it, flicking and sucking and combining his fingers to make the perfect motion. It brought me to the edge of an orgasm within minutes.

"Look at me, Greta. I want to watch you."

And I obeyed. I opened my eyes and held his all-consuming stare when my legs shook as the orgasm shot through me. I cried, words becoming almost impossible. I fell apart in his mouth and barely had time to catch my breath when he stripped himself down. He supported himself on his elbows and smiled down at me. I wanted to say everything, and nothing, so I took his mouth in mine. "Let me ride you."

"Fuck. Yes." He groaned. "Slide down on me...yeah. Just like that."

"Wait—you need a little prepping, yeah? I've missed you too, Ronnie." And I crawled down his body to fit his very large, very happy cock into my mouth. He fisted my hair, the motion getting me hot as hell, and I aimed to give the best blow job of my entire life. I used both hands and took him deep—so deep he let out a loud curse and jerked back.

"Greta! No. I don't want to come yet. I want to be inside you. Please," he begged, and I felt drunk on power. I gave him one last kiss on the head and moved to have him slide into me—bare and all.

"I *love* you," I said as he fit inside me. It was tight — but perfect. "Oh. Oh man."

"Rock those gorgeous hips, baby." He gripped my sides and thrust. "I love seeing you ride me like this. Your tits bouncing everywhere. God. I love this, you, everything."

His words warmed me. Each stroke to my G-spot had me bursting with anticipation and when he brought his thumb to my clit in circling motions… It was too much. I burst again. "Aaron, oh god!"

"Yeah, baby, say my name. I love my name coming from your mouth."

I screamed, throwing my head back as waves of pleasure shook me from head to toe. My body was on fucking fire and I wanted to ride it out. Aaron didn't say a word, just stared at me until I'd finished.

"Jesus, fuck, that was the hottest thing I've seen. I need to… God." He flipped me over and drove into me. I used my hand to hold onto the sheet to keep myself in place. It was a heart-pounding, animalistic act on his part and I loved it.

"Harder, Aaron. Yes!" I screamed when he thrust into me, stretching me further than ever before. His cock throbbed inside me and I swore I saw stars. "Yes, Aaron!"

He grunted and lifted my hips with his hands, the angle making everything more extreme. I entered an entirely different part of the atmosphere — all I saw or heard or smelled was Aaron. His sounds, the subtle scent of his cologne, the way he growled my name in my ear. Each thrust had the perfect angle to hit my clit and the buildup came hard and fast.

Just as he tightened his grip and spilled into me, I held on tight. He let out a carnal groan, the rough sound amplifying my pleasure. Sweaty, unabashed and sedated. He fell to the side of me and brought me with him.

Best. Sex. Ever.

An hour or so later, because time sort of froze for a moment for me, we remained on my bed without an article of clothing or sheet between us. It was perfect.

"I know we didn't talk about it much, but I want to explain the girl." He trailed his fingers down my back, making small circles. I felt high, the aftermath of the lovemaking taking my breath away. "Greta, you still with me?"

"Yeah." I hummed into his chest and heard him out. "Explain that girl."

"She's a pretty well-known columnist for the campus newspaper. I talked to my coach a lot and he suggested getting a step ahead of them. I gave my first in-depth interview."

"Yeah? Wow. Did you talk about everything?"

"Yes. It felt freeing. No holding back. There's been a lot of attention on me and you because of the scholarship, my dad and the photos so I wanted to put an end to the rumors."

"That's frightening, but I'm proud of you." I squeezed him.

"Thanks. She assured me I would see the final draft before she publishes it, so I'm holding her to it. I want you to read it. You're in it, a lot."

"Yeah?" I grinned, feeling giddy as fuck. My air was back, my Aaron. "Of course I'll read it. I'll support you almost all the time. Except when you're an asshole."

"Fair enough." He pressed another kiss to my temple and let out such a deep, satisfying sigh, I felt it in my toes. "I have a real question to ask. And you can say no, but I'll fight you for it."

"I'm listening." And I repositioned my body to face him. The light hit the bracelet perfectly and I smiled when he blushed. "Ronnie, what is it?"

"I bought that for you the night before the charity event. I wanted to tell you that night, but I chickened out." His brow furrowed and I felt awful. Worse than awful.

"I'm sorry I let what I overheard ruin this."

"No, this is as much my fault as yours. I should've told you. I should've fought for you. I get why you lied about Tony —"

"I should've told you. I got scared." *There, I admitted it.* "But we can learn from this. No more holding back."

"Agreed. Look, I have something else to say."

"Shit, that doesn't sound good." I tensed again.

"No. Nothing like that." He groaned. "God, this is hard." He cleared his throat. "This is the first time asking this...for real. But, would you be my girlfriend? For real?"

"Oh my god." I lifted my head and cackled. "Your first time?"

"Yeah, give me a break," he scoffed, and flipped over so I couldn't see his face. I snuggled up behind him and spooned his massive body. "No cuddling until you give me an answer."

"It's a firm maybe."

"Maybe?" He spun around so fast he had me pinned underneath him. "Do I need to show you *again* how good we are together?"

"I think so. I do like a good showing."

"You're a pain in the ass." But he grinned when he said it.

"I'm *your* pain in the ass."

"That you are." He brought his tongue down on my nipple and sucked it into his mouth, the metal ring clinking against his teeth. "Yes or no?"

"Mmm," I moaned and arched my back.

"*Greta*." He bit down on it and I jumped. "I'll make this hard for you."

"Yeah. Give me something hard."

And he tickled me. It was so aggressive and fun and sexy, the way he knew the right spots to hit. I cried from laughter and decided to give in. "Yes. Yes. Jesus, yes. I'll be your goddamn girlfriend. For real."

"Good. My little cleat chaser. I'll make it worth it."

"Yeah you will. You know your way around the bases and how to use a nice piece of wood. It's a perfect combo."

"God, I love you."

Epilogue

Aaron

"Gabs, come here for a minute." I patted my lap with excitement bursting in my belly. Ambar had emailed me the article—and I couldn't have been more impressed. "I want to show you something."

"Yeah? It'd better be good. Last time you did this, you mooned me." She chuckled and plopped down on my lap. It was a typical Saturday morning for us—coffee and time in bed before she had to work and I had to head to the gym. With the season starting in a couple of weeks, I made sure to spend every second I could with her. My *girlfriend*.

She wrapped her little arms around my neck and planted a wet, aggressive kiss on my mouth. *Hot damn.* "You taste perfect. I want more."

I hummed in response and let the kiss last longer than necessary. It was almost too much, because my dick jumped to life. And I knew she felt it. "Ronnie, put him away if you want to get anything done. I get distracted when he's out."

"And I love that you love my cock." I nuzzled her neck and moved my mouse. "Here, the computer's on now. You need to read this."

"Is it sex positions?" She cocked an eyebrow.

"No, don't be an asshole." I poked her side. "Be a doll and listen for once."

"Hey." She spun around and pointed her finger at me. "You told me to wait before coming on your face last night, and I followed your directions."

"Goddamn it. I love you." I kissed her and, with more force, made her look at the screen. "It's the draft of my interview with Ambar."

"Oh, well, shit. You should've said!"

She brought her face inches from the screen and gasped at the title. "Ronnie."

"Give it a chance. I promise." I patted her knee.

A LEGEND, A SCANDAL AND A ROMANCE. AARON HILL TALKS.

I want to point out that Aaron Hill, star shortstop and well-known campus playboy, asked me to pen this interview with the sole intention of speaking the truth. I did the best I could to put his story into words.

Aaron Hill was born with talent. Some say he could throw his pacifier across the room as an infant. Others argue his parents made him practice groundballs for six hours a day. Either way, a legacy was left behind at his former high school, Clintonia. He broke all offensive school records before he was a senior, won the golden glove all four years playing shortstop and was the first player from his hometown to contemplate getting drafted before college. But, as we all know, Aaron, or Hilly to us mortals, chose to come here for an education and more experience. He hit .350 last year and started almost every game at short. And if you know anything about baseball, you know a shortstop needs swagger and confidence to lead. And, boy, Hilly has both.

But, as the story goes, with fame and fortune comes scandal. Hilly became the target of a religious do-gooder this year whose sole intention was to hurt his playing career. Pictures were posted on an Instagram account – they have since been removed but the culprit is still unknown. This is where the scandal and romance come into play, as many of our readers are anxious to learn about. So, I could've written the amazing stats and potential Hilly has to make it to the big leagues, but let's be honest. We all know that already. We've seen him play.

We want the story. You know, the one involving Greta Aske. The stunning blonde who always hangs around with the baseball guys. During this interview, I learned a lot about cleat chasers. These are groups of fans, girls and guys, who follow players with the intention of using their fame for themselves. And, as Hilly made it very clear, Greta is not a cleat chaser. She is his best friend. The yin to his yang, the one who doesn't quite care he's 'good' at some sport. When I asked him about his father's diagnosis and how his life changed, he said one of the only things that held him together was Greta. He said, 'That girl cussed at me. Called me out. Pushed me to keep going. And didn't censor herself around me. She was a friend who is motivated by love and helping others. There are very few people like Greta and I'm glad she's in my life.'

Swoon, right? Well, after the pictures came out the two went into cahoots to stage a relationship. Don't get your hopes up, ladies, because while the faux-couple started out as a PR plan…something else happened.

Aaron Hill fell in love.

The messy, terrifying, beautiful kind of love. The kicker is – the couple hadn't admitted it to each other at the time of the interview. The fear held them back. How could a guy like him – his words, not mine – convince a girl like Greta he was worth it?

She was his game changer.

I concluded the interview with one burning question. Why? Why come out now and tell this story when he's active on social media and could do it any day? His response – because people can say what they want about people they don't actually know. And I wanted to tell my story on my terms. And if it helps me get my girl back, then it'll be worth it."

To read about his family's charity, click here.

I knew she'd finished reading – her body tensed and she blinked quite a bit. My heart pitter-pattered. *Does she hate it? Fuck.* But then she spun around with a watery smile.

"Ronnie...wow." She widened her eyes, the gorgeous brown orbs seeking mine. "That was brave and silly and I'm proud of you."

"Thank you." I knew it was risky but I had no regrets. Coach had my back and even my parents had read it. Of course, they were most happy about me finding Greta, and we'd all agreed to never discuss the pictures. Ever. But Greta's radiant face brought me back to the present. "You're a game changer. A Pita. A gabby Pita, but you're mine."

"Yeah." She licked her lips with a seductive grin. "I am yours. Now, I'm feeling really generous after reading all that, so I say you drop your pants and get on the bed right now."

"God. I'm gunna marry you someday, Gabs. Just you wait." I picked her up and threw her on the bed. She laughed, clawing at our clothes. "And it'll be the best damn adventure of our lives."

Want to see more from this author? Here's a taster for you to enjoy!

Cleat Chasers: Best Player
Jaqueline Snowe

Excerpt

Leaving the home I'd grown up in — the house packed with every memory I had — hurt more than I'd anticipated. My throat burned each time I held back emotion, but it wouldn't do any of us good to mention the overwhelming worry and sadness. We couldn't afford wasted sentiments when every second of every day we worried about our dad — fighting cancer wasn't a single person's battle. It took all our efforts.

"I can't believe our baby girl is going away to college," my dad said from the front seat of the old navy mini-van that smelled like used sports gear. He craned his neck and gave me a weak smile. I returned the gesture, hoping I hid the bubbling anxiety growing in my chest, and raised my fists in the air.

"Yay!"

He coughed, the sound better than it used to be, but I still tensed every time I heard it. Each breath he took was a struggle. "While I'm not thrilled you're going to be living with Aaron and two of his teammates for the summer, they seem to be decent young men. They're better now than they were his freshman year. Good lord, they were hellions. But he promised he'd take care of you for us."

"Dad," I mumbled. "Come on."

"I mean it. Your mom and I are going to be hours away trying out different treatment facilities. Someone needs to look out for you, K-Bug."

I will not cry. Nope. I will not. "I'll be fine. Really. I've been looking forward to college for years."

"But not everyone goes two months early..." My mom let the words hang and our eyes met in the rearview mirror. Hers were tired and gray. My heart hurt for her and how strong she'd been for all of us. She'd been our family rock forever and while the thought of being away from them was freeing, it also left a hole.

"It's better like this, I promise. It'll be a good way for me to get acclimated to the campus and I signed up for two classes already. Introduction to Film and Online Biology. Both sound awful, but it'll help me get ready for my hard schedule this fall."

"K-Bug, you've never had to worry about grades. You're our smart girl," my dad said, not hiding his pride. Another wave of gratitude went through me. Despite Aaron's insane athletic abilities, my parents had never once made me feel less important or talented. Not once. The world needed more of them and the gratitude switched to anger at the injustice of my dad getting sick.

It wasn't fair.

But showing my internal battle would do none of us any good on the already emotional day. I swallowed down the grief and worry, plastered a smile on my face and spoke with a practiced enthusiasm that I'd mastered with all the hospital visits. "I'm just excited for the newness. New friends, new experiences, new things to learn and new mistakes to make. I've always heard about how college is this life-changing experience of fun, embarrassing stories and the place where you meet lifelong friends. I want that. I'm ready for it."

"Then that's what you're going to do." My dad's voice held a finality to it and we all remained quiet for the rest of the drive. The campus was about two hours away from our childhood home — the house my parents had sold — and the moment we left the driveway that morning was the last time I'd set foot there. It was an odd combination to experience — utter excitement about what was next, and longing for what used to be. My constant battle was defining myself. I had always been Aaron's younger sister. The daughter. The girlfriend.

I wanted to be me.

College was my answer.

"Honey, we're going to stop and get some shakes. Would you like anything?" my mom inquired as she pulled into a fast-food place. My dad had a softness for milkshakes and we'd made an unspoken agreement that when he wanted one, he got one.

"Yeah, I'll get a coffee. Want me to run in and buy one?"

"That'd be great, K-Bug."

They handed me a twenty-dollar bill and I grabbed my phone before heading inside the diner. The humid air was hard to swallow, but it was a brief escape from the confines of the car. My dad got cold real fast, so we couldn't have the air on too high. I fanned myself, moving the end of my old jersey-shirt to get air on my midriff. Sweat dripped down my muscles and a cold milkshake sounded perfect. I ordered — my mom preferred chocolate, my dad mint-cookie and I always got banana.

My phone went off and I almost ignored it, since my ex-boyfriend had thought it a great time to reconcile after our disastrous prom weekend. *No thanks, Sean. That ship sailed.* But it wasn't him. It was Aaron, my ridiculous, awesome and obnoxious older brother.

Aaron: Yo, you almost here?

Kenzie: Stopped for milkshakes. Maybe fifteen minutes out.

Aaron: Coach just called and wants to meet me at the field – Tanner is here though. He'll help you unpack. That cool?

Kenzie: That's fine. Mom and Dad will be pissed if they don't see you though.

Aaron: I'll try and be back in an hour. Coach knows they're here but said this is important.

Kenzie: Okay, see you soon.

Aaron: No backing out now, kid. You absolutely sure about living here?

Kenzie: There's no home to go back to. Yeah, I'm sure.

I didn't expect a response from him, and the few minutes I had to wait for the shakes were spent thinking about my future roommates. Sure, it was only two months, but these guys had the personalities of celebrities.

Aaron—my brother who'd slept with countless ladies the past two years and suffered a sex scandal. Zade Willows—the all-star pitcher who had a fan club named after him. Tanner Johnson—the giant center fielder who could make girls faint with a wink. Yeah. It was going to be an adventure living with them until their fourth roommate, Jeff, got back from playing baseball overseas.

Me, the awkward kid without an ounce of athletic ability, was living in the baseball house in the center of Jockville. Life was funny sometimes.

"Order's up!"

I thanked the hostess and carried the drinks back to the car. Too soon, we were pulling into the chipped driveway of my new temporary digs. White house, large porch that had seen better days, overgrown trees in the front and backyard and the door wide open. I pulled my long dark-blonde hair into a high messy bun and took one final breath.

College.

Adventure.

New.

"What's up, Hill family?" Tanner's voice boomed from him. He leaned against the front railing, his height almost putting his head on the roof of the house. His hair was midnight black and it spilled from his head in messy curls, but his light brown eyes were killer. Yeah, I had a little bitty crush on him after having met him a couple times over the past three years, but it was hard not to. He was my kryptonite—long eyelashes, mischievous grin, the perfect dimples and real tall with broad shoulders. I gave him a little wave, hoping I didn't blush too much.

I was going to be living with him, so it didn't bode well for anyone to know about my crush. "Hey, TJ."

"Roomie, let me grab your stuff. Aaron had to head to the field, but he'll be back. Good to see you, Mr. and Mrs. Hill." He swaggered—it was the only way to describe it—to the car and gave both my parents a hug. It pleased me to see how good he was to my family. The warmth on the back of my neck had nothing to do with his fitted shirt and workout shorts that showcased how much time he spent in the gym.

"You're too kind, Tanner. Really," my mom gushed and I had to roll my eyes. Even she succumbed to his charm. She had to know how much he got around… I mean, he was one of two single guys who lived in the baseball house. I snorted into my fist and Tanner slid me a look.

"Laying it on thick there, TJ."

"What? I can't hug my second-favorite set of parents?" He dared to raise one beautiful dark eyebrow, challenging me to call him out. I did.

"They brought you all beer and homemade casserole for at least a week. You don't need to suck up."

His grin widened and, after patting my dad on the back, he walked to the trunk of the car to help get my five bags. It was sad that, moving into college, I only had five bags' worth of stuff. That was one lesson learned after seeing my dad go through his struggle—material things didn't matter all that much. Life was more about the experience.

He walked past me, smirking, and picked up two of the bags. "Come on, Kenny. Let me show you to your room."

He didn't lower his voice or do anything weird, but those words coming from his mouth sent a shiver down my body. I cleared my throat and picked up the final load. "After you, Johnson."

My parents took their time bringing food into the small kitchen while I followed Tanner into the house and up the stairs. I had been there before, but only for a small amount of time where they could hide their craziness. Now, they'd let it all hang out. The mess, the dirty bathroom, the pile of useless things stacked in the corner. Why did they have a stack of empty boxes? And empty cups? They had a kitchen…why didn't they use it?

He led me down the upstairs hallway. There were two rooms on each side, two with their own bathrooms, but I wasn't that lucky. While Zade and Aaron across the hall had one each, Jeff and Tanner shared theirs. And Jeff's was the room I was using…meaning I had to share a bathroom with Tanner Johnson.

Two months was going to be a long time.

"Okay, Kenny. Here's Jeff's room." He opened the door and gave me a bemused look. "He's the neatest out of all of us. I saw you scowl on the way up. We're not total pigs."

"I'll just have to do some cleaning, that's all." *Thank God I brought supplies.*

He chuckled and dropped my large duffel bags on the beige carpet. I took a hesitant step inside the room and sniffed. Nothing smelled off and there weren't any weird stains on the carpet.

"Did you just *smell* the room?"

"Yes, I did." I jutted my chin out at him. "I've lived with Aaron. I know how smelly boys can be. It seems fine so far."

"God, this is going to be fun."

"I'm bursting with excitement," I deadpanned.

It earned me another grin, showcasing his impressive dimples, and I scanned the rest of the room. The walls had various baseball posters of the team and

MLB teams. The sheets had been stripped from the queen-sized bed and the dresser drawers opened and emptied. I placed my bag on the desk and spun around. Tanner watched me with a curious expression and I did not look at his mouth when his lips quirked up on one side.

"We need to talk about some ground rules."

Shit. Butterflies formed in my gut and I felt foolish. I wasn't sure what I'd thought he was going to say, but it wasn't that. Crossing my arms, I scrunched my nose and asked, "About what?"

"Living here." He stepped farther into the room and with that small action, the walls seemed to close around us. He took up so much space and his warmth crowded me. "I know you're pretty chill from everything Hilly's told us, but I want to get it all out in the open, you know?"

I bit my lip to prevent myself from smiling. Was he going to give me the *talk*? *Holy shit.* I hoped he was because I wasn't going to make it easy for him. "Okay. I'm listening. Should I write this down?" I moved toward my backpack, but he shook his head.

"We share a wall and a bathroom. The foundation here isn't great and I don't plan on being a saint just because you're here." He winced and moved his hand to his neck, stress lines forming around his eyes. "I mean, I'll be more discreet about it. I won't...you don't have to see anything."

"Tanner, what are you talking about?" I asked, successfully keeping my face blank. He had to know what my life had been like with Aaron. Hell, everyone knew the baseball house was notorious for hooking up. I wasn't dumb or naïve. But watching him struggle through this was worth it. "What do you mean by *saint*?"

"Christ," he said, then rubbed his hand over his face. Gone was the playful expression—uneasiness replaced it. "I don't want you uncomfortable, but you might run into girls who…spend the night."

"Ohhh, you have a *girlfriend*?" I whistled, getting another worried look. "Do I get to meet her?"

"Kenzie." His cheeks turned just a little bit red and I pressed my lips together to prevent breaking character. "You might hear…stuff. I don't want you to… *Shit*. I don't know how to do this. I didn't think it through."

"Okay, enough. I'll stop." I laughed and enjoyed the myriad expressions crossing his face. They ended in curiosity and I closed the distance between us so we stood a foot apart. "I know you'll have hook-ups. That's fine. All I ask is that she doesn't hog the bathroom the morning after and that you don't fuck *too* loud."

He blinked. It was slow and telling, and I bit my lip, but it did no good. I burst out laughing at how uncomfortable he was and I hit his shoulder without real force. "I was messing with you before, but I appreciate you trying to warn me."

"I thought—Aaron said… Never mind. I didn't want to shock or upset you."

His comment warmed me, but his use of my brother's name did not. "Whatever warning Aaron gave you, forget it, okay? I'm not this naïve, innocent kid."

"Okay."

"Your tone doesn't agree with your word." I pursed my lips and gave him my best leveling stare. "Mean it."

He gave me his signature crooked grin, narrowed those baby browns just a smidge and lowered his voice like a soccer coach. "*Okay.*"

We stood, not in a face-off or battle, but in a weird bubble of not really knowing the other person. He was the playboy with a bright future. I was the *innocent* younger sister of his best friend. Two months living with him, good or bad, would be an adventure, and my excitement for something new overshadowed the awkwardness. I held out my hand, grinning, and broke the tension that had formed in the last two minutes. "Thanks for letting me live here, roomie. I think we're going to have a hell of a time."

He placed his large hand against mine and shook, a slow smile forming on his too-handsome face. "I already regret agreeing to this."

About the Author

Jaqueline Snowe lives in Arizona where the 'dry heat' really isn't that bad. She enjoys making lists with colorful Post-it notes and sipping coffee all day. She has been a custodian, a waitress, a landscaper, a coach and a teacher. Her life revolves around binge-watching Netflix, her two dogs who don't realize they aren't humans and her wonderful baseball-loving husband.

Jaqueline loves to hear from readers. You can find her contact information, website details and author profile page at https://www.totallybound.com

Home of Erotic Romance

Sign up for our newsletter and find out about all our romance book releases, eBook sales and promotions, sneak peeks and FREE romance books!